LEO KANE

JOURNEY THROUGH THE VEIL

BY

MICHAEL SLOAN

To my wife Odell. Our many travels together have brought us a long way through life. Let's continue making memories.

Chapter 0 – Prologue

Tonight, look out into the stars, look into infinity, and dream of worlds beyond our own. Multiple worlds, similar to our own, contain realms as varied as our own nations. Now, take a step forward. Did you feel that? No? That's too bad. Perhaps there are other worlds closer than you think, separated and unseen by the human eye.

The Spring Crow, a beautiful ancient realm can be accessed by only a very few, and those few are of an ancient Jinn decent, born of a world beyond our own only to be cast out. Throughout the millennium these decedents have grown, lived, and died protecting the realms and worlds they now traverse. This is one of their stories.

He refuses to do it. The lineage is over and there will be no protection, I may be the last.

Sir Joseph Kane, a Jinn descendant of the Kane Warriors spoke softly to Lady Cybele, the ruler of the Spring Crow. The Spring Crow, one of the many realms hidden in the multiverse outside of most human's perception, is protected by a veil separating our reality from theirs. Only a few, to include Joseph, could pass between the veil and walk in both worlds.

"What do you mean he won't do it?" asked Lady Cybele. "There has always been a Kane protecting the Spring Crow. It's his heritage, he must know that."

"I've explained it to him and have made every attempt to train him, but he refuses. I will not in good conscious force him to do something he does not wish to do, that is not the way of the realm, and I will honor his wishes," replied Joseph.

"Sir Joseph, he is your son; he must carry on the tradition. How else will we ensure our safety from the other realms?"

"He has a young wife with child. While unconventional, I have an idea. I will find a way to protect the realm."

"Sir Joseph, the realm trusts you with its life. I trust you with my life, but you can't be serious. By the time the child grows he or she will not understand. It will be too late to start training."

"I'll think of a way; it's the only way around this mess."

"Think about the years you spent with your own son. Even before training began, he knew you were different, that he was different. Do you believe that will carry over to this child?"

Joseph thought about this for a moment. He recalled the years spent with his son, cultivating his beliefs and responsibilities to one day take over as the protector of the Spring Crow, only to have the hard work and love that he poured into his son shunned by stronger beliefs in his earthly world.

"First and foremost, I must ensure the child is brought up in a loving home. My travels here will remain the same as they are now and when I'm away from the realm. Back in the other world, I'll treat the child as my own. The child will be of my flesh and blood, so that will be the easy part. The hard part will be making up for lost time... to teach him in the ways of the Jinn, of the Kane Knights."

"It is possible," said Lady Cybele. "The child will be years behind, but what other choice do we have. Go with my blessing, Sir Joseph, and do be careful."

Chapter 1

Leonardo Joseph Kane, or Leo as he was called by friends and family for as long as he can remember, sat in the second row on the polished glassy finish of the wooden church pew as his best friend was eulogized. His grandfather, his only true friend, was gone.

The local church was a sight to behold, not something you would expect in a small town in Ohio. The outer shell was built from old grey stone that, when viewed from a distance, gave it a medieval appearance. Two spires rose up well above the small A-Frame houses surrounding the area. Inside you were greeted by marble floors that were well over one hundred years old, but gave the appearance of being laid just yesterday. Inside the sanctuary were two rows of pristine pews, sealed and polished to an extent that Leo could imagine sliding off when taking his seat. Surrounding the sanctuary, stained glass windows were commonplace, but in this instance, gifted by a wealthy benefactor. Imported genuine Tiffany Stained Glass, constructed in the old standards of channels filled with bone, wood, and sealed with lead. Each window depicted Old Testament stories, daily life of the times, and stories told by Leo's grandparents.

While Leo and his family did not attend on a regular basis, he knew that his mother and father were happily married in this very church and someday, he was expected to do the same. At sixteen years old, marriage was the furthest thing from his mind. Leo was in the tenth grade and had become interested in girls, but at this point in his life—while he definitely noticed the girls his age beginning to change, to grow hour glass figures and were getting taller, nearly the same height as his five- foot eight build—he only had a slightly greater interest than he did when he was younger.

Leo leaned back and listened to his grandfather's friends recount stories of the Great War, his love for his wife who passed ten years prior, and how he would do anything for family and friends. Normally, the splendor of the church and its medieval appearance would have fascinated Leo, but today was no ordinary day.

Leo's Grandfather, Joseph Kane, or "Grandpa Joe" as Leo knew him, had been a drinking man, a working man, and a gentleman. Grandpa Joe was perpetually well dressed, from his starched collared shirts, vests, and pressed pants—all the way down to his shined shoes. Occasionally, he wore a tie, but Grandpa Joe's signature look was neatly pulled together without, only his top button remaining unfastened. He'd finished his classic look with dark slick hair and an amulet depicting a black crow on a blue stone hanging from a beautiful silver chain.

Grandpa Joe had lived in a typical house for the area of town. The simple dwelling that was smaller than Leo's house, but had a grand, wraparound, wooden porch that extended from the front north side to both the east and west. The siding was a worn beige, but still in surprisingly good shape for vinyl. Inside, Grandpa ensured his house was always clean, but it had the unmistakable aroma of books with a hint of mustiness, even when the house's few windows were flung open to let in the fresh air. Old leather-bound books were scattered in random locations and piled on bookshelves, tables, chairs, and the floor. It never ceased to amaze Leo how Grandpa had been able to always flip to exactly where he left off in any of his readings, almost like magic. During the spring and fall, when the weather would be pleasant, Leo would sit on the porch with Grandpa Joe in the evening. They would watch the sun set on their sleepy Ohio town, while Grandpa Joe read passages out loud from one of his many books.

Almost every day during fall, winter, and spring Leo would run to Grandpa Joe's house to hastily finish his homework and listen to the extravagant stories that he would seemingly pull from thin air. The stories were so vibrant, lifelike, and unchanging that, as a younger boy, Leo never once doubted the validity of the fantastic lands of far away and long ago. Once Leo's homework met Grandpa Joe's standards, which were not always necessarily up to his school's standards, Grandpa Joe would pour himself, in his own words, "three-fingers of the nectar of the Gods" over a single ice cube rattling in an antique crystal glass and sit comfortably in his favorite, beat-up brown leather chair. Leo knew this tradition and verbiage was a veiled attempt to hide the fact his Grandfather enjoyed Scotch, preferably something from the Islay Region, over ice, and was an excuse to rest a bit. The bite from the liquor would always bring a satisfied smile to the old man's face, while the ice slowly opened the peaty flavor. It would also relax him and put Grandpa in the mood to spin whatever tale was closest to the surface on his still sharp, seemingly never aging, mind.

That afternoon, just a few short months ago, was no different. Leo had finished his last homework assignment, which in this case was literature. Leo's teacher assigned the class to recount the meaning behind a book that either the school, or state, had charged the class to read. Being that Leo was a sophomore he was thankful that literature at his age consisted of interesting books such as *The Great Gatsby*, *To Kill a Mockingbird*, and his favorite *The Catcher in the Rye*. They were all books that he could, and often did, become lost in... although he wouldn't share this fact with his peers. No, at his age it was deemed uncool to spend an afternoon reading rather than playing the latest first-person shooter video game with all the false glory, blood, guts, and action normally appreciated by, seemingly, everyone aged forty and under.

In his assignment, Leo recounted what he thought to be the meaning of *The Catcher in the Rye*. It was, in his opinion, a well thought out report, detailing the growing into manhood of Holden, the main character, and how changes in one's self and others affects us all. Normally, Grandpa Joe would take a passing glance over Leo's work, but this time he took a particular interest in the symbology of childhood and Leo's spin on death. Once Grandpa finished reading the report, he placed it on the table sitting beside his leather chair, took a slow sip, and smiled at Leo.

"Once, a very long time ago," began Grandpa Joe, as he fiddled with the amulet around his neck, "friendships, family, and turmoil didn't affect us in the same manner as today. Wars were waged to protect family honor, brother turned against brother for the approval of the father, but friendships were never wasted.

"This life, our world, was not the end of all possibilities, and the people of long ago knew, and agreed, that our world was merely the beginning of another. The gateway into a world set apart by a veil so thin—that if it were known—could be broken with the slightest touch of the lightest feather. This world was hidden but known, it was looked upon as something to look forward to, and to smile when thought about.

"As the years went on, stories of this world were passed from generation to generation, changing a little each time as ideas were lost, facts altered, and untruths told. These variations in the story caused mankind not to revere the possibilities and the prospects of passing into a new world. No, mankind today views leaving our Earthly dwelling as the ultimate end, something of darkness and despair, something to be fought with every fiber of the living soul. Because of these falsehoods, the world set apart went into hiding behind the very darkness that man created. Behind this thin veil, the symbols of wonder and magic became dark and foreboding, rather than of light and prosperity."

"Grandpa Joe," Leo said with eyes wide, "the report is only recounting a story of growing up, lost youth, and someone who sees himself as better than the rest—nothing more, nothing less."

Grandpa Joe gave a weary smile. "Leo, my boy, someday when you are able, I hope you can discover the path to understanding the light and love in the symbology of transitioning; the ultimate journey of transitioning from boy-to-man and from man-to-warrior."

Grandpa Joe, still sitting in his worn leather chair, leaned left and with nimble hands, thrust his right hand into his worn jeans pocket and drew out—what appeared to be—a worn piece of rounded copper. He again, with surprising agility of an elderly man, leaned forward, took Leo's hand with his own, and passed the rounded copper to his grandson.

"Leo," Grandpa Joe said looking into his grandson's eyes, "I don't have much in this world, but I have you and the necessary fee for Charon, which came to me after generations of sacrifice. The fee is passed down and not discovered. I will always have the necessary fee and this coin, this fee, is your start." Grandpa Joe closed his eyes and his smile returned. "When it's your turn, remember that at the start of any great adventure, the belly of the whale can take many forms."

Leo stared at the large copper coin his grandfather had given him and didn't understand. Grandpa Joe's stories were normally filled with action and adventure, stories that could only have happened years ago when Grandpa was a young man. They were also filled with sense, not nonsense. "The fee for Charon? The start? The belly of the whale? Grandpa, it is only a report on a book about a boy growing up." Never in Leo's life had Grandpa been so... strange... and he moved not with the stiffness of his years but, for some unknown seemingly mystical reason, even while sitting, Leo could tell all the years drifted away when he decided to place the coin in his hand.

After the funeral procession, Leo and his dad, Robert Jr, Bob to his friends—and, much to his chagrin, Robbie to his grandfather—and a handful of longtime and faithful friends, paid their very last respects to Robert Joseph Kane. Six of Grandpa Joe's oldest friends were a sight to behold as they struggled to carry the casket to the final resting place. In reality, the casket set on a collapsible aluminum church truck to ease the movement from hearse to grave, but it still posed a heavy load for the grieving gentlemen. A few final words were given by the preacher before two out-of-place burial-ground custodians in jeans and colored shirts unceremoniously lowered the casket via two lowering devices. As the casket sank from sight, Leo's father turned to him and stated, "That's it, ashes-to-ashes and all that goes with it. If everyone is ready, let's make an attempt to salvage the rest of this miserable afternoon."

Leo wanted to make the most of the afternoon, he really did, but he couldn't shake the crass, uncaring way his dad offhandedly shrugged of the death of his own father. Even so, Leo had absolutely no idea what he would do in order to salvage the day, even if he hadn't just come from his best friend's funeral.

Leo pondered this for a moment... best friend, he thought. Sure, Leo had friends, just like any kid his age, but his friends didn't seem as close to him as they were to each other. He was cordial with kids his age, nobody was out to bully him, and he occasionally shared a laugh with other boys in the class. *That's friendship isn't it?* Leo asked himself. When he was younger, he had never been invited to a sleep over, to a movie, not even a birthday party. *Perhaps*, he thought, *perhaps I have acquaintances, but do I truly have a real friend? Did I spend so much time with Grandpa that I've missed out on forming lifelong bonds with my peers?*

625 Knoop Avenue sat at the end of one of the most sought-after cul-de-sacs in town. His father always kept a comfortable home and he always felt safe in the house where he spent restless summers waiting for Grandpa to return from his yearly business trips.

Once inside, the house opened into the living room—obviously decorated by either a bachelor or a widower. In this case, it was the later as Leo's mother had passed away some time ago. A pile of newspapers grew ever larger beside the front door—a strange habit his father apparently inherited from Grandpa Joe, as this was customary in his house too—and the carpet was in need of a good run of the vacuum. Beyond the living room sat what was once a cozy dining room that now sat empty, and yet further beyond was the unremarkable kitchen. To the left of the dining room was a set of brown shag carpeted stairs that led up to Leo's room, his private sanctuary in the house he dwelled.

Leo, much like his dad, picked up habits from Grandpa. For one, his room was always neat, his clothes folded in a specific fashion, and his bed was always made. Another habit he picked up was dropping his schoolbooks wherever they may lie; although, that didn't work to his advantage as he would occasionally forget his homework within the random stacks. Unfortunately, he did not inherit his Grandpa's knack for always choosing the exact wanted page from the books he read, or to remember to bring the books with him to class for that matter.

As he sat on his neatly made bed in his room, he realized that in all his years, he never asked questions as to Grandpa's occupation. It was an unspoken rule in the Kane household that the subject was never to be discussed. As he continued to think about all he knew about Grandpa Joe, and all he did not, he rose, walked to his dresser, and opened the top drawer. Folded neatly in the bottom of the furthest white sock on the right was the large, round copper coin Grandpa had given him. *What did he call this again? The fee for Charon? Of all the things Grandpa told me maybe I really didn't know him at all... or perhaps he was getting older and losing his mind and I was just around too much to notice.*

Leo put the coin back into the white sock, folded it neatly, and placed it back in the bottom of the drawer, ensuring it remained furthest on the right.

"Dad, I'm going out for a walk," Leo yelled down the stairs from his room. He knew his voice wouldn't carry far in the house, but in this instance, due to the stark quiet of arriving home only a few minutes ago, it rang clear.

"Take your jacket, it's still chilly for this late in spring," his dad responded.

Once outside, Leo looked around his small street in his small town. Unlike his Grandpa's house, Leo's was slightly larger, of newer build, and was constructed of brick. The brick was quite befitting for the neighborhood; in fact, this neighborhood was one of the better in town. Occasionally, Leo would feel self-conscious about living in such an affluent area because he knew his parents couldn't really afford it. His mother—when she was alive—swore that they were the luckiest family on the block.

His mother, *God rest her soul,* Leo thought, was a kind woman taken too soon. She "succumbed to heart failure" is what his dad had told him, corroborated by Grandpa Joe. Leo was young when she passed, too young to remember details, but he did remember her kindness. The kindness she showed in those few short years almost made up for the fact that he never had a feminine figure in his life.

The house didn't have a wraparound porch, making it a little less inviting than Grandpa's, but it did have a large, grand, bright red door that, upon installation by his dad, Grandpa exclaimed, "Why, that may as well be the gate to all of eternity! God and Lucifer themselves will use it as a beacon to navigate their way." From that point on Dad hated that door, but refused to replace it because, as Dad put it, "Spent too damn much of his hard-earned money and time to be concerned with the ramblings of an old man who isn't around enough to appreciate it'." Deep down Leo knew his dad loathed the door, but Leo smiled, he absolutely loved it. From what he remembered, so did his late mother, giving Leo the impression that his dad really kept it more for her than to spite his own father.

Leo's house was just a house, but the area—his area—was, in his mind, the most beautiful spot on the planet. The lush maple trees that lined the road had just finished budding and were turning a bright shade of green. Each tree was as large around as a small car, perhaps half the size of a Volkswagen Beetle, and the roots of the trees were so old and strong that they caused the once pristine sidewalks to bubble and bow in ambitious directions, reaching out as though each new shift was the start of new growth.

Every year Leo knew when he saw the first leaf turn, the slightest hint of gold or red, his Grandpa would soon return. Leo would examine the trees, wishing and praying every fall for a glimpse of color in the lush green canopy that covered each side of his cul-de-sac. In this case Grandpa had only a few weeks left before he would leave for the summer, but this year he was mercilessly taken away from him, early—forever—a fact his family attributed only to age and drink. Leo continued to scan the roads, the sidewalks, and the row of houses on either side of his world.

All the houses were similarly built: brick, small front yards, slightly bigger back yards, and just enough space, in Leo's opinion, between them. Far more space than that of a larger town, where the houses seem to sit so close you could hand a cup of sugar to the neighbor, if people still did that sort of thing.

From this location Leo could also see his school and the church where, just this morning, he paid his last respects. Behind the church, roughly a mile to the south, was the Rosehill Cemetery, named after one of the towns earliest founders and Mayor, former Army Sergeant Anthony Rosehill of the 3rd Infantry Regiment, Regular Army Infantry, a fact that he had picked up from Grandpa during one of their talks.

Leo shoved his hands in his denim jacket pockets and slowly started towards the cemetery, subconsciously counting his footfalls; he needed time to say a proper goodbye to Grandpa Joe without the boorish comments and stares of his dad. *On second thought,* Leo thought to himself and reversed direction. *Grandpa gave me that silly piece of copper without so much as an explanation. If he thought so much of it, he can explain it, I don't care if it's from the grave.*

In reality, Leo wasn't upset and knew the piece of copper coin wasn't silly, it was a gift; he knew that he needed to cling to anything that would bring him closer to Grandpa, in order to honor his memory. He vowed that the church and his father at the cemetery would not be his final memory or last respect. With that, Leo turned around and quietly went back to his room, as not to disturb his dad—who may have made him stay in for the rest of the evening—and retrieved the copper coin piece. Only then did he start on his way again.

By the time Leo arrived at the cemetery the spring evening was settling in, making the air cool and damp. As Leo walked to the freshly dug and covered grave of his grandfather, he marveled at the differences between the headstones in the vast cemetery. He could tell it wasn't always so large, that it must have started off as a small plot, probably in a farmer's field bought or acquired by the town and expanded as the years ticked by. The older section consisted of rough stone or sandstone grave markers marking the deceased's name, age, and year of death. Some contained an epitaph—or a few words written by family—regarding the deceased, but most were difficult to read due to advanced age.

Further beyond the entrance, the headstones became larger and made of slate, again marking the memorialization of the dead and a few kind words for the departed loved ones. Dotted on the outside most edges of Rosehill Cemetery were the mausoleums and monuments, constructed by those with the foresight and means to mark a final resting place for the deceased and provide a lasting tribute for the bereaved.

Finally, there were the markers... the markers. The markers always made Leo a little sad for they were normally simple bricks placed at the head of the grave with a small brass plate affixed that merely stated the name, age, and year of death. These were always selected by one of two classes of mourners: those who couldn't afford the elaborate headstone or mausoleum, but still wanted to honor their lost love; and those who didn't concern themselves with the human soul who was lost to this world forever. Leo's dad, of course, had chosen the latter—probably for both reasons—which, in Leo's opinion, was the most depressing of all reasons.

Leo sat beside the newly placed stone at the head of Grandpa Joe's grave. He could smell the damp grass surrounding him, covering most of the cemetery, but the sight and smell of the freshly stirred dirt covering the remains of Grandpa Joe remained prominent against the otherwise green landscape. The earthy scent of the turned soil filled his nostrils and brought him a surprisingly peaceful feeling knowing that his grandfather had returned to the Earth. Deep down he hoped that he was reunited with his grandmother and the mother that he barely knew.

As he sat and contemplated returning to the earth, he reached into his denim jacket and withdrew the copper coin Grandpa Joe had given him. *The fee for Charon*, thought Leo, *Grandpa, what in the world did you mean? Never in my life, for all the hours that we talked, that you told me stories of what I assumed were of your youth, adventures that you seemingly made up on the fly to entertain and mystify, never once did you speak in riddles.*

Leo began flipping the coin, catching it each time in his left and placing it again on his right. As Leo flipped the coin, a large crow swooped down and grabbed the coin, mid-flip, in its large black beak. The crow had to swoop so low that its right-wing grazed Leo's face, stunning him for a second. Only after the crow zipped towards the west side of the cemetery did Leo snap out of his temporary daze and realize what had happened.

"Get back here," he yelled in an absent-minded attempt to get the coin back. He knew that yelling at a bird was the absolute last way to get the crow to sit still, but it was the first thing that came to mind; rather, it was a natural reaction to having his coin swiped. He also knew that the crow was probably attracted by the shiny object flipping up and down and that he was partially to blame for its loss.

The crow alighted at the entrance of one of the ancient mausoleums at the furthest edge of the cemetery. The large, black bird was bounding up and down the three steps leading up to an iron gate, which separated the inside of the mausoleum from the outside world. As Leo tiptoed closer to the crow in order to catch him—which he knew would be near impossible—the crow slipped between the iron bars.

Okay Leo, he thought, *the crow is in the mausoleum and is trapped on three sides, if I can get in there, I may be able to corner it.*

Leo approached the mausoleum, which seemed to grow in age with every step he took. Unlike the others in the cemetery, this one wasn't built with the grandeur of marble, sandstone, and brass. Rather, it was constructed using what appeared to be five roughly cut stone slabs, each eight feet in height, sixteen feet in length, and two feet thick. The stones were placed with two on either side, one that served as the back, and the fourth and fifth large cut stones capping the fortress and provided its floor. The iron gate seemed to be rustier than it originally appeared from a distance and there were no signs of an epitaph whatsoever. Leo inched closer to the now more ancient-looking building, reached out from the bottom stair, and gave the iron gate a shove. It was so timeworn that the lock no longer worked and swung roughly, as if it were in a tight bind, but made little to no sound.

Leo eyed the bird, who was happily staring at him with the copper coin in its beak, taunting Leo with its black pearl eyes and—uncharacteristic for a bird—standing quite still, only cocking his head from side-to-side.

Leo saw his chance and from the bottom step, he lunged after the crow. As he dove his left foot cleared the first two stairs, but his toes caught the top of the third. He was now crashing face first and headed directly for the crow. He threw out his arms, closed his eyes and, forgetting all about the crow and coin, braced for impact.

A second passed, then another, then another. The impact was impending now... another full second ticked by, and yet another... the impact wasn't coming.

Leo opened his eyes. There was nothing but darkness and a sense of falling. The smell of the air rushing past reminded him of the earth covering Grandpa Joe's grave as it careened by. He knew he was falling, but didn't understand, he was in the mausoleum—he must be dreaming. As soon as Leo let his guard down and wonder why he hadn't made impact with the hard-stone floor, he landed face first, on a hot, black, sandy shore.

Chapter 2

Leo stood up. There on the shore, next to his left foot, was the copper coin. He bent down to pick it up and dusted sand from its edges. Leo looked around, half-expecting to see someone but knowing he probably would not. The shore below his feet was black sand, but not as fine as the sand he pictured at a beach, this was different, much more course and it shifted with every step he took. It was also hot, so hot that he could feel it though the soles of his sneakers, but not so hot that it burned to the touch. Leo began to walk the shore, a black sulphuric river wound lazily off to his right, nothingness but the expansion of black sand to his left. He was surprisingly not scared, in this vast nothingness he felt nothing but confusion.

As he walked through the emptiness next to the dark river, sand crunching below his feet, he listened to the sound of the water slide across the shore. He could tell the water ahead made a slightly different lapping sound and he eventually came upon a dock, hidden in its dark color just like everything else around him. *The river Styx*, thought Leo. *Isn't that what Grandpa Joe and every other mythological book called it? I guess some religion had to be right, might as well have been one of the older stories. Wait, if that's Styx does that mean I'm in Hell? What did I do? I've been a good person—didn't cheat, didn't lie. Well, there was the one time in fourth grade where I used my calculator in math class during a test when we weren't supposed to... No, I can't be sent to hell for cheating on a math test, there must be some other explanation.*

As Leo was contemplating his faith and the absurdity of being in Hell, he didn't notice the flat-bottomed, two-chinned hull boat, slowly make its way to the dock. It hit the dock with a small, almost inaudible thump, which was just enough to pull Leo back from his internal thoughts. A figure, a tall, slender man, dressed in black, was holding what appeared to be a chain that stretched from one end of the murky water to the other. The foreboding darkness that stretched to the opposite side made it impossible to see the distant shoreline. The figure stood, waiting for Leo.

Leo walked towards the boat, eyeing the figure the entire time. As the figure came into better view, he could tell that the black cloak covered the figure's shoulders and sides. The cloak draped down far enough to sweep the bottom of the boat and covered the head. It did not, however, cover the torso or face. The figure's face was sullen, not quite a skull, but the skin was stretched so tight every feature of the possibly once human head was quite visible. The eyes and mouth were stretched open, never able to close, with dark-black barbed wire—that showed in sharp contrast to the putrefied white skin—clung tightly. The torso was also gaunt, showing signs of what appeared to be an old operation or autopsy scars and stitches, running from each shoulder down to the lower chest, meeting, and forming one jagged vertical line down to the waist. Where the waist was supposed to be, there was a gaping hole, allowing the figure's intestines to swing freely. The black, infected intestines were dotted with small, putrid white maggots. The maggots inched and crawled their way around the decaying entrails. Leo came to rest his eyes on the arms. The arms were cut deeply and through the rancid flesh he could see the muscle below ripple and tear with every slight movement. Around his slit throat hung a dark-brown amulet, barely visible from underneath the cloak. The figure could not speak, for the barbed wire holding its mouth open prevented words from being formed, but it did give a gesture of the head signaling to Leo that it was time to come aboard.

Leo, carefully, so as to not tip the boat, climbed on. Scared, it was odd that the only thing he could think about is not touching the figure and, strangely enough, not tipping the boat as to cause him and the figure to fall into the black and murky stench below. The figure held out its hand as if to request something.

Leo looked at the figure and, in almost a whisper—out of fear—and with his parched lips asked, "Charon?" The figure nodded with outstretched hand. Leo placed the copper coin, *the fee for Charon*, into his hand. With that, Charon turned towards the far bank, took hold of the chain linking the two sides, and began to pull.

Seconds turned to minutes, minutes into hours, and hours seemed as days. Leo was tired but could not close his eyes. He was thirsty, and while there appeared to be black and murky water all around him, he could not drink. All he could do is continue staring straight ahead. He couldn't think... he tried to recall the great times spent with Grandpa Joe, but he couldn't grasp a single memory. He tried to remember some of the names of friends, strike that, acquaintances from school but nothing would solidify in his racing mind. He couldn't even recall the face of his mom, who was the first person, as far as he knew, who held him to her breast and caressed his newborn head. Time continued on, and time was taking its toll in the form of faulty memory and the slip into madness.

As Leo stared in the distance, something caught his eye, *there right below the edge of the boat, was that blue? Blue water? I must be completely losing my mind. I'm dead, I can't remember anything. My life is definitely NOT flashing before my eyes. I'm seeing blue water in a sea of darkness, and my only company is Charon, who, for all intents and purposes, is going to torture me when we get to where we are going. Charon, with his taught face, his... wait, what happened to the barbed wire on his face? He's, he's, is he blinking? His mouth is closed, and he now has an almost human expression on his, well to be frank, his almost normal-looking face. The body is healing, yes, it's definitely healing, or is it changing? Do the dead heal?*

There was a splash to the right. Leo looked beyond Charon and there, in the distance, in silvery blue water, was a school of fish jumping from the surface. Leo turned back towards Charon who, by this time, was dressed in a sharp black suit, accompanied by a sky-blue vest, and matching tie. Leo was taking note of the contrast of Charon's appearance from just moments ago. The closer they got to their destination, the grander the transformation of Charon and the world around them.

Charon's face was beautiful with chiseled features, strong and perfect in size and shape. Within the light blue and flecks of deep green in his eyes, he felt he could see white clouds surrounding beautiful, lush, rolling hills. His coat was now neatly pressed, as were the slacks that adorned his legs. Everything was beautiful, right down to his polished black cap toed shoes and the expensive looking watch on his wrist. The boat itself was now a sight to behold, gold railings, cushioned seats, and a foldable footrest that could be flipped down from the inside of the seat.

Charon smiled. "The veil is thick today, but it is lifting. We're almost there."

Chapter 3

Charon slowed the small boat as it skidded up to the freshly painted white dock. The dock was only the beginning of the magic around him, without the hint or speck of debris or dust the simple structure seemed as though it was an impossibility. Leo looked down to the water lazily lapping up and down on the piles, not a single indication of wear or algae. Charon brought the boat to a stop with the ease of a skilled sailor. He jumped from the vessel to the dock and tied it to a single post with a length of silver chain.

"That will hold fine," Charon said with a smile and a wink in Leo's direction.

"What is this place," Leo said as he stepped up onto the dock. "Have I died? Is this Heaven? Purgatory? Who are you? And what happened to you? You were... you were..."

Charon laughed "It's not often we get visitors, normally only once in a generation. Trust me, I know. I've seen thousands of generations come and go, but only one at a time from your world. Each one having the same questions, and each one answered in all due time. Follow me, I don't have to be through the Veil again for... let's see..." Charon caught himself and trailed off before he said anything else.

"At the very least, tell me where we just came from. What was with all the darkness, doom and gloom, and YOU? You were hideous."

"Well, that's hitting below the belt now, isn't it," replied Charon.

"Don't get me wrong, the way you look now... well... now, you're definitely not hideous," Leo said in an apologetic manner. "It's just, you scared the Hell out of me across the river, or lake, or... or... what in the world did we just cross? At least give me something."

"Don't sweat the hideous remark." Charon laughed. "I'm meant to be hideous across and through the Veil."

"That again," remarked Leo. "Is that what you called where we came from?"

"Surely, Joe told you about it. At least, he told me the last time I spoke with him that he was going to. In fact, I absolutely know he told you about it, otherwise you wouldn't have had the fee to cross.

"Joe told you that there was a 'world set apart by a Veil so thin that if it were known, could be broken with the slightest touch of the lightest feather'. And he gave you my fee knowing that once you had the fee, you would always have the fee. Exact change, if you will. Of course, throughout the millennium the Veil has been thickened, quite a bit, actually. As you can tell, it can no longer be broken with the slightest touch of a feather."

"Am I dead? I seem to remember he said something about the Veil being a symbol of death."

"You're only remembering half of the story, my boy. I believe he said the Veil became a symbol of death, rather than the thin line separating your world from ours. I think he actually used the term 'light and love'. That Joe, he always could make things sounds more glamorous than I; he sure had a way with words."

"So, I'm not dead? What about my family? They will eventually come looking for me and when they can't find me, they will start canvasing the area, my school, call the police, call out the dogs... well, maybe not the dogs... but I'm sure they will look for me. When they can't find me, I'm going to be in more trouble than you could ever imagine. If I'm not dead, then I must be dreaming... that's it... I knocked myself out chasing that silly bird and I'm out cold on the floor of that miserable mausoleum."

Charon laughed. "You're not dead, Leo, and I wouldn't worry about your family trying to find you just yet. And for the love of all that balances your world and ours, don't call it a silly bird."

"Charon, what am I supposed to believe if I'm not dead, not knocked out, and not supposed to worry about the consequences when I get home?"

"Oh, there are always consequences to worry about, but don't think of that now. Once we get where we're going, all the pieces will fall neatly into place. AND, before you ask, just follow me and don't worry, you can trust me; your Grandpa Joe always did."

Leo followed Charon as he jumped off the dock and casually made his way towards the town. The street was paved with highly polished green bricks, with mesmerizing black lines strung through. There was no pattern to the black veins, but they always met uniformly brick-by-brick. Leo stood in the middle, staring down in wonder. Confused and intrigued by the simple complexity.

"Polished chrysoprase," Charon called back from a few yards ahead, "very common here. Now come on, I can't explain everything you see during your first ten minutes."

Leo kept pace and caught up with Charon but continued to scan the wonderous new world that was beginning to feel oddly familiar. There wasn't a single car or any other type of motorized transportation, rather, everyone either walked or rode what appeared to be horses of various shapes and sizes. The largest horse-like creatures were no less than four meters high, with thick muscles, short manes, and hooves the size of large dinner plates. They pulled heavy wagons that, at first glance, appeared to be armored but in reality, were fortified to handle their heavy wares. Smaller horses seemed to be the common mode for personal transportation. Sleek, well-behaved, and with a gait smoother than anything Leo had ever seen on wheels.

Leo jumped as one of the horses passed and turned its muzzle towards its rider. As it did, flames shot out over the rider, who unlike Leo, didn't flinch. "Did you see that?" Leo marveled at no one in particular.

The buildings were made of a rough, antiqued wood, thick enough to withstand a gale-force wind, and were a beautiful contrast to the highly polished road. Most appeared to be shops and their lead crystal windows advertised the merchandise within: Mr. Perennials Amalgamated Herbs; Livret's Libraries: Libraries fixed while you wait; Owen Commissary & Supply; and The Aesthetic Citizen. They were adorned with freshly cleaned entrances surrounded by strange, brown and pink flowers that would follow the passersby, as though the flowers were people watching. None of the buildings stood more than a few stories high. For the most part, the buildings were so short that all of the shadows were small, allowing for the most beautiful and velvety sun he had ever seen to warm the area around each corner. In fact, as Leo marveled at the buildings and contemplated the shadows that were being cast, he began to wonder if the shadows were playing tricks on him. *How could one shadow face one direction and face another?*

He scanned overhead and saw a second sun, just as beautiful as the first. They weren't the same brilliant yellow that he was used to; rather, they were a soft yellow with a hint of violet and silver encircling both.

The inhabitants of this strange and beautiful world were diverse, just like back home... old, young, various colored hair and skin, but back home everyone was human. Giant men and women walked amongst the human forms, being careful not to knock anyone over or to break any of the solid thick wood buildings. The buildings, although low, were just large enough for giants to be comfortable when doing business. There were also smaller creatures—roughly the size of a loaf of bread—both flying and walking the streets in a manner so nimble they would make even the smoothest of flowing water envious. A few of these minuscule creatures were flying alongside the giants; holding conversations and laughing, as old friends do.

Overhead, large scaled birds—of every color of the rainbow—swooped in and out of the community and occasionally went into one of the many shops. Leo peered through the window of The Magpie as one of the hued, scaled birds entered. Leo watched as the bird picked up a white apron with his beak, expertly threw it over its long neck, gave one of the humans a thumbs— or rather, claws—up, and proceeded to blow fire into the bottom a large cast iron stove, in order to bake the fresh pastries that left a glorious smell wafting through the air.

"Dragon," shouted Leo, "tiny dragons!" Turning his head to look for Charon, who was by now, far ahead. Leo took one more look before turning to catch up to Charon, who was happily strolling along and greeting everyone with a friendly wave.

As they turned a corner past a populated area, he caught glimpse of a lush city park. There ladies walking together were giggling and smiling, as they walked along the most gorgeously manicured grass, he had ever laid eyes on. With each barefoot, he could see that the blades of grass seem to come alive and tickle the feet of the park's well-dressed visitors. The middle held a grand carousal. As the carousal rotated, Leo could see contained carved wooden creatures of both beauty and terrifying beast that would have given him horrid nightmares as a child.

As Leo walked and continued staring at the strange and wonderful sights, he momentarily forgot he was trailing behind and ran smack into the back of a stopped Charon.

"Here we are," exclaimed Charon. "Isn't it a beauty?"

Leo gathered himself from the abrupt halt and peered skyward. There standing before him, stood a building that extended far into the sky—much higher than the modest shops along the street—designed in the shape of a perfectly round sphere, completely constructed of polished stone, similar to the streets below. The magnificent speared structure was a highly polished light brown—almost tan—emboldened with veins of garnet and gold, with an ancient aura surrounding it. It had the same windows as the other buildings but were convex to meet the form of the structure. Although they were curved, they moved in a way that allowed for whomever was on the other side to view the world from different angles without the need to move themselves.

"Heliotrope, also known as Bloodstone," commented Charon, smiling as he enjoyed watching the young Leo take in the sights. "It's one of the hardest substances in the Realm, yet surprisingly easy to use in construction as long as you apply the right magic. Let's go in, shall we? There is someone who would like to meet you."

Leo followed Charon up the polished stairs into an arched doorway that above read, "AMICORUM OBLITUS PROELIO CARLUXS BELLO NOLI OBLIVISCI".

"What does that mean?" Leo asked, pointing upward toward the words engraved in the archway.

"Oh, it's our motto written in Latin, a popular language at the time. I suppose the founders of the Realm decided it sounded like words to live by and the architect must have agreed. It translates loosely into *Never forget our friends in battle; never forget our enemies in war.* It reminds us to treat all with basic dignity. I wouldn't worry too much about it; we haven't seen conflict since before my time and I pray we won't see it again during my lifetime. Come on, we don't want to keep her waiting."

If Leo thought the outside of the sphere was beautiful, the inside was breathtaking. A large hall gilded with the same type of stone—but this time silver—adorned the great room. A fountain of polished silver stood in the middle with three figures: one male, one female, and one androgynous; facing one another and holding hands, while crystal clear water poured over their bodies. The water seemed to appear from nowhere—as Leo could not see its source—and it pooled ever so calmly in the center of the twenty-meter circumference pool. Koi fish lazily swam around the bottom, seemingly in ignorant bliss of the artistry surrounding them. On all sides of the hall were large wooden doors with brass handles, dotting between the glorious windows. The wooden doors were the first porous building material Leo remembered seeing in the hall, but he had a feeling that they so heavily polished that they were had become stronger than any timber from his world.

"Over here," pointed Charon, as he made his way to the large wooden door at the far side of the hall and ceremoniously pulled at the handle and stepped away.

Leo entered, ensuring not to trip over his own feet.

"May I present to you, the magnificent, Lady Cybele."

"Sir Leonardo, it's an honor and privilege to finally meet the grandson of the Great Sir Joseph Kane," Lady Cybele said with a gentle smile.

Lady Cybele was older, but not so old that Leo couldn't put a guess to her age. She appeared to be roughly seventy, standing dignified and moved with the grace of royalty. She was dressed in a dark amber dress, that effortlessly clung to her, and a black cape around her shoulders, providing both warmth and practicality. Accompanying her was a girl Leo's age, and at first sight Leo's heart jump into his throat, his face grew flush, and his knees became weak as a newborn. She had long dark hair, tanned skin with a beautiful glow, and deep brown eyes that seemed to look right through him.

Lady Cybele glided towards Leo and embraced him in a brief, but heartfelt, hug. When she released her embrace, she turned towards the girl and smiled. "Leo, please meet my ward, Angel Dianna."

Angel gave Leo a friendly enough wave, but made it apparent she was already bored with his company.

"Please, sit," she instructed, as she motioned to three chairs that, upon her command, glided towards them.

"Whoa," Leo exclaimed, jumping back. "What was that?"

"Magic, of course."

Lady Cybele and Charon sat beside each other, leaving the third chair—situated across from them—free for Leo. Angel snapped her fingers and a fourth chair appeared before her. She sat at a distance in order to listen, having no desire to participate in the conversation.

"Tell me Sir Leonardo, what has your grandfather told you in regard to your lineage and powers?" Lady Cybele asked with an inquisitive look.

"Lineage and powers?" Leo repeated part of the question.

"Why yes, dear. Oh, I was afraid of this. Sir Joseph didn't have the time needed in order to complete your training. Oh dear, oh dear, indeed. I suppose he had only begun to start when he was taken from your world. I had better start from the beginning, and we can hopefully catch you up in the end."

Leo looked between them, more confused now than when they arrived.

"There are multiple worlds Sir Leonardo; in fact, more worlds than even I know. In this world, Elysium, we are comprised of four realms. You are currently in the Spring Crow, and our realm attempts to balance life with work and enjoyment. Nobody is forced to accomplish a task or profession that he or she wasn't born to do. Some take over for their parents, some are set upon their own path, but all professions are enjoyable to the individual and all are needed for daily life," Lady Cybele explained. "Not only are individuals born to perform certain tasks, once an expert, the fruits of their labor assist in our magic."

"That explains a little of where I am, but why am I here and what about the magic? How did I get here and how did you know Grandpa Joe?"

"Oh my, you really did just start your training didn't you," sighed Lady Cybele with obvious concern. "Your Grandfather, Sir Joseph of the Knights of Kane, was a Jinn Knight. His son, your father, was meant to be his successor, but he wouldn't answer the call. He instead turned his back on your grandfather's tales and guidance and sought out what he believed to be his own path in your world. Perhaps, I had better go back further than the beginning—to the birth of the Jinn."

Leo sat in confused silence.

"Years ago, maybe three-quarters of a billion years or so, give or take, when the Earth was cool and harbored life in its densest forms, an internal struggle was happening in the first realm, the Cardinal Realm."

Charon sat back and smiled.

"In the Cardinal Realm was a great leader, wise and as old as the universe itself, whom had three sons, Theiler, Garaile, and Kane. Each of the three was Jinn from birth."

"Jinn?" asked Leo.

"Yes, Jinn," she continued. "There are three orders of Jinn and each son was naturally born into one of the orders, and each of different mother. The orders include conquerors, dividers, and intelligence—all with walker ability. All Jinn are walkers, and all walkers can traverse worlds. For example, the journey from your world into ours.

"The three brothers all wanted to seek the favor of their father in order to control all four realms of Elysium. The first, Garaile, was born a conqueror. None, save the Cardinal Leader, was a true match for his swordplay. His brothers, being of the same blood, could survive his brutality, but never overcome his skills. He believed in ruling with an iron fist, and that he would someday rule in his father's place.

"Theiler, the second born, was a divider. In an attempt to gain favor, would spread lies and rumors about his brothers to his father. He felt that if he divided his brothers from his father, and his brothers from each other, he could gain favor and one day rule the Cardinal Realm and Elysium.

"Finally, Kane was an intelligent soldier. He looked at both the strengths and faults of his brothers and reported to his father. Their father—knowing that there would be internal strife and bloodshed within the family so long as he lived—decreed that each son, each sect of Jinn, only be able to travel to one of the four realms as well as one of the many worlds on another plane. This, he felt, would provide separation and time for each brother to control his own destiny rather than attempt to control all destinies. Your Jinn ancestor, Kane, was given access to the Spring Crow Realm and your earthly world.

"Finally, all Jinn can travel back to the Cardinal Realm with the permission of the Cardinal Leader. While the fighting between Jinn continues, an uneasy peace has been preserved for millions of years. Jinn are warriors, magicians, protectors, and on occasion, enemies."

"How does that explain my presence here?" prodded Leo.

"Haven't you been listening, Sir Leonardo? One of the sons, Kane, was born into the order of intelligence. You, Sir Leonardo Joseph Kane, are a direct decedent and member of the Intelligence Jinn. That gives you the ability to travers into our world, specifically our realm and your world. Only one Jinn from each sect has power at any one time, so at the time of your grandfather's passing, the responsibility was passed to you."

"Me?" exclaimed Leo. "What about my Dad? Why isn't he here instead of me?"

"Sir Joseph attempted to pass the ways of the Jinn, and its magic, to your father but your father refused the call. Instead he chose to focus on the ways of the physical world that he could touch and see. As he grew, he told your grandfather that he had no need for fairytales of other worlds, magic, and higher learning on a higher plane. He pursued the path of mortal man."

"Is that why their relationship never seemed like that of father and son?"

"Yes, and it is also the reason Sir Joseph needed to train another Knight of Jinn, before it was too late. What normally takes decades would have to be compressed into very little time. Unfortunately for Sir Joseph, his time ran out as he was just beginning your training."

"Okay, if I'm in this intelligence business and can perform magic, why am I just an average student with no special abilities?"

"Because Sir Joseph had not yet introduced you to your library," Lady Cybele stated. With that, she raised her right hand, waved it from the middle of her body and slightly to the right, and said the words, "*Forthwith Knowledge*," and a door appeared before her. "Follow me," she smiled. "We need to start your training immediately."

Leo, Charon, and Lady Cybele walked through the door into the most beautiful and expansive library Leo had ever laid eyes on. Comparatively, the library at his school was a closet full of near worthless paper. Leather-bound books of Earthly classics lined the walls, accompanied with what he assumed as other world classics. Books of spells, potions, herbology, weaponry, and war also dotted the room. Finally, hundreds, if not thousands, of other well-worn books in languages Leo could not understand finished the collection.

"All the knowledge you will ever need is located in your library. While here feel free to browse, but only I can open my library. Would you like to see yours?"

Leo, still wide-eyed with amazement, nodded.

"Good," she said. "Shall we?"

The three exited Lady Cybele's library and re-entered the hall. Leo had not forgotten about Angel who was still in the hall, but she seemed to have forgotten about Leo. She was now preoccupied with the hem of her dress, as if all of was boring her to tears.

"Complete," Lady Cybele stated, waving her hand and closing the door, which simultaneously disappeared from sight.

"Now, do as I do. Sometimes it's easier to start with the words out loud, later you can just think of the proper incantation when you summon your library. Raise your right hand to about eye level, wave it slightly to the right, and say *Forthwith Knowledge.*"

Leo did as he was instructed. Nothing. As he was about to try again, a single page of paper appeared, floating to the floor from above.

"Bravo," exclaimed Charon.

"I don't understand," Leo muttered as he bent down and snatched it from the marble floor. "This is just an old scrap of paper."

"It's your library contract," explained Lady Cybele. "Charon, summon a blood pen so we can finish the agreement."

As instructed, Charon waved his right hand up, muttered something Leo couldn't understand, and before him appeared a silver pen placed vertically on a shimmering blue disk. The disk had a small hole where the pen was inserted, and the side of the disk also had a small hole. He held the disk holding the pen in front of Leo.

"Place your index finger into the hole on the side of the disk Sir Joseph," instructed Lady Cybele.

Leo placed his finger into the hole and a needle shot up, sticking into his finger "Ouch!"

Leo instinctively started to pull back from the stick, only to be stopped by Charon. "Stay still, let the pen do its work" stated Lady Cybele.

Leo watched in amazement as the pen began to draw his blood into its chamber through a thin cavity.

Once the pen was filled, the needle released and Leo could withdraw his finger, which he promptly put into his mouth to ease the pain.

"Fantastic," said Charon. He presented the pen to Leo and exclaimed, "this is your blood pen, now and forever. Whatever you sign will become binding by your own will."

Leo took the blood pen and instinctively knew what he was to do next. He glanced back and forth from Lady Cybele, Charon, and Angel—who still didn't feign the slightest interest—and with as much concentration as he could muster, signed his library contract, and it faded into a memory right before his eyes.

Charon grinned. "I'd place the pen in your jacket pocket... well, we will get you a jacket. For now, please keep it in a safe place until you need it again."

"Now, Sir Leonardo," Lady Cybele looked at Leo with all seriousness. "I want you to understand that you now own your library. It has been passed down through the Kane family for over a millennium. Summon your library as taught."

Leo raised his right hand again, waved right, and said the words "*Forthwith Knowledge.*" Immediately, a single non-descript, brown leather-bound book appeared in his left hand. *My library is one book, thanks Grandpa Joe*, thought Leo, as he gave a disappointed sigh.

Charon gave an audible gasp. Angel, suddenly interested, jumped from her seated position and put her hand over her mouth, her eyes wide.

"Oh my," whispered Lady Cybele. "This is much better than I had hoped for, you are more powerful than I ever imagined."

Chapter 4

Sometime following the lesson on summoning his personal library, Leo and Charon made their way to Charon's house. Not unlike the other buildings from the outside—save a nautical themed door knocker—inside the main quarters, reminded Leo of an eighteenth-century Victorian lounge. The walls were adorned with sea foam green striped wallpaper and between the stripes green circular designs laced a white border. The floor was covered with lush red carpet laid out in a large rectangular pattern, and the furniture... *Oh Lord, the furniture.* An upright piano sat in one corner and a large, polished, wooden wet bar in the other. Opposite the entrance sat a grand fireplace adorned with a mantle constructed of the same material as the road, which—thankfully—matched the wallpaper, in an odd way. The art which decorated the room depicted ancient wooden ships, both trading and whaling vessels of the late seventeenth century, some with two masts and rigged sails, others lumbering with full sails. Finally, several Rococo-styled chaise lounges adorned in mahogany and covered in thick brown leather—a stark contrast to the rest of the room—tied the eclectic style together.

"Make yourself at home," Charon said. "Would you like anything to drink?" Charon paused and considered his question, "are you old enough to drink?"

"Well... I," stammered Leo.

"Wait, I have just the thing." Charon disappeared down a winding staircase Leo hadn't noticed before and returned a short time later. "I have a barrel of fine, freshly squeezed mapleberry juice in the cellar. Here, you should have a glass."

Leo put the glass of orange and brown, hypnotically swirling mixture to his lips and took a small sip. "Wow," exclaimed Leo, "this is one of the most delicious things I've ever tasted."

"Should be, it's been fermenting for over fifteen hundred years." Charon smiled. "It will help you keep your strength up. You must be tired, but I need to finish explaining how you arrived, in accordance with of Lady Cybele's wishes."

Leo knew it was pointless in arguing and he succumbed to the fact that he was not in a dream, so he settled into a chaise lounge and prepared for an explanation.

"In order to get to Spring Crow from your world you first off must be a Jinn, which Lady Cybele has already explained, and as you now know there can only be one Jinn from each sect or order, which is now you."

Leo nodded in understanding

"In order to find the opening to Spring Crow, the process is simple. When it's time the Crow will find you. He will get your attention in any way possible and lead you to an area where you are alone, with no one in sight or within earshot. Then, all you do is close your eyes and dive in."

"Dive in? What are you talking about? Dive into what?"

"The mausoleum, of course, you dive into the mausoleum. Just like your Grandpa Joe said, 'the belly of the whale can take many forms', and in this case, you entered the gateway accessible by the mausoleum. That is the gateway into the veil and then onward to the Spring Crow."

Leo's head began to reel, either from the mapleberry juice or the fact that he had been informed that he entered into a hidden world through the ancient mausoleum. "You mean to tell me that I physically went through the solid stone of the mausoleum? That's impossible, it's physically impossible."

"Of course, it is," winked Charon, "unless, of course, you have magic and the fee." "Speaking of magic," Leo continued, "Lady Cybele said I was descended from the Jinn. If that's true, are there more? Where are they? Are they family? Did Grandpa Joe know them?"

"Ah, jumping right in, I see. Good. I was wondering how I could explain where Lady Cybele left off. We knew you would have questions." Charon took a seat on the chair opposite Leo, leaned back, crossed his legs and began.

"Years ago, before we could measure time and some say, before time as we know it existed, there was a king, King Acadamel, of the Cardinal Realm, the oldest of all known realms. King Acadamel had three sons: Garaile, Theiler, and Kane. All three sons grew up mastering the art of magic under the watchful eye of a tutor—whose name has long been forgotten to history.

"The tutor was, at the time, the most powerful magician in the land. It is told that there is nothing he could not do and nobody he could not teach. Both dark and light magic was taught, but the brothers were as opposite as three can be. The eldest brother, Garaile, believed in only victory through conquer and conquest. He wanted, or felt that he needed, control of the Cardinal Realm and all realms, as such, he attempted to destroy his brothers any way possible. When he was younger, his choice of weapon was poison. As he grew older, his rage became more evident and he would battle his brothers with both weapons and poison whenever he had the chance. He not only learned the art of magic, but also the art of the sword and shield, wielding each with such power and accuracy none, save his brothers, came close as his equal. He believed that if his brothers no longer existed, he would be the sole heir and ruler of the Cardinal Realm and all other realms."

"Theiler was the second brother and a loner. Theiler was a man who relished in the division of people, the realms, and worlds. While he tolerated the company of his brothers, while he was at home in solitude, he reveled in being served by others for all of his desires. He truly believed that all should be controlled by one but meant to divide all for his personal pleasure and gain. He grew powerful in his beliefs and spread rumors of deceit about both of his brothers and the realm to his father. Theiler thought that if his father trusted him, he would gain control of the realm and use the citizens of the realm to do his bidding, to do everything he commanded, and rule with an iron fist. He would be content with power when nobody else was content... division of all, ruled by him."

"Finally, there was the youngest, Kane, who was an intellectual, studying military strategies, weaponry, and war. While simultaneously practicing magic and weaponry like his brothers, he also read and experienced all that he could. He was the people's soldier—believing if all fought for the same cause of righteousness, all would be free. He truly believed that if the Cardinal Realm could learn to be victorious in any cause, any war with the worlds could result in peace. He would inform his father of his brother's strengths and weaknesses in order to strengthen the realm."

"So, the brothers weren't close?"

"On the contrary, they remained close while studying magic, but only to understand the others' weaknesses. Years, hundreds of years, some say thousands, went by and each brother became stronger and more convinced of their own power and beliefs."

"I have a feeling you're not going to tell me they get together for family picnics"

Charon chuckled. "Not quite. In fact, their love of power and want for control of the Cardinal Realm ultimately tore them apart. Following a spectacular dinner one evening, Theiler, the second born, began discussing heritage with his brothers and—Theiler being Theiler—devised a plan to further divide his brothers by pulling at their hearts. He began by speaking lovely words and phrase of how he adored his mother. His mother, he said, was the most righteous, beautiful, and well-respected woman in all of the realms."

"That's an awful thing to say to a brother. If the king had three sons from three mothers, I'm sure each were equally as righteous and beautiful."

"Theiler further elaborated that this was easily proven and without question. He could argue that as his mother was the second choice of Acadamel, as she was chosen and required to replace the first and inferior wife." Charon paused and shifted his weight. "It is said that Theiler told his brothers that his father had personally confided in him, that when he first laid eyes on her beauty, he knew that no other could ever take her place and that she alone would bear him a son worthy of the Cardinal Realm"

Leo contemplated this. She was, after all, Theiler's mother, *why wouldn't he express his love towards her to his brothers?*

Charon continued, "Theiler didn't stop with only loving words for his mother. He turned to Garaile and then spoke of *his* mother."

"Garaile, your mother is a handsome woman, a handsome woman indeed. There is no doubt that she was built for work, with her stout legs, her ample hips, and arms as strong as the mightiest of all the men in the realm. I'm sure Acadamel found use for her in the fields as well as in the bedchamber. Yes, I'm sure you were birthed first to provide over watch of my armies once I ascend to my rightful place."

Theiler then turned to Kane. "And *your* mother, as unassuming and submissive as they come. Acadamel found her one day buried in her own thoughts, neither eating nor drinking. She took no sustenance whatsoever for she feared the time to pause for such activity would take away from her education. Poor soul, the only reason Acadamel took her under his roof was to ensure her survival. Yes, when she gained her strength, she thanked him in the only manner she knew. As with all of her learned ways, she did not know love; only to resign to others wants. How else do you think you were conceived to understand so much about everything, yet nothing all at once?"

"How would that place a divide between his brothers?" Leo asked.

"Easy," said Charon. "The love they had for their mothers and the words of Theiler caused a divide by planting a seed of doubt, by the thought that each son alone loved their mothers and that Acadamel never did and never would. If he didn't love their mothers could he truly love them as sons? Theiler was like the snake, staying low in the grass, claiming his territory and spouting venomous words in order to twist his will."

Leo began to see how this simplistically well-thought-out plan would work based on the emotions of the brothers. While he knew his mother loved him while she was alive, even if she didn't always show it as Leo had wished, he would never tolerate anyone speaking ill of her.

"While the divide grew, Garaile," Charon continued, "the warrior of the family, believed the only way he could truly become the heir to the Cardinal Realm, was to prove to Acadamel that he, and he alone, was strong enough to rule. On the morning of the first day in fall following his middle brother's hurtful words, he arose and decided to take one of his steeds for a run through the forest surrounding the Cardinal Realm. He saddled the beast, sheathed his weapons, called his hounds, and began his journey east into the Autumn Suns.

"It sounds like he wanted to cool off a bit," Leo said.

"Not quite," Charon said. "As morning turned to afternoon, Garaile came upon a brook where his brothers were sitting, talking of philosophy and arguing as to how civilization should live by their specific rules. Garaile, seeing an opportunity, dismounted some distance away, snuck up on his two brothers, and struck each with blows to the head and shoulders so fast and fierce that any mortal would have had their life forces drained away into the babbling brook."

"But they were okay? They didn't die?"

"Theiler was gashed in a way that blood poured from his head into his eyes and could not see where the attack originated or were the next may come. Kane, although wounded, slashed from stem-to-stern, was able to summon a spell to heal himself enough to transform into a crow and took flight to fight another day. Perched in a giant oak tree, still thick with golden autumn leaves and hidden from Garaile's wrath, he summoned a spell to force the brook to wash up onto Theiler, clear his eyes from the spurts of blood, and whisked him away from the danger. Kane knew Theiler was in no condition to fight and that his middle brother cherished division, by sweeping him downstream, he created the division Theiler craved. Garaile, thinking that Theiler had succumbed to his wounds and Kane a coward, rode back to Acadamel to inform him of his brothers' weaknesses and insist that if they were not strong enough to defend themselves, they should never be in control of the army nor the realm."

"So that means Kane is the good guy."

"None of the brothers were without sin. Kane, being a learned scholar, but not as experienced in combat as his brothers, devised a plan to teach his brothers a lesson. While they slept soundly in their separate chambers, he plotted his revenge. First, he crept into Theiler's slumber, whispered, "*Limpid Serpentia*", causing his brother to transform into a translucent snake. He then went into Garaile's room and whispered, "*Snow Crocodylidae*," in which he turned into a snow-white crocodile as he slept. The next morning when the two brothers woke for their morning rituals with their father, Acadamel not seeing his sons but wild animals, attacked each with such veracity that each brother fled, not knowing any other course of action as their father had never raised a weapon towards them in anger. Kane, standing beside his father, laughed and told Acadamel how foolish his brothers were to allow an intruder into their chambers. If they were so careless then how could they rule? Upon finally witnessing the disastrous results of his sons' arguments, King Acadamel confined each brother to separate palace towers while he consulted with their tutor, telling the tutor all, which had never done before outside of the bloodline."

Leo thought about the decision to go outside of the family for advice, "If Acadamel were to go to anyone, why not the mothers?"

"You have to remember that the mothers would not have been an honest broker for any of the three as they were too close. The tutor, on the other hand, was the perfect arbitrator and he knew the sons as well, if not better, than their own father. The tutor advised Acadamel to slay each of his sons and create a fresh bloodline free from strife."

"But he didn't do it, right? Otherwise, why would I be here now?"

"The story is far from over Leo. After hearing the advice to destroy his kin, Acadamel dismissed the tutor and contemplated his next decision. After months of thought he banished the poor tutor away to an unknown realm; for it was improper for an outsider to know of intimate details of the royal family affairs. He appreciated the tutor's past service and current candor, so he gave him enough for a modest life and ordered that he not return to the Cardinal Realm until summoned. After banishing the tutor, Acadamel decreed that no brother was worthy of rule and banned each of his sons to one of the three remaining realms; allowing only one brother at a time to return to the Cardinal Realm and only then with his permission. As a father he could not bear the thought of killing his flesh, as they rightfully deserved, but he could no longer allow them to remain."

"That's horrible, he had to tear his own family apart to save them from themselves," said Leo.

Charon continued, "Being compassionate to their Jinn and walker birth, naturally going from realm-to-realm and world-to-world, he banished each son to a separate realm and allowed for travel to one world of their choosing, which were separated as well. He summoned each individually from their tower to administer his ruling and he presented each with a choice. To either live under his rule, to never again fight within the Cardinal Realm, or to be banished to roam their own lesser realms, possibly never to return. This gift from the father, the gift of a choice, was met by all three with the same denial. All felt he should be the next ruler of all the realms."

"That must have been extremely hard for a father," Leo stated while thinking of his own father in a world far away.

"I'm sure it was heart-wrenching, but Acadamel was furious. As a leader, his word was everything to him and was his reputation. He scourged all for their decisions and reminded each of their actions, of why they had been chastised, and to ensure they contemplate their actions and consequences. One-by-one he banished his flesh and blood as well as their descendants to come."

Leo started to speak, but Charon held up a hand.

"Taking what little pity he had left in his heart, he banished his youngest, Kane, last. Before he sent the weaker warrior to a possible lifetime away from the Cardinal Realm, he presented the youngest with a gift. His intelligent soldier received a black crow on a shield of blue, clutched on a silver chain, to be used when Kane learned control over his wisdom. Your ancestor Kane was banished to our realm, so named the Spring Crow Realm, and he chose your world to dwell. Once separated, King Acadamel created the veils, thin enough to protect the realms, worlds, and his subjects, but magically strong enough to prevent the crossing of realms by those forbidden. Each Realm is protected by multiple veils and the Spring Crow is protected by the Water Veil, the Mountain Veil, and the Forest Veil. King Acadamel granted crossing powers to very few in order to keep a link between the realms, I am one of those special few, a Gadaseer, a trait passed down through family. Supposedly, all realms have one, but it's a very rare trait and I've never met another. Although I can adventure into other realms, I prefer to spend my time in the Spring Crow."

Leo stared at Charon, not quite understanding what he was being told.

"I digress," Charon said. "The veils are protected by forces unseen until they themselves desire to be seen, forces that are meant to protect the innocent, and, some say, warn of the future. Even with the veils and their protections, the fighting continues today and the ancestors of Theiler and Garaile are still attempting to control the Cardinal Realm, to break free from their assigned realm, and control the Cardinal Realm and in time, all the realms and known worlds in existence. War still continues even if there is a tentative peace. Some say the ancestors of Garaile are plotting revenge through war, but none have appeared since the banishment. Others say Theiler is building an army to divide and rule through lies and fear. Most agree that both are honing and practicing their magic. I can be certain that the ancestors of Kane, your ancestors, have continued to learn, but the rage within, while not gone, has subsided."

"But I don't have rage," Leo began to argue.

"Today," continued Charon, "the realms continue in separation but stories of long ago have been either forgotten or twisted. The world you know, for example, has portrayed all other worlds as evil, torturous, or make-believe. This is obviously untrue. You have witnessed our realm and know our hearts are true, we live in balance and appreciate and seek knowledge. In the distant past, some have tried to break through to our realm in order to destroy us out of fear. Due to these attempts meant for destruction, the veils, once thin, have grown, expanded and made so fearsome that all, save the rightful Jinn, cower and flee at its very thought. This is one of the veils you witnessed today"

Leo sat for what seemed like hours, trying to understand his lineage passed from his grandpa, through his dad, and had allowed him to find himself here in the Spring Crow. "I'm a Knight of the Jinn, descendant of Kane, and my specialty is knowledge. I have family who wish to destroy me, and I can walk through the Veil from my world to yours."

"That sums it up."

"But, I'm average. How can knowledge and warrior blood be part of my power, of my past?"

Charon sighed. "It's not just your knowledge; it's the knowledge and warrior responsibility of all Jinn. Summon your library, let me show you something."

Leo raised his hand. "*Forthwith Knowledge.*" The leather book appeared.

"Now, think of something you want to know, concentrate on the question, and open your library."

Leo thought. He opened the book and read. "*The realm will rumble, the unity will split, the tutor and student will be as one again.* This is nothing but a riddle, how can I understand my lineage and interpret the library if all it's going to do is give me gibberish?"

"Not quite," smiled Charon. "When the time comes, you will understand. Your library will always tell you what you need to know, and it will always give you the answers you need. Trust it and be specific with your questions. You don't need to tell me what you asked, I'm sure it's correct."

"Why do I only have a single book when Lady Cybele had a beautiful room?"

"Because her library is formed and appears to supplement the magic in her, that's the way it works. All have libraries of a certain size and her library is amazing. With your library, on the other hand, all information that ever was, can be found in a single book, a single turn of the page. Powerful magic indeed, that of which I've never seen. Why, even your grandfather had a small oak shelf with at least a few dozen volumes."

Leo, seeing enough for now, with eyes drooping, thought *Complete*. The library disappeared.

"You've had a big day, bigger than most, and you need to rest up for tomorrow's gala."

"What gala?"

"Why, the annual Jinn Ball? It's the biggest event of the season and you're the guest of honor," Charon smiled. "As I said, you've had a long day Leo and don't worry about the gala, it's going to be great and I can answer any questions you have tomorrow. If I don't have the answer, you can always consult your library. Now, it's time for me to show you to your room."

Charon led Leo to a door, covered in the same wallpaper as the walls, and pushed it opened to reveal a small room. The room was not nearly large enough for someone to be comfortable in, even for someone Leo's size. "There you go, I'll get you in the morning for breakfast. We're having cotton muffins with cream."

"W-wait," Leo stammered. "Where is the bed? Do I lie on the floor?"

"Silly me, I don't normally have guests, and I've never hosted someone who is still learning magic. Simply state *Eventide Slumber*, while giving a wave."

"*Eventide Slumber*," Leo repeated and the room, as though in slow motion, duplicated his room back home. His clothes and bed—even his books—where all right where he left them. He reached for one of his books, thought of what he wanted, turned the page, and... *nope, still not the right place.*

"Very nice," said Charon as he peered in. "Although, it could use a theme, pirates maybe. I have a few pictures of some of my old friends, folks who would make your Black Beard look like a Baptist Minister in your world."

"No, that's alright, I think it's good the way it is, for now. Thanks for the offer, though."

"How about a framed photo of your grandfather?"

"That," said Leo, "would be a perfect addition."

Charon snapped his fingers and a gilded frame of Grandpa Joe, dressed in his typical impeccability, appeared on the chest of drawers.

Leo smiled. "Goodnight, Charon."

"Goodnight, Leo."

Leo readied himself for bed, lied down, and closed his eyes. Visions of brothers fighting, gore, and bloodshed ran through his mind, making it hard to sleep even through his exhaustion. Finally, his mind drifted to the last thing Charon said in passing, something about a gala, a Jinn Ball, and that he'd be the guest of honor. *How can he say not to worry after everything I've learned tonight?* His mind drifted. *I wonder if Angel will be there. I don't think she likes me, but she is so pretty...* Leo fell into a deep sleep.

Chapter 5

Charon made the second-best cotton muffins with cream in Spring Crow, second only to the Magpie Bakery. "Due to the fact," Charon stated matter-of-factly, "that the Magpie is able to better control the temperature because Clivelhorn—their finest employee and a very detailed oriented dragon—would ensure just the right amount of caramelization on top." The simple concoction consisted of eggs from the sonkress bird whipped feverishly with mikva cheese and placed in pans and set to bake for forty minutes. They finished light as a cloud and when topped with the cream Charon had on hand. Leo couldn't help himself but to ask for seconds—and thirds.

"You must have slept well; you definitely woke with your appetite."

"Yeah, I didn't think I was that exhausted, but I don't remember falling asleep, let alone dreaming. How long was I out?"

"Not too long, although you did miss the morning sun rises... you should have seen the first. Normally, at least one of the four moons are still reflecting, but this morning none were visible; the colors over Spring Crow gave me the chills. But you woke just in time to get cleaned up, so we can head into town to buy some clothes for tonight's main event."

Leo suddenly remembered thinking about the upcoming Jinn Ball, as well as other things, as he was drifting off to asleep. He had angst about going to a formal event where he barely knew anyone and would be the guest of honor. *Oh God, Angel will probably be there too*, he suddenly worried. *I'm going to look like a complete idiot in front of her, I just know it.* From what he understood, it was a Jinn Ball and for all he knew he would be the only Jinn in attendance AND he had the feeling he had a crush on someone who showed little interest, perhaps even distain, for his presence.

"The water closet is through those doors," Charon pointed to a room in the corner. "I set it up just as Joe had his configured, I figured that way you would know where everything is and wouldn't have to rely on magic to take care of any of your needs."

Leo made his way to the bathroom, or as Charon called it, the *water closet*, and he had to admit that Charon did a great job of making it a typical bathroom that Leo could navigate. The double vanity sinks, mirrors, toilet, and walk-in shower that mimicked Grandpa Joe's—were all a welcomed sight. As he stood in the shower to let the previous day's grime wash away, refreshing himself in the warm water, he wondered why Charon would need to make it look like a *typical bathroom*. His thoughts soon turned to excitement, as he and Charon would be going back into town very soon, which meant he could take in more of the wonderful sights of its structure and citizens. As Leo finished up and found a fresh towel hanging on a warm rod just within reach of the shower, he noticed a neatly pressed pile of clothes on a tabletop just to the right of the vanity. *I wonder if he knows my size?* thought Leo. As soon as he was finished outfitting himself with the jeans, green V-neck t-shirt, and a new pair of sneakers—that completed the look—he didn't wonder any longer. Everything fit perfect and he didn't look half bad for jeans and a simple shirt. He brushed his teeth and hair and presented himself once again into the nautical-themed sitting room.

"That will do well, very well for now," Charon viewed Leo with approval. "Once we stop by Joe's house to retrieve his bank information, we will set you up with everything you need."

"Grandpa Joe has a house here?"

"Of course, you didn't think he would just bum around and rely on the kindness of strangers, did you? I suppose once all the legal work is complete, both the house and Joe's assets will be yours to do what you wish."

"I can't have a house here. If I stay any longer, I'm going to be missed. As I told you before, my dad probably already called the police and they are looking for me."

"I told you not to worry about that; you won't be missed. I suppose, I did forget to give you an explanation, though. You see, from what I understood from your grandpa, time moves slower in Spring Crow. He would stay for years at a time, normally between six or seven, and then say he had work to take care of back in your realm and leave for a month, or so. He said he wasn't missed and told his family that he was away on business all summer."

"But he was only gone during the summer, for about three months, and always back by the first turn of the trees in autumn, through Christmas and spring, and then back on business again the next year."

"Well then, that proves my point. If he were here for roughly six or seven years and you only missed him for three months you can see that Spring Crow time is on a different plane of existence. If you're away for a few days or weeks, it will only seem like minutes to your dad so nothing to worry about."

This eased Leo's mind. If his dad wasn't out looking for him, he could settle into a bit of a routine here in Spring Crow, at least for a little while until he figured out how he would be able to juggle this realm, his world, and school simultaneously.

"You mentioned Grandpa Joe's house; can we see it?"

"Of course, Joe gave me access in case of an emergency and his unfortunate passing—rest his soul—certainly constitutes and emergency; let's head over."

Grandpa Joe lived just on the outside of the main square of Spring Crow. Far enough away to enjoy the privacy of a lush garden, beautiful koi pond, and the quietness that came with living away from most of the population, but close enough to be anywhere you needed to be within a twenty-minute walk. Leo marveled at both the differences and similarities Grandpa Joe's Spring Crow house had with his house back in Ohio. Rather than a typical A-Frame house that was common in his Ohio town, Grandpa Joe's Spring Crow home was roughly the same size, but a magnificent polished golden fruitwood structure trimmed in light red mahogany. It had two stories, what looked to be a freshly painted black tin roof, and a wraparound porch. What Leo wasn't expecting was a solid red door that was a perfect match to his own father's door.

Inside was typical Grandpa Joe. His leather chair, the faint smell of his favorite Scotch mixed nicely with the smell of the often-used fireplace, and windows that were worn from being frequently opened. It hit Leo hard as to how much he already missed his best friend. It had been such a short time since Grandpa Joe's passing, and so much has happened since, that Leo hadn't even had much time to properly mourn.

One item, or rather, *items*, were obviously missing... Grandpa Joe's collection of books placed and piled as he liked. This, Leo assumed, was because Grandpa Joe must have finished with his library in Spring Crow prior to his return to his world. Grandpa Joe had family portraits throughout the house, to include older, rather worn photos of himself and his late grandmother, photos of Leo, and even photos of residents of Spring Crow that he considered family. Leo drew a sigh of relief when he also saw photos of his own father, proudly displayed with the others.

"Got it," Charon stated, as he returned from a room; Leo didn't even see him enter. Charon was holding, what appeared to be, a banking book typical of those his own father kept from the late nineties.

"Take a few minutes to look around; the place will be yours once everything is settled by the town. Don't take too long, though; I'd like to get to the bank before lunch so we can grab a bite before we head to the Aesthetic Citizen. Hopefully, they have a proper selection left; it is terribly close to festivity time."

"Charon, before we go, what exactly did Grandpa Joe do in the Spring Crow?"

Charon paused before speaking thoughtfully. "I hadn't realized that when Joe started your training, he didn't let you know what he was training you for."

"I didn't know I was being trained; I was only confused."

"Your Grandpa Joe was the protector of the Spring Crow and the veils warding off attack from the other realms. As you now know, there are protective barriers between the Spring Crow, other realms, your world, and the worlds outside. Joe was a scholar and would research both the strengths and weaknesses of each particular veil. Why, it was his idea to advance the water veil by darkening the other side. He believed it would ward off any accidental visitors."

"That makes sense," said Leo. "When I arrived, I thought I was dead. I would have done anything to get out of there."

"We've never had to worry about it, but it is a precaution."

"So, besides researching the veils, what else?"

"Oh, Joe had his hands in so many things in the Spring Crow. He was an engineer as well, you know."

"I had no idea; my dad never spoke of anything grandpa did."

"That's too bad. Joe was brilliant, as were all of the Kane Knights. The Kane Knights discovered how, without magic, that the glass in the town hall could be concaved in such a way that no matter where you need to look you have a clear view."

"Let me guess," said Leo. "The proper amount of heat to concave the glass coupled with the magic walls allows the person inside uninterrupted views."

"Yes!" Exclaimed Charon. "The Kane who brought this to the Spring Crow did say it was an easy feat that he learned in your world. Imagine, combining the mundane with the magical to create something so useful and beautiful."

"What, specifically, did Grandpa do?"

"Other than engineering and research of the veils? Well, he was a protector."

"Protector?" Leo asked.

"Why, of course! Many times, he would accompany me through the water veil and as far as he could through the mountain and forest veil. You see, he could only go all the way through the water veil because that was the path to your world; and only so far into the other veils."

"Why would he go at all?"

"If something ever broke through, it would be up to Joe to slay the beast. The Veils absolutely keep out the other Jinn ancestors due to its magic, but sometimes nature has its own way around such protection."

"So, he was an engineer, researcher, and warrior? Wow, what a renaissance man! Why didn't he ever tell me?"

"He tried, but unfortunately he passed before your training was complete."

"Did Grandpa ever create something from my world?" Leo asked.

Charon paused while he watched Leo. "Of course, he did, Leo. He created your dad, who in turn created you." He paused again before continuing, "do you need a little time?"

Leo wiped his nose with his shirtsleeve and fought back a tear. "It's okay." He stood tall and stoically, "I've been to Grandpa Joe's house in Ohio hundreds of times. I know my way around and I'll explore upstairs tonight or tomorrow."

"Suit yourself; now, let's go *suit* yourself," quipped Charon seeing an opportunity to lighten the mood, and was obviously cracking himself up with the awful pun.

Chapter 6

Leo and Charon walked into the front door of the Aesthetic Citizen; Leo had never seen such a store in his life. If Charon was worried about not having a selection, he need not worry any longer. Mannequins of sharply dressed males, females, giants, fairies, dragons, and trolls lined all sides of the store; each displaying the latest in creature fashion and all top-lighted in order to show all of the best features.

"Camille, my love," exclaimed Charon as a dark-haired fairy decked out in a bright red blouse, black slacks, wearing a thin gold, crossbones necklace, and black high-heeled stilettos flew towards them.

"Charon, what a nice surprise. Why, I assumed you already had all the proper items for tonight? And, who is this fine young man you have with you today?"

"Camille, I would like you to meet Leonardo Joseph Kane, grandson of Joseph, the reigning Kane Jinn."

"Please, just Leo," Leo replied as he extended his hand and was met with a surprisingly strong handshake in return.

"What can we do for you today? Perhaps a dressing robe or the latest in footwear? I understand your boots are becoming shameful from the back and forth through the Veil. It's so damp, I'm surprised that they have lasted this long."

"Nothing for me today, although keep the boots in mind for later this week. Today, we need to fit Leo with a tuxedo of your finest satin and wool. I'm picturing a five-piece classic model, double vented, and, of course, a typical Kane vest of solid blue, with matching tie. Leo, what size shoes do you wear?"

"Uhh... nine... regular," stammered Leo.

"Fine, fine, and leather cap-toed Oxfords to complete the look... for heaven sakes, not boroughs. Make sure we have some leather in those soles too. We can't have a Jinn showing up with rubber or plastic footwear."

Camille snapped her fingers and another three fairies—all dressed similarly to Camille—went to work measuring, poking, and prodding at Leo. Once finished, they proceeded to peel off his shirt and shoes, while the written measurements took flight and fluttered to the back, where Leo could only assume the tuxedo was being created to his very own specifications.

"I think I can handle that myself," stammered Leo a little embarrassed at the attention, and the simple fact that he was being dressed like a boy on his first day of kindergarten. "Just tell me when the clothes are finished and then show me the way to a dressing room. I'll make sure I'm presentable."

"Why, it's complete," Camille said proudly, as a brand new, one-of-a-kind tuxedo floated their way. "Right over there, dearie, pull the door if you would like some privacy."

Leo had never been fitted for a tuxedo or put one on for that matter—tailored or not. After some time and trial— *who knew cufflinks could be so hard to figure out*—he emerged from the changing room to be critiqued.

"Very good Leo," Camille said with a smile. "And you put the cummerbund on correctly; always remember, pleats upwards."

Leo looked at himself in the mirror, "Perhaps this isn't going to be so bad after all, maybe I can pull this off without completely embarrassing myself."

"You about ready?" Charon shouted from the sitting room of his house, where he had been waiting on Leo after the two had returned from lunch. "We don't want to be late, there are a lot of people who want to meet you, and the ceremony can't start without you."

Leo, who was just finishing the final touches on his outfit suddenly felt sick, his stomach dropping from its normal resting place down to his toes. "Ceremony? You didn't say anything about a ceremony."

"Didn't I? Maybe, Lady Cybele mentioned it? I'm sure we told you, it's the highlight of the evening and it's not something we have the opportunity to do often. I've only seen it seven times; the last was your grandfather, and that was years ago."

Leo was beginning to think that besides his bad jokes, Charon was also getting forgetful. "Charon, exactly how old are you?"

"By your timeline, six thousand and thirteen years old," Charon grinned, "almost middle age already, boy time sure does fly. Are you ready for your carriage, my good sir?"

By carriage? Leo assumed that Charon had a car, which he thought odd because he hasn't seen or heard one thus far. Charon waved his hand, said

Kaleso, and outside in the distance, Leo could clearly hear the clip-clop of heavy hoofs.

"You meant an actual carriage?" Leo asked in awe, as he knew they only had to walk ten minutes to get to what Leo considered City Hall, the round Bloodstone building where he first met Lady Cybele and Angel.

"Can't chance ruining the shine on our shoes, my boy. Come on, time is wasting."

Charon and Leo hastily exited Charon's house and climbed into the open-air carriage, which was pulled by one of the larger horses, but not the largest he had seen in the Realm. The carriage was driven by a naked gargoyle-coachman in a top hat, who tipped his hat in their direction. Once securely seated, the coachman gave a flick of the wrist and they were off.

They arrived at the ball as the clock on a newly visible tower was striking six p.m.

"Was there a clock tower yesterday? How did I miss that?" questioned Leo as they pulled alongside of the other carriages dropping of passengers of all shapes and sizes.

"I don't remember, but probably not. Lady Cybele and the town council don't normally have it erected unless something special is going on. I can't imagine that it was up yesterday."

Inside, the hall was bigger than Leo remembered, much bigger. What he equated to the size of his school's gymnasium, was now twice the length of a football field and just as wide. The doors, that had surrounded the hall, were replaced with rich tapestries that depicted long ago battles of, what he assumed, to be the founding of the realm. Tables were arranged in twelve rows around three sides of the giant room, providing enough room to navigate between. Each was covered in a shimmering white tablecloth, set with twelve perfectly white place settings, more gold flatware than Leo had ever seen, and crystal glasses of various shapes and sizes. At the front of the hall stood a grand stage, with yet another larger table set for eight individuals and a polished black podium placed front and center, a stark contrast to the rest of the room.

Above was a terrace that hung over the stage and on it sat a full orchestra of gargoyles, this time, thankfully, dressed in shirts and ties, holding brass and woodwind instruments. The floor was polished to a glass finish that was so intimidating Leo felt sure he would slip and fall on its surface with his brand-new leather soled shoes. The only recognizable feature in the vast hall was the fountain, still fixed in the center, complete with figures and flash. Finally, the lighting would have made one think that he was inside a medieval sanctuary during the blessing of birth. He looked both left and right and realized that both suns, now miniature and more silver than gold, were casting their warm glow over everything and everyone contained within the boundaries of the hall.

"Come on, there are some people who I'd like you to meet," Charon stated as he grabbed Leo's arm and escorted him over to a group of seven individuals; Lady Cybele laughing in the center.

"Sir Leonardo," exclaimed Lady Cybele, "so nice of you to join us. Please let me introduce you to the town council. This is our Treasurer, Mr. Tomas Forswear; the Planning Commissioner Ms. Laura Parish; our Commanding General of the Army, General Ontario Carlux; the Manager of Creature Occupation, Honorable Lester Morphon; and finally, Councilwoman Sylvia T. Korpus.

Before Leo could properly introduce himself, a band of what appeared to be sasquatches, on the upper level began to play their instruments while Lady Cybele raised her hands and, as if she had a public address system, stated, "Ladies and Gentleman, please take your seats, the feast is ready to begin."

Leo, Charon, Lady Cybele, the town council and others made their way to the table set upwards on the stage. Lady Cybele took the seat at the center.

"Leo, please, sit to my right, everyone else, please take your places."

Leo complied, and while doing so, scanned the crowd for Angel. He caught sight of her at a table down and to his right. She was wearing a beautiful black and gold dress, cut just above her knees, and hanging slightly below her shoulders. Her hair was put up into what he could only describe as someone getting ready for a school dance, and on her wrist were silver bangles that moved as beautifully as she. The only thing missing, and now that he was fully aware of everyone around in attendance, was the fact that everyone, except the two of them, were wearing amulets, the type that Grandpa Joe always wore around his neck.

"Ladies and gentlemen, let the feast begin," announced Lady Cybele.

Large trolls, dozens of them, navigated their way around the room with agile precision, each carrying two large silver and bronze covered platters to the center of each table. Once in position, each held their station, hand over each cover, and with a simultaneous nod, lifted the covers. On the platters on the right-hand side, the trolls had revealed an impressive assortment of fine meats, breads, cheeses, and dressings; while the left-hand side contained all manner of cake, pie, and pudding. Leo stared in amazement at the delicious looking food and realized that the afternoon did pass so quickly that his stomach was turning over with hunger.

"Leo," called Ms. Parish from two seats down, "do try the corned game hen with a little of the stuffing; it's quite delectable."

"Stay away from the stuffing lad," retorted the General Carlux. "It will quite literally stuff you to the point you won't be able to walk right for a week."

Ms. Parish gave him a whack on the shoulder, "Oh General, how do you come up with these outlandish ideas?" She gave him a wink.

Leo ate his fill, and then some, satisfying himself with strange and wonderful meats and a sampling of every dessert set before him. When he felt that he couldn't eat another bite, he thought, *don't be silly, there is always room for more pie.* As he reached for what could only be considered one piece too many, he looked over at Angel, who had daintily completed her meal, neatly folded her napkin, and was looking in his general direction. *Well, maybe I have had enough, he reconsidered. Perhaps I can ask to take a piece home and have it for a snack after breakfast.*

"Ladies and gentlemen, now that we have eaten our fill, I'd like to call your attention to the center of the stage," Lady Cybele announced as she stood and made her way to podium. "As you all know we have recently loss the companionship of our good friend, Sir Joseph Kane, to the ages of his chosen world. Age doesn't come upon us the same in our Realm, as can be attested by his many years among us, but his family, in his chosen world, were just as much a part of his heart as we."

"Finally," Leo thought as he listened to the fitting eulogy, "a proper remembrance."

"Sir Joseph Kane was an honorable man, armed with the knowledge of the Jinn, a walker amongst us, and a friend to all. In his passing he has ascended and has passed his Jinn nature to the next in line. Tonight, we honor Sir Kane's memory as well as welcome the newest Jinn to our fold."

Leo sat frozen, eyes wide, as General Carlux rose and accepted a black velvet box from a petite troll, who glided gracefully onto the stage from somewhere behind. General Carlux accompanied Lady Cybele to the front, turned, and in an authoritative voice heard by all, requested Leo's presence.

Leo carefully made his way to the podium, unsure of what was to come.

"Sir Leonardo, grandson of Sir Joseph Kane, Jinn, Walker, and Friend, your education is ongoing and will never cease. Learn all you can from the Spring Realm and all the worlds you have yet to travel. Be wise, learn our ways, and protect your heritage as well as the good name of your realm."

Lady Cybele ceremoniously opened the box still perched in General Carlux's outstretched hands and retrieved an amulet depicting a black crow, sitting on a blue stone, hanging from a silver chain.

"As all citizens know, the soul is the source of our power and the assigned amulet, color, symbol, and meaning, amplify the soul and, therefore, the power that can be wielded." Lady Cybele turned to face Leo, "Your amulet, passed down through the generation of Kane Jinn, is the only known amulet to be touched by Acadamel himself. Only a true Kane can bear the true weight of such a piece, learn to use it wisely and learn to use it carefully."

Lady Cybele slid the silver chain around Leo's neck and kissed him once on each cheek. The crowd erupted and cheered, raising their glasses of assorted drinks, and toasted the memory of Joe as well as to the arrival of Leo. The celebration was short lived.

"Do you feel that?" Leo whispered to Lady Cybele, still standing center stage with General Carlux. "It feels like the building is shaking."

Tremors, slight at first, growing stronger by the second, grew into an earthquake, violently shaking the tables and their contents. The only items that stood stationary were the Suns themselves, now casting strange shadows on the items as they shook below. One second, five seconds, fifteen seconds. All it took was fifteen seconds to put the revelers into a panic, now all collecting their belongings and making haste to the doors, pushing and shoving on their way.

"Charon," Lady Cybele, visibly concerned in all manners, called to her worried friend once the quake had subsided. "Please find Angel and escort her and Leo to your carriage. Meet me and the rest of the council in the tower."

Charon did not waste time pulling Angel from a crowd of panicked creatures and led both to a side door. As they hurried, Leo could not help but to turn and look over his shoulder. The room was no longer in its splendid beauty but looked as though there had been a brawl. Plates, glasses, and cutlery strewn about, upturned chairs from the hastily retreat, and many of the once happy party goers had forgotten jackets and coats. There was also a crack... a small but perceptible crack around the once solidly held hands of the figures on the fountain.

"Angel," Charon ordered, "take my carriage and go directly to Joe's... Leo's house, don't stop along the way, and keep Leo in your care. Don't let him out of your sight." With no further explanation or instruction, Charon turned and re-entered the hall to take his place with the rest of the council.

Chapter 7

"Come on," whispered Angel as she grabbed Leo's hand, while he was walking towards the carriage. Much to Leo's confusion, Angel looked back over her shoulder before darting and pulling him towards the back of the building. "There's a back door leading up to the upper part of the tower, we can listen from there."

Leo, head spinning from confusion, didn't argue and let Angel lead the way. Angel pulled open the maintenance door revealing a wooden staircase, dimly lit by ambient light that shone through from the suns still burning in the hall.

"Find a light switch."

"No! What's wrong with you? They may see us," scolded Angel in a whisper.

The two crept up the stairs into the tower attic, which was now used to store artifacts and documentation from the town's past. The crowded floor was not polished like the rest of the building and the wooden slats making up the floor were worn, causing space between the boards to allow for sight and sound to penetrate.

"The tremors are getting worse," Leo and Angel heard Ms. Parish state matter-of-fact, in a worried tone, as she paced the council meeting room.

The room was similar to what Leo imagined a court room to be configured. There was a high judge's bench that contained enough seats to accommodate each council member, with two lower tables on each side. Across on each side were two tables, clear of work, and to the left a jury box with twelve empty wooden stools. The room was split by a bar and opposite the bar were seats for spectators. Leo was surprised at the starkness of the room and its condition. The wood, old and dull, not as he had imagined a court room would be, looked as though it hadn't been used in quite some time.

Everyone began talking at once:

"Did you see? Tell me! Did you see the crack in the fountain?"

"They are definitely happening more frequently now."

"What will it take to continue making repairs?"

"How are we going to explain the latest one to the town?"

"It can't be possible; it's too thick now."

"Can we keep it a secret much longer?"

"What are we going to do if it's true?"

"I told you something was happening; it's not a coincidence."

The last two statements made Leo and Angel listen more intently.

"We don't know if it's true or not, but the crack in the fountain does indicate that there may now be an opening in the Veil," Charon stated, quieting down the rest of the committee. "We have known that he has been trying to get in for quite some time, but we don't know how powerful he's become, or if it's really him and not some other simple explanation. We can't jump to conclusions and must look at the facts rationally."

"What other explanation can there be," shouted General Carlux. "We need to prepare for a fight in order to maintain our way of life. I don't care what the fairy tales say, he's dangerous and knows more about warfare than any of you can imagine."

"Who?" Whispered Leo.

"Shhhh," Angel scolded with a finger to her lips, still listening.

"Ladies and gentlemen, please listen, and listen well." Lady Cybele was taking control, clearly frustrated with the lack of unity. "I believe we have come to the crossroads that we all feared would one day be upon us and I, for one, believe that he is attempting to gain access to the Spring Crow Realm in order to drive a wedge between us and our ways. We must review what has previously been discussed, ensure that our proposed courses of actions for safety are implemented, and develop a plan to counter his attempts before he is successful."

"Now someone is talking sense," agreed General Carlux, pounding his fist on the nearest table.

"General, we mustn't rush in," continued Lady Cybele. "First, we must assess the damage from this latest event while ensuring the citizens of the Realm don't panic. Keep this and our actions to the confines of this room. Ms. Parish, please have your office survey the town to determine the extent of damage, report your findings to Mr. Forswear so we can create a planned budget in an attempt to repair what we can. Start with the roads, shops, and any municipal necessities of the realm, and work your way outwards to the houses and farms. Mr. Morphon, gather as many of the work creatures, especially the trolls, giants, and gargoyles that you can enlist and bring them to General Carlux for conscription."

"Conscription." General Carlux stated, a little confused.

"We need to re-enforce our army in the future. General Carlux, I need you to start training as soon as you can, preferably as soon as tomorrow. Tell your men it's a new creature integration initiative so rumors don't spread. And finally, Mr. Morphon, while you are gathering work creatures go with Charon to survey the veils on all sides, most of the creatures can be found in those areas. Charon, pay special attention to the forest and mountains on the perimeter of the veils, they would be easier than the water crossing due to the proximity of his realm."

"Cross a veil?" Mr. Morphon retorted. "The only person who can successfully cross any veil and survive is that boy and Charon, and the boy is so clueless that we might as well put a bell on him to make sure he doesn't get himself hurt. Why, even Charon only ventures to the edges and look what it does to him every time he goes out. Why did Joe have to go back to that other world? He should have stayed right here, where he was needed."

Lady Cybele contemplated this for a moment, choosing her words carefully. "That's not quite true, Mr. Morphon. There is one other who can cross, someone who isn't fully aware of her potential and power; although, she doesn't realize it and I've kept it from her for as long as she's been in my care."

Ms. Parish looked wide eyed. "Angel?"

"Angel?" asked Mr. Morphon. "Why, she doesn't even rate a library of her own. And if she were to have one, there isn't a library in all of the realms to teach her anything she would be capable of remembering for more than an hour. She's uninterested in anything that doesn't fit into her own little head. Besides, not having her own basic library, she doesn't even rate an amulet. She's as worthless as a gargoyle who can't dress himself before breakfast."

Leo stared wide eyed at the council members below, had he heard right? Was Angel the only being without a library or amulet? He turned to Angel, but she was no longer in the attic. Slowly, as not to be heard from above the council, Leo tiptoed to the exit and down the wooden stairs.

Leo found Angel in Charon's carriage, visibly upset and the remnants of dried tears channeling down her cheeks.

"Angel..."

"Don't say anything, it's not worth it."

The two rode back in silence, each lost in their own thoughts and staring out into the dimly lit night. Once they arrived at Leo's, Angel exited without a word and with a wave of her hand, flung upon the door seconds before she entered and slammed it shut, before Leo even had a chance to thank the coachman and dismount.

"I don't understand, what was all that about?" Leo said when he made his way into the house to find Angel pacing, "Why did the general say the story was a fairy tale? And why does Lady Cybele believe you can make it through the veil when nobody else can?"

"Don't forget, you can," she said, still visibly upset.

"Forget about me; start from the beginning."

"Charon told you the truth, the tale of the brothers, all Jinn, all walkers, and all wanting to control the realms. He told you the story in a manner that we tell all the children as not to frighten them."

Leo sat in confused silence.

"Look, the brothers did fight, and they did tell stories to their father, but the fighting was

74

worse than you can imagine. What he told you about Garaile was sugar coated and was only the climax of their hate, only a small part of their story. Garaile, Theiler, and Kane were all great warriors, with even greater tempers. Theiler's favorite weapon was a war ax, given to him by his father and believed by him to be able to split any thought or anyone who disagreed with him, for that matter. He supposedly imbibed it with the darkest magic he could summon and used it to slash and dismember all that disagreed with him. He built an army hell-bent on dividing the realms; he thought nothing of dividing his army when it pleased him as well. None of his soldiers or citizens stood a chance, and he happily used his war ax to bend his will."

"That's not quite the story of motherly love and brotherly loathing Charon told."

"No, not by a long shot. Garaile, the oldest, was the strongest of the bunch, when it came to warfare. He would slice and dice his brothers with a gifted broadsword on a regular basis... he also sliced and diced his mother as he saw fit. Being powerful beings, each survived but anyone else who confronted him was not so lucky. Even Theiler's army en masse, was no match for Garaile and his dark broadsword. For fun, he would ensure any army or foe who faced him would be incapacitated, only then to slowly and unmercifully fileting them until they eventually perished."

"And Kane?"

"I'm not sure you're ready for Kane, just yet; let's just say his gift was knowledge, books, and was too smart for everyone and his own good. Kane was just as evil and cunning."

"I need to know."

"You will, you will see how Kane lived as well as how his brothers were even worse than I can explain. There is more, much more, and you will soon see once we cross the veil."

"Are you out of your mind? The last time I crossed I thought I'd be sick; now you want me to do it again."

"It's the only way, Leo, and I'm coming with you."

"No, I absolutely won't be taking you, even if I do go."

Angel put her hand up to her hair, picked out the pins holding it up, and shook it out, "You don't have a choice."

"But I, I mean you..." Leo started.

"No more thinking. You heard them, something has to be done and if we stick around here... we are going to continue being treated like kids. And who does that Mr. Morphon think he is? Who cares if I don't have a library or an amulet? I'm a strong woman! And what right does he have insulting gargoyles like that? I don't care if he does consider them lower than us; they work hard and deserve every right that we do."

"I believe you; I do." Leo said, trying to calm her down.

Angel continued, "I can't begin to tell you how pointless it is to try to have civilized conversation with half the people in the realm. Sowing the seeds of misguided truths, keeping everyone happily in the dark, dim-witted, and blissful in their own ignorance. All creatures were created with the intention of enabling everyone to do what they were placed here to do, without someone thinking they are better. Without keeping creatures down, wielding power over others because they think they are smarter or better educated because they have a stinking library. What is with the prejudice over an amulet? Why, if half the people here weren't created the way they were, I'd swear they were to be as useless as the ear on a bug. Is it no wonder Theiler thinks he can waltz into our realm and divide us, we've already begun to divide ourselves."

"Theiler?"

"Of course, Theiler. Who else do you think would split the ground, the fountain, the very Veil protecting us from his presence? We haven't made it hard for him either, oh no, not us, not with our holier than thou shiftless attitudes towards individuals not like us. We might as well have rolled out the red carpet and invited him to the Jinn Ball. It wouldn't surprise me if he was the guest of honor at the next Jinn Ball the way we have been carrying on."

Angel paced back-and-forth, fists clenched, shoes kicked off, and looking like she was ready for a fight. Leo knew there would be no talking her out of going.

"Fine. Which way?" He sighed.

Angel gave the first smile Leo had seen from her, "I knew you'd see it my way. You tell me. What does your library say?"

"*Forthwith Knowledge.*" The book appeared, still shocking Leo each time it did. He closed his eyes, thought of his question, and turned the page. "Be cautious of your wooded route, the forest is fraught with perils."

"Of course, the Forest Veil," exclaimed Angel. "It's easier to break the trees of the forest, than mountains of stone; Theiler would more easily find a path there."

"*Complete,*" commanded Leo and the library disappeared.

"Now, what to do about this dress? This will never do. *Modekleider.*" In an instant Angel was decked out in army battle dress uniform pants, a long sleeve black shirt made from a synthetic material, and hiking boots.

Did a girl just dress in front of me? thought Leo. "*Modekleidervos,*" Angel pointed in Leo's direction.

Leo's tuxedo and all its accoutrements were now neatly hanging on a cedar hangar, shoes below, and he was dressed in sturdy, but comfortable jeans, a long sleeve brown shirt, made from the same material as Angels, and tan boots.

"I wish people here would stop dressing me; I can do it myself."

"Shut up," Angel said with another grin. "I know where the veil in the forest begins."

Chapter 8

Angel led Leo to the freshly planted field behind his house. The furrows had just begun to sprout with new life and Leo tried to navigate between the ruts as best he could. "This would be much easier if it were flat land," Leo said.

"I wouldn't normally walk through the field at the beginning of spring, I hate disturbing the work of the farmers and I feel bad if I don't step lightly. I know I'm destroying a tiny root system, and the innocent plants won't have a chance to get back their footing, they have to start all over again to survive. If it were daylight, at least I could be more careful; hopefully, I keep step in the furrows." Angel said as she stepped more gingerly than Leo.

"I had never considered plants working to grow, nor working for anything for that matter. Do you feel the same about all inanimate objects?" Leo replied, himself stepping in the furrows.

"They're not inanimate. Sure, they don't have feelings like you and me, but everything struggles to survive, and the seedlings never did anything to you or me. I just hate disturbing anything innocent."

Leo had the feeling they wouldn't be discussing innocence much on this journey.

The end of the field was lined by large, old trees that Leo assumed had been standing for as long as time itself. Through the darkness of the night, he could still make out the mixture of buds and green leaves, signaling the beginning of both spring and the forest veil.

"This isn't so bad; like a walk in the park."

"I don't think it's going to start bad, we're technically still in Spring Crow," replied Angel, "but I've heard stories from Charon about traveling some distance; that the deeper you go, the creepier the forest and its inhabitants get."

"Hopefully just squirrels and rabbits. I can handle squirrels and rabbits."

The moonlight peaked between the leaves and branches, illuminating their surroundings to include the path that Charon obviously followed during his time in the Veil. As the two walked in silence, Leo kept a watchful eye towards the dark distance, where the moonlight washed away, leaving nothing but night. The deeper they traveled, the more Leo became sensitized to the smell of the earth and of the decomposing leaves of last year's fall. The scent took him back to autumn in Ohio, when Grandpa Joe would take him trick-or-treating when the weather cooperated, and of the prospect of Grandpa Joe being Leo's to converse with for the next eight months. Autumn gave way to winter, and winter to spring, and the remnants of last season's decaying foliage in the dark night comforted Leo.

"The trail leads this way." Angel's whisper pulled him back from his thoughts into the spring night. "It's not as clear, but I can still make it out."

The trail, once a wide path that would accommodate the two, was now narrow, branches giving way as they passed between the ever-closer trees.

"For what is it you search, my children?" a low voice sung out.

"Did you..."

"Shhhh," Leo could hear Angel, but could not see her.

"You must be very beautiful children in your world," the voice continued.

"Who's there?" stammered Angel.

"We rarely get visitors and all visitors this far out are never nearly as handsome as you two. Don't you agree?"

All around Leo and Angel could hear whispers of 'yes', 'quite right', and 'very beautiful, indeed'.

"Who's speaking? Who's out there? Show yourselves," Leo demanded, trying show bravery, but didn't feel very convincing.

"Show ourselves? Why, we are all around. We've been watching from the beginning, yet haven't made a sound."

Leo backed away from the ever-narrowing trail and leaned against a tree in order to seek protection, in the event a fight was to break out with the unknown and unseen voices. He thought he'd heard that in a movie once, to protect your back to ensure you only have to fight in one direction. A boney hand stroked his shoulder and Leo jumped, moving to the protection of a larger tree.

"Show yourself," Leo demanded, now obviously more afraid than courageous.

"Why? We're all around. Don't you see and feel our beautifully barked skin as well as our moon bleached canopy above?

"The trees," said Angel, as if she were talking to both herself and Leo under her breath.

"Of course, it's just us, silly girl. Who else do you think would be this far into the forest? What is it you seek, or are you lost and waiting to become a meal for one of the creatures we shelter within?"

"No, we're searching for the path to the next realm. We know there is a crack and we must hurry," Leo said matter-of-factly with as much bravado as he could muster.

"Hmmm, the Carved Realm is what you seek is it? It's at least a day's travel from here. Total darkness is what you will find this far out, only to become somewhat lighter at the end of your journey, should you make it that far."

"And how exactly would you know if you can't move further than the spot your standing?" questioned Angel.

"Why, our roots, of course. Look around, do you believe our roots are not connected, that we don't communicate with our brothers and sisters as you would communicate with yours?"

"Such beautiful children, it would be a shame if anything were to happen. We sense Jinn... we can understand why the boy can cross, but you, girl, how have you remained? You must be very pretty in your realm to have made it this far. Why, the only visitor we receive is Charon and he's in no fine shape to gaze upon this far in," stated a sweeter, more feminine voice.

At these words, a soft greenish golden glow began to emit from below Angels collar bone, faintly lighting her now slightly blushing face. Lady Cybele was the only person who had ever called her beautiful and she wasn't used to the compliment. Leo stood, not knowing what to say, or if he should say anything at all. There was a wind, a rustle in the treetops that spread to every tree in the forest.

"Ahhh... now all is explained. The scholarly Jinn and the teacher who nurtures, both of high-born lineages. We will ask no more questions and tell no one unless asked."

"What do you mean?" asked Leo.

"We will ask no more questions of you and we will offer your presence to no creature. Please, you have had a long journey thus far; sleep and we will ensure you are not disturbed until it is time to continue."

Leo and Angel didn't understand the statement regarding being special beings and wanted to ask questions but were exhausted.

Leo gazed at Angel, the glow in her chest now fading. Rather than question her new appearance, he sat, exhausted both mentally and physically. The questions could wait until his mind was clear.

Angel followed suit, but still wary of their new foliage acquaintances, ensured she stayed clear of any branches or roots that may come into contact with her as she lay down next to the path.

When Leo and Angel woke, it was still dark deep in the forest. The suns were now high overhead, but the thick canopy above blocked almost all the light. Leo could better make out the black trunks mixing and merging into a dark background. Leo looked for Angel to wake her, but she was already stirring and, in fact, eating a piece of fruit.

"Where did you get that?" Leo now realizing he hadn't eaten since last night as his stomach gave a low growl.

"Bower gave it to me."

"Who's Bower?"

"He's the first tree creature we were talking with last night. He's actually quite nice, once you get to know him. Did you know his family has occupied this very spot for more than one thousand years? Why, he is only fifty years older than I. I was skeptical at first, after all, who can you really trust in the Veil, but he seems an honest guy, for a tree, that is. Would you like a piece?"

"I thought you'd never ask," Leo took a piece and began to dig in.

Leo and Angel sat in the cool shade of the forest quietly eating the fruit provided by Bower, not questioning its origin, contemplating their next move and direction. Leo thought they should stay on the path in order to ensure their arrival on the other side, but Angel decided against it. Her logic was that if they stayed on the path, others could also be on the path. If they stayed within the shadows of the trees there would be less of a chance of being seen.

Now off the path, much to Leo's chagrin, the two continued for the rest of the morning and well into the afternoon in silence. The only words said were the occasional warning of an obstacle that hindered their path—the odd rock, log, or ankle-twisting burrow from a long-forgotten animal.

Leo couldn't stand the silence or his own curiosity any longer. "What was that in your chest last night? You started to glow. I mean, physically and literally glow," he blurted.

"It's only happened a couple of times," Angel replied sounding slightly embarrassed. "Lady Cybele says it's because I have a big heart and that the glow won't hurt me; although, she wouldn't tell me what it is. She said it was for my protection, for my own good, and that someday I would understand. I hate it when I'm told that *someday I will understand.* I wish I were treated with the same dignity and respect as everyone else. Lady Cybele is the only one in the Spring Crow who is truly honest with me, but in this case, she holds back. I don't have another explanation for the glow other than it seems to happen when I'm happy, which unfortunately doesn't seem too often. It also happens when I'm helping someone in need, which also brings me occasional happiness. Not too many people in the Spring Realm like me, in fact I truly believe most only tolerate me. Let's just say, I'm not summoned to help with anything on a regular basis."

"I don't understand, why wouldn't people like you? Sure, you seemed a little standoffish when I first met you, but once someone gets to know you, you're not the same person. I've really started to enjoy our time together."

"I know you heard the council; I'm not like the rest and I know there is something wrong with me. I'm the only human creature in the Spring Crow that hasn't been presented an amulet and, try as I might, I can't summon a library of my own. I can perform other acts of magic, in fact quite a bit even without a library to guide me, but that's the only reason I'm paid any mind.

"Lady Cybele allows me access to her library whenever she's present and using it. Charon has let me browse his a few times, and each time I do I find myself becoming bored, as if I've already read the book, or all of the books. Other than Lady Cybele and Charon, nobody else pays much attention to me. If it weren't for Lady Cybele watching over me and Charon's kindness, I'm sure I would have been sent away to fend for myself long ago."

"So that's why you were so silent during the Jinn Ball. We're a lot alike in that way, you don't have many friends either."

"If you haven't noticed by now, you'd be more clueless than most. The Spring Crow prides itself on ensuring everyone accomplishes the job that they were created for by birth, if you will, but certain jobs aren't as glamorous and creatures in those jobs aren't always treated well.

"You heard Mr. Morphon, he's the Manager of Creature Occupation and he's supposed to respect and ensure everyone is doing their part—even he shows animosity towards others not like him. To make matters worse, he's the norm, not the exception."

Leo thought back to what he heard in the tower attic, Mr. Morphon did have a lot of unkind words about the creatures not like him, and he definitely showed his true feelings towards Angel. Perhaps the Spring Crow wasn't as wonderful a place for everyone as it appeared on the surface.

"Stop! Get down," hissed Angel, breaking Leo from his contemplation of the Spring Crow inhabitants. "Something is moving in the woods, off to our left."

Angel and Leo hit the ground, lying as low as possible on the damp forest floor, trying to control their breathing and not make a sound. Carefully lifting their heads, their eyes already adjusted to the dark, they watched as a team of four warriors on horseback came closer to their positions. The scarred beast of battle—clad in medieval armor, carrying thickly muscled pale riders—shook the ground as they plodded.

The riders wore their hair long and braided, each dyed a sinister blood red, contrasted by their coal black sclera-less eyes. The riders, like the beast they rode, were clad in black and silver medieval armor, protecting their vital organs. Each carried with him sword, war ax, and crossbow, complete with a quiver of glowing arrows. The four warriors stopped, turned inwards, and slowly circled. One battle horse turned and looked directly towards the two lying prone in the wet leaves, neither the horse nor the two made a sound. They only stared, one daring the two to move, the two wishing the warriors would take their leave.

The horse was the first to break the stalemate, giving a horrifying whiney and suddenly rising to his rear legs and lunging his upper torso towards the two. Leo and Angel, knowing that their positions were compromised, bolted in the direction in which they had traveled, only to be closely pursued by the four warriors.

Leo skidded to a halt, Angel crashing into his back. Two heavy laden warriors were now in front, circling sinisterly and silent around to encapsulate them on sides, front and back. There was nowhere left to run.

One warrior turned his horse away, gently blew into his pale muscular hand and a dim orange yellow orb, not completely formed but fragmented, appeared in his palm. In a low, inaudible, but sinister, guttural sound he began to speak into the orb, occasionally listening, as if informing someone of something and taking commands in return. The other three warriors tightened the circle— there was no escape, no time to summon or consult the library, and nowhere to hide.

A crushing sound could be heard behind Leo and Angel. First a slow crunch, followed by a louder squeeze and audible popping of bending metal. The warrior holding the orb closed his fist, his black eyes grew wide and wild. Leo turned to see the second warrior's horse falter, but it was too late for the escape. Branches from the trees twisted, bent, and descended upon the remaining warriors, lifted them from their steeds, and began crushing their armor, holding the figures aloft in an unbreakable hold. For a time, the warriors struggled but the stranglehold was too strong, no escape was possible. Not dead, but in enough pain to kill a mortal, the warriors hung silent, clenched in the grips of the powerful limbs.

"Take the weapons you need, I'd recommend the lightest of the swords, and mount two of the horses and release the others. Ride your beast to the edge of the Veil, ensure you keep off of the beaten path and don't stop for anything or anyone," a tree ordered.

"Who are they? How are you doing this? Why are you helping us?" cried Angel into the forest.

"Warriors of Theiler's army presumably sent to scout a path, as we don't have any reason to believe they were sent in search of you. We are beholden to no one, which gives us power over most, to include the armies of many. As for the why... it's our way of saying thank you for the kind words you said in the field."

"What words in what field? You must be mistaken; we haven't been in a field for at least a day.

"In the field on the way to the Forest Veil. You showed compassion by your worry of the young and innocent, which shows a heart that cares for not only your kind, but for all forms of life. You are truly the one who nurtures, and we welcome your return as well as the Jinn's"

Angel's chest, again right below her collar bone, resumed its faint glow.

"We are not beholden to you, but we are appreciative and word travels fast through the expansive roots of all we touch. We have been watching from the beginning of your journey, long before we knew your identities. Now hurry, we will hold these men until our brethren at the edge of the Veil inform us that you are at a safe distance."

Leo and Angel pulled the heavy armor from the remaining horses and set them free. No longer beast of burden, the two bolted in the direction of the Spring Crow, unsure of their newfound freedom, but making no effort to question their release. Once out of sight, Leo and Angel pulled the weapons they could easily handle from the eerily still warriors as instructed, Angel seemingly taking extreme pleasure in procuring the crossbow and two quivers of glowing arrows. Now armed, the two mounted the remaining horses, while gently communicating to them that they meant them no harm. The two rode in their intended direction of travel. Onward to the Carved Realm.

Chapter 9

"What do you mean, missing?" ordered Lady Cybele. The council members were busily accomplishing their assigned tasks when Ms. Parish, who had been surveying damage, reported back to Lady Cybele following a cursory check on the two teenagers at Leo's house.

"My team had finished the main areas, the shops, businesses, and utilities when I split them into two in order to begin conducting checks on the houses and outbuildings. I personally went to each of the council members' homes to find the extent of any damages. I knocked on Leo's door, when there wasn't an answer I peeked into the windows and didn't see anyone. Thinking they must be asleep, I knocked harder but there was still no answer. At this point, I was slightly concerned, but not overly because the carriage was still out front. To ensure their safety I went around to the back, out by the field, to knock on the back door and I found it unlocked. I went inside, called their names, but nobody answered and that's when I saw Leo's tuxedo neatly hanging. This gave me relief that he must have changed to go to bed, but I wanted to be sure. I went upstairs and neither of the beds in the master or guest room had been turned down. I ran to each room just to be sure the two didn't fall asleep somewhere while talking, but nothing and no one were anywhere to be found."

"I'm sure that the two are exploring the town; Angel wouldn't lead Leo into trouble but keep an eye out for them while you finish your survey of the town," Lady Cybele said. "Let Charon know the two are not in the house, he's more familiar with the landscape and the outer boundaries of Crow Spring than anyone I know."

"What about Mr. Morphon? He's with Charon checking the perimeter of the Veils, he's bound to know something is up if I pull Charon to the side."

"Yes, let Mr. Morphon know as well; he could glean valuable information from any creature that may have seen the two." Lady Cybele considered her decision and thought it best to continue on the current path, and before dismissing Ms. Parish she felt the need to inquire further into the discovery of the unaccounted-for adolescents. "Ms. Parish, your team has already conducted a survey of both the town and the outlying buildings? How long did it take?"

"Well, my team is technically still working on conducting checks on the houses, I believe that the main town has already been completed, but because I went to Leo's house, I can't be sure. Once I discovered that they were gone, I wanted to tell you straight away, just in case they were in trouble."

"Why would you believe they may be in trouble?"

"Why, they are just children, and Leo is now in possession of the Jinn Amulet. And who knows what Angel may convince him to do, now that he has so much power."

"But Angel doesn't know the extent of Leo's power," Lady Cybele reminded. "She's never seen the power wielded by Sir Joseph, and Sir Leo hasn't been in possession of the amulet nearly long enough to discover his new abilities. Why, it's been such a short period that I assume he hasn't even opened his library or practiced a solitary incantation or spell."

"But..."

"Thank you, Ms. Parish, for informing me that they are not in their designated location. I'm sure that they will be fine, and I'm sure Charon and Mr. Morphon will keep an eye out once you inform them. In the meantime, have you spoken to Mr. Forswear on what you have found thus far? I would like to have an initial planned budget by morning."

"No, Lady Cybele, I have not had the opportunity."

"Please, find Charon and Mr. Morphon, get an update from your team, and inform Mr. Forswear on the damages. That will be all for now, Ms. Parish."

"Right away ma'am."

Ms. Parish, feeling as though she had been chastised in public as if she were a child herself, left Lady Cybele in order to find Charon and Mr. Morphon. On her way she plotted exactly what she would say to the two once she did. *Just because Lady Cybele is one of the original members of the Crow Spring, she thinks she can just boss me around. She has no idea what I bring to the table— or what I will bring to the table.* With that, her hand began to tingle, a sure sign that someone was trying to send her a message. Checking her surroundings and not seeing a soul, she ducked into an alleyway tucked between Madame Muncie's Medications and the town theatre and peered into the orange shimmering ball summoned in her hand. She listened... the forest... She replied to the shimmering ball, "take both alive and bring the boy to the master, leave her for me," but before she could continue the light disappeared without a warning. *So, that's where they wondered off to*, Ms. Parish gloated internally as her mood lightened. *I'll be sure to let everyone know they are being well taken care of.*

Charon and Mr. Morphon had finished exploring the outskirts of the Mountainous Veil, beginning with the western most point, Mr. Morphon not daring to go more than a few meters past the peak of the foothills in fear that he would not make it out the same. Charon, on the other hand, forged ahead, approximately one quarter of a mile in. When they were in position, while still maintaining sight of one another, both began walking east in a methodical manner in order to catch any inconsistencies in the landscape—such as cracks or other magical anomalies. Finding nothing on their first pass they turned, still within eyesight, and they began the trek back west, again looking for any anomalies before they tackled the Forest Veil.

The Mountainous Veil was uninhabited, and Mr. Morphon was less likely to recruit a creature from this area. Save the occasional giant who may tear a rock from the landscape in order to fashion a mill stone for the baker, very few ventured in this direction as there was little need. Mr. Morphon initially balked at starting at the mountain region rather than the forest, because he knew he would not find members to draft for the army, but Charon won him over when he explained that that is the exact reason they should begin at the mountain. If someone were to slip through a crack in the Veil, what better place than an area where very few traveled, it was less likely that someone would see and report an intruder. Following the first painfully slow search east, the two men turned their sights west to begin the search again.

"Mr. Morphon," Charon called and pointed towards the town. Ms. Parish was on her way towards them, looking very determined and obviously had something on her mind.

"Mr. Morphon, have you or Charon noticed any changes in the Veils that we need to report to Lady Cybele and Mr. Forswear? My team has nearly completed the town, and I thought it might be prudent to include all findings in a single report."

"Ms. Parish, we are only a quarter of the way done. Why, we've only now just begun our second pass on this side and have yet to start the forest, which will, in all probability, take at least twice as long. There seems to be something on your mind, is everything okay?"

"Yes, yes, it's just those two insulant children, Leo and Angel."

"Leo and Angel? It's only been a couple of hours since they took the carriage back home. What trouble could they have possibly gotten into in a short period of time? Not too much I imagine."

"No trouble, they just ran off and gave me an awful fright when I couldn't find them. While conducting our rounds, I personally checked Leo's house to ensure their safety and when I arrived, they were gone. I, naturally, let myself in because I was concerned, and when I found them missing, I didn't know what to do. I immediately told Lady Cybele who asked me to ensure you and Charon were informed, you know, to keep an eye out, but on my way over here I caught them in an alleyway playing with Leo's library as if it were a toy. When I confronted the two, he said he was trying out some simple spells that he had always been interested in, common follies known to him from his world, and that he was trying to educate Angel on a few, as well. I told them to run along back to the house, as we don't know if it's safe to be out tonight, but I can't confirm that they paid me any mind. The last I saw of them, they were heading in the direction of the house, but you know young ones, they think they know best and never listen to their elders."

"I wish I knew what Lady Cybele saw in that Angel girl she's been keeping around and taking care of," Mr. Morphon snickered, while replying to the information regarding the two. "I imagine it was her idea to run off, and I bet it was also her idea to toy with Leo's library since she doesn't have one of her own. Why on Earth wouldn't they stay at the house to play games, instead of running off to an alley?"

"Who knows, maybe they wanted to ensure that nobody would interrupt them and figured someone would be around to check on them. As I said, Lady Cybele wanted you and Charon to keep an eye out for them, but I wouldn't worry too much, I'm sure they are either at the house or playing in another out-of-the-way corner of the town. Either way, please continue your survey of the Veil; I'll see you later back at the Town Hall."

With that, Ms. Parish turned and quickly walked away, keeping the same pace of frustration that she arrived with. Charon, watching the exchange, gave a confusing look towards Mr. Morphon, who in turn gestured by waving both hands in the air as a signal of 'nothing out of the ordinary' and the two continued their search.

"Men, listen up. As you all know and have laid witness to, the tremors have gotten worse and this last one was the worse yet. I personally would describe it as a full-blown earthquake... something we haven't felt in the Realm for thousands of years." General Carlux paced, arms folded across his chest. "I know some of you may have heard stories or maybe fairy tales of the past, of how our enemy had tried and failed to tear a hole in the very fabric that protects our Realm on all sides. Gentlemen, those fairy tales are meant to teach us a lesson, a lesson of the clash of battle, fighting and overpowering the enemy as is our sense of duty to the Realm. A lesson to train and be prepared in the event we are called upon to protect our Realm, whether that be proactive defense or in glorious offense."

The creatures of the Spring Crow army shifted uncomfortably in their formations. "Gentlemen, take a seat." General Carlux waved his left hand and his amulet gave the slightest hint of a glow. As he did, chairs appeared behind every man in the Spring Crow army, several hundred in perfectly aligned rows.

"We have all benefited from the rules and regulations of the Spring Crow, each man, woman, and child have the honor to pursue their naturally born and instilled occupation. You repay the kindness and safety of the realm by acting as a team, by drilling, fighting, eating, and working as a team. I don't care what your day-to-day responsibility is to the army, we are going to train each and every one of you as combat fighters, and every one of you will continue your day-to-day role as well. Each job, all responsibilities, is of the upmost importance to ensure we are a well-fed, well-hydrated, and well-trained army... but first and foremost all of you, from florist to blacksmith, will become a warrior."

General Carlux retrieved a handkerchief from his uniform, patted invisible sweat from his brow and paused a moment, for melodramatic effect, before continuing.

"There is the possibility that our enemy is trying to bring war to our home. If that does happen, all the families in the realm are in perilous danger. It is thought that the enemy, in this case is Theiler, one who would think nothing of splitting our souls, while simultaneously splitting our heads."

At the words 'splitting our heads' a noticeable rift went through the seated formation. "Sir," one of his ranking giants stood up, "how do we know it's Theiler? The stories of the past tell us he is trapped within another realm with no way of escape."

"I'll tell you how. Over thousands of years he's been growing in power, never venturing past his realm, never aging, and always seeking revenge in hopes to please his father in the Cardinal Realm. Think of it this way, who else would cause earthquakes in order to split our society, or families, our faith, and the very Veil that protects us from intrusion? It could be nobody else other than Theiler. Theiler is a tricky one, and he's been educating himself on warfare and our forms of protection for years, mark my word. We don't have spies, we don't have information from the other side of the veils, and we don't know the capabilities of his armies. What we do know is this is exactly how we think he would start an invasion, by playing on his strengths of division."

"Yoo-hoo, General," Ms. Parish was walking towards General Carlux, her demeanor changed as to reflect nothing out of the ordinary had happened that night. "I had a productive visit with Lady Cybele earlier and my inspection team is nearly finished. I also ran into Mr. Morphon and Charon who are taking their sweet time in surveying the Veil. In fact, they weren't even half finished when I left them. I swear, I don't know if they are taking this seriously or not." She looked over the men still shifting uncomfortably in their seats, "How is the training going?"

"Well, I'm giving a pep talk to our men, I think we will be ready to start training bright and early. I don't suppose Mr. Morphon has found any recruits for me yet? I'd like to get the new members paired with my seasoned veterans to begin as soon as possible."

"Oh no, the pair decided to start on the mountain side. I personally wouldn't have suggested that because, of course, there isn't anyone on that side. It's as if those two don't want to find volunteers to help protect us. I'm so glad that you are taking this seriously, look at the men you've already assembled for our protection. Why, this must be the greatest Spring Crow Army in a millennium."

General Carlux found it difficult not to blush. "Why yes, they are a strapping bunch, and I'll have them trained for our protection in no time flat."

"Well, personally, I think that the tremors are a result of a new Jinn coming through the Veil. Think about it, Leo came through the Water Veil with Charon right before the largest, most recent activity."

"That's a coincidence; the tremors have been happening for some time."

"Yes, but I think Joe might have been sick and wanted to pass in his other world, surrounded by his Earth family. Perhaps it was the veil paying tribute to one of our finest Jinn. Speaking of the finest Jinn, or in our case an untrained Jinn, Leo has been playing with his library instead of staying home as instructed. Who knows, maybe he was playing with it right before the latest event, before the amulet was placed around his neck. It could have been the library's way of telling him he wasn't ready."

"He's not at home? He could be in danger! I'll send a team to scout the town, we won't leave any stone unturned..."

"That's very thoughtful, General, but I don't believe that's necessary," Ms. Parish laid a calming hand on the General's shoulder. "I found him and Angel and told them, very matter-of-fact, to head home. Whether they heeded my instructions is to be seen, but I have every faith that the Spring Realm is a safe place for them, even if they didn't go straight home."

"Did you inform Lady Cybele of your interactions?"

"Not yet; although, I did tell her that when I went by the house to check on them, they weren't there. I only found them after I left her side, and before I spoke with Mr. Morphon and Charon at the Mountain Veil. She didn't seem pleased with their disappearance. After I consult with my team one more time, to ensure that they have thoroughly inspected the town, and I report to Mr. Forswear so he can begin a budget plan for repairs, I'll let Lady Cybele know that they are fine. Kids just being kids, in this case a kid Jinn."

"If you believe they are safe where they are, and as long as they are still within the Spring Crow, I suppose you are correct. As of this moment we are in danger of a possible raid, but I don't see any danger in the foreseeable future." General Carlux sighed. "Leo has only been here for a couple of days, it would do him some good to be away from the house for a bit, and to see some areas of the town he may be unfamiliar with. He is going against Lady Cybele's wishes but as you said, kids being kids. I'll be sure to tell my men to keep an eye out for them, but I won't send a party specifically on their behalf. I'm sure you're right and they will eventually tire and make their way back to Leo's."

"Quite right, General. Now, what are your plans for the army?"

"They have a long day ahead of them tomorrow and I don't see a reason to keep them any longer than needed. I expect that they will want to be with their families tonight and we can start the training late tomorrow morning. I can at least give them a little extra time."

General Carlux addressed the army. "Men, as I stated, we drill, fight, eat, and work as a team, but I've been remiss on another aspect of our team. Your families are the lifeblood of your dedication. Tonight, go home and spend time with your wives, sons, daughters, mothers, and fathers. Report back in the morning, one hour past the start of the normal duty day; this is my gift to you in preparation for training. Group, ATTENTION." The army all stood in perfect unison. "DISMISSED."

"What a kind and thoughtful gesture, General. I'm sure the men appreciate it and I feel that the training will go well; however, long and slow you feel that you need to take it on behalf of the new troops you will receive."

Ms. Parish turned to take her leave from the General. She smiled to herself, *only one council member left to visit.*

"Ah, Ms. Parish, what news and information do you have? I need to complete the financial plans for Lady Cybele before daybreak. You know how she is insistent on ensuring the Spring Crow be in tip-top shape, in order to ease the minds of everyone," Mr. Forswear began, greeting Ms. Parish as she walked into his office. The office was an organized chaos, files and books lay in piles on the floor and a spare chair. Calculators, antiquated adding machines, and half-finished reports filled the remainder of the space available on the worn wooden desk. It was set up just how Mr. Forswear liked it.

"So far, no major damage; the big-ticket item will be repairing the crack in the fountain, but you know how things are, the fountain is old and delicate. I'm sure once that is repaired the rest can be done in no time. A few broken shop windows make up the remainder of the damage; I don't believe there will be a need for too much worry. As long as the citizens know that they are safe, I believe we can come out of this as if nothing happened within a few days, hours even."

"Please, have a seat," Mr. Forswear offered after realizing he had not properly welcomed Ms. Parish, while clearing a pile of last year's finances from his spare chair. "What have the others found and how are preparations going?"

"Everything is moving along smoothly. Charon and Mr. Morphon should be finished with the review of most of the Veil by now, General Carlux has given quite the pep talk to the army, and I've been briefing Lady Cybele whenever I get the chance. Leo and Angel gave me a scare earlier tonight, but I've sorted that too. All in all, it's been a productive but exhausting night, but it's our sworn duty, isn't it? To protect and advance what we feel is important."

"Quite right, quite right. What type of scare did the children give you?"

"They weren't in the house earlier tonight, but I was able to locate them and give them a little motherly advice. I'm sure they are back by now, as it is late and I know they have had a hard day, bless their hearts." Ms. Parish stood, stretched, and yawned. "I'm sure you have some work to finish before morning, so I'll let you get to it. If there is anything else you require, just let me know. I'm going to give Lady Cybele one last update before

I'm off to bed myself. Is there any other information you need from me now, or can the rest wait until morning?"

"I can put together my initial proposal and estimation, just write down how many windows and I can pull together historical data on past repairs of the fountain. It should be fairly accurate, and I can fine-tune the amounts once we begin repairs."

Ms. Parish wrote down the figures, said her goodbye to Mr. Forswear, and left the office, all while trying to hide her sly smile. *Too easy*, she thought to herself. *Bringing everyone onto the same page will make ripping the page that much simpler.*

After she exited the building, she made her way back to Leo's house, ensuring she mentally remembered every store and alleyway she passed, in case she was questioned later. She would pause occasionally to give the appearance that she was surveying damage and jotting down notes. She knew that Leo and Angel would not be at the house, it was the perfect place to finish for the night.

When Ms. Parish arrived at Leo's she remained outside as not to further disturb the interior, in case someone did notice the children were still missing. She didn't want to be caught knowing they were gone by entering a second time. She brought her left hand, palm up, to eye level while gently touched her amulet with her right. The amulet began to glow a golden gray as she peered into the orange sphere taking shape in her palm.

"Master, the young Jinn and the girl will be delivered to you and all is going to plan in the Spring Realm. Yes, thank you, Master. All I ask is that the girl be given to me. Of course, Master, once you have deemed her worthiness first, thank you, Master."

Chapter 10

Once across the tree line at the end of the Forest Veil, Leo and Angel dismounted their horses, peeled off the heavy armor, and released the beasts into the woods. Again, not understanding their freedom, Angel whispered encouraging words to each. As if in complete understanding, the magnificent animals took off towards the Spring Crow, enjoying the first taste of freedom in their tortured lives. Angel watched for a moment before placing her hand on the closest tree. "Thank you, my friends, I don't know what we would have done without you."

Leo stood, not knowing what to say. Just days ago, he was content in his father's house in Ohio, going to school, finishing book reports, and missing Grandpa Joe. In the time since, he has traveled through a passage to a new world, paid a skeletal boatman—whom he now considers a friend—to take him across a vast waterway, and arrived in a realm that he assumed was another dimension co-existing with his own. In addition, he attended a ball in his honor—something he never thought possible—met and befriended a girl who on the surface seemed very brash, but was truly gentle, learned of magic, and finally crossed another passage where he was saved by animated trees. "What now?" Leo asked when Angel was finished with her thank you.

"I think we need to get closer to the town, but we need to stay hidden. It wouldn't hurt to try to blend in too, just in case. We can keep to the edge of the Forest Veil for now but once we get into town, we will have to lay low and gather any information we can."

"Information about what?" asked Leo.

"About Theiler and his plans, of course. I'm sure we are up against something that hasn't been seen in years. If I'm right, we need to find out what's going on and warn the Spring Crow. If I'm wrong, well, let's just have an adventure. No matter what, keep low until we find out exactly what we are dealing with."

Angel spread her arms and brought them together with a silent clap. The weapons she acquired from the warriors disappeared, as if she never possessed them.

"How did you do that?"

"Bring your hands up and then together while saying *Obscure Armory*."

Leo complied and his weapons vanished, as well. "Where did they go?"

"They are safe in a world of our choosing. Everything we have, our weapons, our large and small possessions, even your library, can be locked into a world of your own making. You won't be able to physically visit the world as it is... how can I explain it... well, it's an imaginary world, if you will. You can't visit, but in your mind it's as real as you and me. You store items and if you can picture the places in your imaginary world where the items are stored, you can more easily summon them when needed. For example, when summoning your library, it takes a second or two, right?"

"Yes, but only a second."

"Now imagine a bookshelf in a room that you are familiar with. Think of as many details as you want for your bookshelf, what's on it, where it is placed, if it's clean or dusty. On that bookshelf is your library, and you place your library on that bookshelf, the same way each and every time. If your subconscious knows where to find the library it will come to you faster, you won't have to mentally look for it each time."

"How do I get the weapons back?"

"Think of what you need from your imaginary world. It becomes easier if you name your world and ask for it by name."

"Crossbow," Leo commanded. Nothing happened.

"You have to ask for it, not just blurt out a word" Angel explained. "Move your hands in a requesting gesture too, like this, *Forthwith Bow.*" The crossbow appeared in her hands. "When you say the words, you must be specific on what you want and picture where you left it. For example, if I said *Forthwith Bow* and my mind is distracted by my hair or a gift, I may end up with a ribbon for tying a ponytail or a package wrapped in crossbow printed paper. That wouldn't help me in a dangerous situation at all, now would it? Be specific, move your hands to summon the energy around you, use the energy in your amulet, and think of what you truly need. When you get into a jam and you don't know what you truly need, or the proper words or phrase, consult your library. If you need something that you don't have, and you need to make something—let's say a potion to ward off fleas from a pet girnocerous—ask your library for the formula and then seek out the ingredients."

It was all starting to come together in Leo's racing mind, all except the part about the girnocerous, which he made a mental note to ask about later. "*Forthwith Bow.*" Leo concentrated and shifted his hands up and out, giving a small clap. The crossbow, complete with arrows, appeared in his hands. He looked at Angel, gave a slight smile, and concentrated on a shelf in his father's garage, a shelf he knew well because he kept his seldom-used baseball bat, glove and other normal adolescent sporting equipment on it, "*Obscure Armory.*" The weapon disappeared, put away on the garage shelf in his mind for the next time he would need it.

As Angel patiently waited, he did the same for the rest of the weapons he acquired from the warriors, ensuring he placed them all on the shelf in his mind so he could easily retrieve them if, God forbid, they were ever needed.

After the impromptu lesson, Leo and Angel made their way towards the town, keeping to the outskirts of the forest. The landscape outside of the forest was nothing like the landscape of their own Realm. It was hot, brutally hot. While the Spring Crow's environment matched what Leo was accustomed to in his world, this was different. The slight wind provided no relief and he felt as if every step he took was into the fan of the hair dryers he had seen in commercials on television. The ground was hard and covered in a yellowish-brown dirt that had not seen rain in quite some time. Rocks protruded in every direction, some small, some large, and all jagged.

Surprisingly the landscape wasn't completely flat, there were multiple hills to make their way across, making the hot journey more tiring than they initially expected. Their legs burned, the oxygen ripped from their lungs, and every breath they took felt like sandpaper filing down the inside of their chest cavity. The air had a dirty smell, not that of the fresh forest directly next to them, but instead of burning embers consisting of waste with the hint of despair. No sign of life was around.

"I need to sit down. How long have we been walking?"

"It feels like forever," answered Leo, sweat dripping down his back, "and the sun here seems bigger, as if it were closer to the surface. Thankfully, I only see one... I hope that means a moon will follow eventually."

Angel plopped down and sat cross-legged in the dirt, head held down to shade her face from the onslaught of the sun's relentless rays.

"We can move into the forest for some shade. I don't think we should be out here for much longer, we can't afford to get sick from the heat." Leo pulled at Angel's arm and led her to the edge of the forest. "There, we can rest here for a minute. It's out of the heat and we will be hidden."

"I've always loved this forest, but I never realized how thick it is. Oh, how I wish we could just stay on its edges, but we would lose too much time. How long do you want to rest?"

"Just long enough to get our heads straight again."

"Heads straight?"

"It's just an expression... just long enough for us to feel better, in order to keep going for at least as long as we've already traveled. Then we can take a break again."

"Leo, wake up," Angel hissed in an urgent whisper. "We fell asleep."

Leo, groggy-eyed, raised his head from a mossy log and looked around, nothing but blackness and an unworldly cold emanating from the golden moon.

"I can't believe we fell asleep; we were only supposed to rest until our faces were square."

"Head straight," corrected Leo.

"Whatever, we need to find the town and figure out what we can about Theiler; come on."

Leo gathered himself and prepared to continue their journey. The moon was out now, a single moon to match the single sun that was visible earlier, both matching his world in shape as well as appearance, but slightly different by the extreme heat emanated by the sun and a palpable fridge somehow radiating from the moon. Leo shivered. "*Modekleidercold*," he guessed as he waved his arms out slowly to gather his magic. Leo was now standing in flip-flops, board shorts, and a tank top looking as he were ready to take on the waves he's seen in postcards from Hawaii.

"Are you crazy, what do you think you're doing?" hissed Angel. "It's freezing out." She pointed at Leo, raised her right arm. "*Modekleidercushvos*." Leo was now more appropriately dressed in warm boots, long black pants, a black overcoat with hood, scarf, and gloves. She said the words again, "*Modekleidercush*." This time, she was decked out in warmer clothes to fit the environment—dark like Leo's, with a splash of color in the form of a dark blue scarf.

"I was trying to keep warm, I figured I needed to say I was cold."

Angel sighed. "You're getting the hang of it, but you have to be specific on what you need, not what you feel or just want. Come on, we must be nearly there."

The two walked for another hour in silence, warming themselves as they traveled, until they reached the first glimpse of civilization.

Sun dried earthen cob structures constructed of ashen dirt, mixed with all manner of other organic material, dotted the landscape. The design wasn't haphazard, but instead laid out in neat rows, and the construction varied from low buildings with no windows or doors, only portholes to enter and exit, to higher buildings supported by both dry mud, straw, stone and wooden beams. Small fires burned within metal hearths on the outside of what appeared to be living quarters, and large caldrons of a rancid boiling concoction of what could only be some type of sustenance for the inhabitants of this realm.

"Over here," whispered Angel, "this hut is empty, and we can see who is coming and going."

The two ducked into the hut, each taking an open, glassless porthole, and peered out at the people living in the Carved Realm. All were dressed in black cloaks that would not have been able to warm even on the mildest of nights. The heads of the figures were covered with a hood attached to the robes, and all were cinched together with dark chains overlapping to keep the fabric in place. What was most noticeable from this vantage point is that everyone was barefooted. Leo looked at Angel. "They must be freezing," he whispered.

"I don't think they notice the cold... in fact, I don't think they feel anything, anything at all. Look at their faces."

Leo spotted the figure closest to him. Rather than the gaunt face he expected to see, there was emptiness. Not an emptiness you would commonly associate with someone who was forlorn or full of doubt, but pure, wispy smoke, emptiness.

"What is this? Are they alive?"

"I don't know," replied Angel, "but I don't think we should stick around to find out. It must be almost dinner time and I, for one, don't want to experience how they eat. Come on, we need to go back to the woods."

"But we haven't gotten any real information. What about the warriors in the forest? They didn't have empty faces and they were decked out in armor and weapons, not robes and chains. And they certainly had footwear under their armor; I didn't notice any bare feet when they were being dangled mid-air by the trees."

"What other info do we need? We have a population of zombies and I don't see any..."

Four large, iron clad hands, grabbed Leo and Angel from behind, one arm around each waist and the other covering their faces and holding their mouths in a crushing manner. Only their watering eyes were visible from the top of the gruff hands.

"So, what do we have here, little mice perhaps? What are you doing here little mice, do you make it a common practice to go into other people's dwellings and spy? Do you know what we do with those who keep secrets from the Master?"

The two warriors who had grabbed Leo and Angel squeezed harder and turned them around until they were face-to-face with a third larger-than-life warrior, just like the others, tar-like eyes with long, blood-red hair.

"Take them to the dungeons until we determine who these two are and how they re-obtained their souls," ordered the third warrior. "Don't be gentle, if they want their vital forces so bad, they should experience every hardship along the way." The warriors holding Leo and Angel turned, no smile or expression, and marched to their own cadence out into the night.

The journey to the dungeons was short, but every bit as painful as the warrior had requested. Never letting their large steel-like hands drop from Leo and Angel's covered face, the two warriors carried Leo and Angel—more by their necks, rather than their bodies—through the realm, past the cob huts, and towards the only truly solid constructed, stone building in the Carved Realm. No matter how Leo and Angel kicked, bit, and tried to resist, the grips were no match and just got tighter the more they fought.

The structure was a mix of a medieval stone castle and fortress. Large and imposing, it was twice the size of the Spring Realm Town Hall and was protected on all sides by gruesome antique cannons and warriors of all shapes and sizes, but none would be considered small. Once through the heavy thick door hung with massive iron hinges the two were taken down a narrow stone staircase. At the bottom were a row of stone floored cells, each chamber no more than three-foot-long by three-foot-wide but over ten feet tall; little room for a normal-sized man and no chance of escape through the tall, thick ceiling.

"We are feeling kind-hearted today," one of the warriors spoke, shocking both Leo and Angel, "since you are small little mice, we are going to let you share a cell." The warriors shoved the two into the cramped cell and shut the gate behind.

With no room to lie down, the two could only stand, close enough that each could feel the other's heartbeat in terrifying fear.

"What now?" Asked Leo.

"Try your library."

"*Forthwith Knowledge.*" Nothing happened.

"Try again, you must not be concentrating hard enough. Think of your shelf and try again."

Leo tried again, and again, and again for a fourth time, but the library refused to appear.

"Your magic won't work down here, believe me, I've tried," came a voice from a cell just opposite of Leo and Angel.

"Who's that," asked Leo, as brave as he could, while waiting for his eyes to adjust to the lack of light.

"The names John, Iron John."

"Iron John, where are we?" stammered Leo.

"Just John is fine. You're in the Oubliette, of course, the Forgotten Dungeon. Where did you think you were? Everyone knows about the Forgotten Dungeon; don't tell me you've never heard the stories? You're either uninformed, stupid, or new... and nobody in the Carved Veil is new, so I'm going to go with incredibly stupid."

Angel replied, "Think of us as uninformed. If you're so smart, what is the Oubliette, or as you called it, the Forgotten Dungeon, and if you're so smart how did you end up here after you knew about it?"

Leo could tell Angel was frustrated and that she wanted to be able to sit or shift into a position that would relieve the extreme cramps in her shoulders and legs. He was feeling the same.

"Ah, you have spunk, I like that, and it's something I haven't seen or heard in hundreds of years. The Oubliette isn't like what you have heard in the stories, or in your cases, what you haven't heard. An Oubliette, by normal description, is a dungeon that is only accessible from a single point in the ceiling, but this is much worse. You were taken down the stairs into your cell, were you not?"

Leo and Angel nodded, unseen in the dark; John took the silence for agreement.

"If there were stairs, wouldn't there be some form of light from the direction you came? Look, absolute nothingness. Once you are a prisoner in the Oubliette the entrance works in one direction only, down. Remember, by description there is a single point of access, in reality once you are a prisoner, there are no points of access. Why, even when you were brought down the stairs didn't appear to me, they are single and appear once for every creature."

With that John fell silent, contemplating his own fate, as he often did, while Leo and Angel now contemplated theirs.

Minutes turned into hours; Leo continued to attempt to produce his library to no avail, while Angel shifted from foot to foot while simultaneously trying to conjure any type of tool that would aide in their escape in their time of need. All attempts were fruitless.

"Why squander your energy?" asked John, who had throughout the years become accustomed to silence. The captured souls surrounding the Oubliette block most magic, even most light and dark. You won't be able to use any power but your own physical power, believe me, I've tried, and your physical power will feign over time."

"What do you mean, souls surrounding the Oubliette?" asked Angel.

"My God, you really are new; how do you not know about the Cellar of Souls?"

"Cellar of Souls?" asked Angel.

"I have to assume you were outside at one point before you were prisoners, you had to have seen others, besides Master's warriors, the soulless creatures wandering from place to place."

"We did see people dressed in black, and their faces seemed empty," answered Leo.

"Their faces weren't empty, my boy, they are soulless creatures, created in a Realm that strips everything after creation." John sighed. "You see, in order to build his army, the Master..."

"You mean Theiler," corrected Angel.

"Yes, Master Theiler," John continued. "Theiler, through his learned knowledge of dark magic, has found a way to create living creatures out of the very ground we walk on. Nobody knows how he does it, but the creatures, in Theiler's opinion, are in near perfect form save for one problem. When you create something, anything out of dark or light energy, there is a soul attached. Upon creation, Theiler will snatch the soul through Eidolon, capturing or carving the soul and encasing

114

it in catacombs built to completely surround the Oubliette on all sides, save the portal used by the warriors to enter and the ground below. The soul absorbs the magic, as does the dark and cursed ground below, making your attempts futile."

"Why would he take their souls if he needs to build an army?" asked Angel.

"When a particularly violent creature is created and its soul is taken, Theiler will personally torture that soul, day and night, until it becomes even more violent and completely obedient to him and only him. Only then will he return the soul to the creature who then becomes a great and powerful warrior serving only the Master. The other weaker creations aren't so lucky, their souls are split for eternity and the poor creatures are put to work doing any and all tasks required in the Carved Realm, all in service to the Master."

"And how do you still have your soul?" Angel continued to pry.

"I've been here almost as long as the Realm itself, before it was the Carved Realm, before the great split of the Jinn. I'm a prisoner just like you, as my soul is ancient and too much a part of me and cannot be carved. After Theiler took power, he attempted to recruit me as his first warrior as I have always been a warrior at heart from birth. I am always prepared for battle, especially as a captive, but I also have free will, something Theiler could not take away. Therefore, I've been a prisoner for a millennium. My armor does not rust, my legs do not grow weary, and my mind is sharp, therefore I'm too much of a threat to Theiler's beliefs."

John grew silent, as did Leo and Angel.

A millennium, Leo thought. Time is of upmost and simultaneously of no importance in the realms, it ebbs and flows differently than in his world and a millennium to him may be hours in his world... how long would he be gone and how long would he survive. Would his father remember him if he somehow escapes, would school continue on, or would he be forgotten to history as so many others in the past? His mind raced when he heard a small voice coming from Iron John's caged cell.

"There you are, the beautiful children we seek. We were worried about you."

Leo and Angel could hear Iron John's armor scrape the walls as he sprang in his tiny cell. "Who's there," Iron John demanded.

Chapter 11

Safe in the Spring Crow, Ms. Parish woke at her normal time, sleeping surprisingly well after setting Master's plan in motion. Perhaps it was the comforting calm that she would be rewarded by the Master in the future, that helped subside the excitement she felt that helped her fall into a deep sleep throughout the night. She went about her normal routine of preparing herself for the day, brushing her long blond hair before pinning it up into a tight bun, leaving a few strands to hang down the back of her neck, dressed in her usual smart attire of black pencil skirt, white button up blouse, and black heels. She finished he ensemble with her amulet, dangling from a delicate but surprisingly strong gold necklace. After a quick breakfast of coffee mixed with dragon butter and heavy cream, she gave her spotless white kitchen a quick wipe down, placed her mug in the sink, and headed for Town Hall.

"Good morning, Ms. Parish," Mr. Forswear greeted her as she walked through the door behind him. I trust you had a good night's sleep after all of last night's excitement."

"Absolutely the best." She replied

"And what of the children, did they heed your advice and go back to Leo's for the night or did they continue to wander the streets like vagabonds?"

"I walked around the house again and it appeared they were safe and sound. Afterwards, I went straight home. I trust my team provided you with the full report last night?" Ms. Parish asked.

"Ah yes, not quite as bad as we had thought it might be. I think we may have a budget that will stretch far enough to work on all damages within the town and may even have some left over for the families and creatures on the outskirts to help with their damages too."

"That's wonderful, I'm so glad my team could be of help."

Mr. Forswear and Ms. Parish passed the fountain in the center of the hall. The hall was re-transformed into its normal and fully functional grandeur following the Jinn Ball and the abrupt ending following the earthquake.

"Sylvia," called Ms. Parish as Sylvia Korpus entered the Hall.

Sylvia, the only non-appointed councilmember on the committee, was responsible for general oversight and advice to the members as well as being a trusted confidant to Lady Cybele. She was a tall, thin woman, very plain in facial appearances with black framed glasses, with her dark hair always pulled into a ponytail, and she wore her signature custom-fitted, cream colored business suit that gave her a polished and professional look. Always in possession of a clipboard, as she found she could easily and quickly work with any information after documenting data she needed from her library, she was consistent with her mentorship and very matter-of-fact with her information.

"Good morning, Ms. Parish, Mr. Forswear. Has everyone arrived or are you the first?"

"Good morning to you, too, Sylvia," greeted Mr. Forswear. "I believe we are the first, we just arrived, but we haven't seen Mr. Morphon, Charon, nor General Carlux. I'm sure they will be along any moment."

"Well, we don't want to brief Lady Cybele without having our ducks in a row, do we? We can wait in the reception café, if you like."

With a wave of both hands in a parting motion and a glimmer from Sylvia's amulet, glass doors appeared to the left of the Hall and the aroma of fresh baked goods and Kopi Luwak coffee from the Magpie Bakery filled the air.

"So, tell me," Sylvia began as she poured cream into her coffee and sat at a table, while Mr. Forswear filled a plate with assorted breakfast pastries, "have you two worked out a plan to pay for the damages?"

"Ms. Parish's team gave me the numbers yesterday and as I was telling her before you arrived, I believe we will be okay this time. But, if the earthquakes keep coming the monetary situation could, and probably will, worsen."

"I see," said Sylvia as she sipped her coffee, "and what do you propose we do in that situation?"

"We haven't completed a solid plan, but my first thought would be a tax on municipal services," answered Mr. Forswear between bites of dragon cruller.

"But we don't want to put the community into a situation where they can't enjoy the necessities of life," countered Ms. Parish.

Sylvia, seeing that the problem had not been adequately discussed, offered her advice. "We need to think of this as a game of chess, always looking a few moves ahead in case of a worst-case scenario or in the case we find a permanent resolution, a checkmate in our favor that will be agreeable to the community."

"Well, I... I really haven't gotten that far," mumbled Mr. Forswear, not bothering to finish chewing. "I suppose we would need to tighten our belts in other areas, perhaps start a creature tax, maybe ration the army a little tighter... I'm sure I can come up with more than a few ideas before the end of the day, once we see exactly where we sit regarding the size of the expanded army and any news from Mr. Morphon and Charon."

As if on cue, General Carlux, in full-service dress uniform, sharply pressed with decorations and highly polished boots, entered the hall reception café. He acknowledged the three with a nod and went straight for the coffee, loading it with enough sugar to turn the bitter black liquid into a sweet syrupy concoction.

"I didn't sleep a wink last night. After I gave my speech, I was so motivated that all I could do after I laid out the training plans to my officers, was lie in my bed and imagine the glorious training and possible battles that will take place. Ah, it's going to be one for the books if someone or something attempts to disrupt our way of life. Generations to come will tell stories of our good works." General Carlux began pacing with his coffee and he smiled at the three.

"General," started Sylvia, "I believe we need to gather and compile all our information and then formulate our plans in a cohesive manner first, before we get too far ahead of ourselves. Once approved by Lady Cybele, we shall proceed with the rebuilding and training efforts. Until then, we need to think of worst-case scenarios, as in your glorious battle, but we must also consider more simple solutions."

"Always the voice of reason, aren't you, Silvia." Ms. Parish smiled. "Why, as far as we know, this is just nature being nature and we have absolutely nothing to worry about. The veils all around have protected us for almost as long as stories have been written, it's probably nothing to worry about and a little elbow grease and paint will make everything right-as-rain."

"I'm not saying that at all, Ms. Parish. I'm saying we need to look at every angle, good and bad, before we jump to any conclusions. Don't get me wrong, I do hope you're right and that we have nothing to worry about, but I'd be a fool to consider a recommendation to Lady Cybele without first looking at every possible cause and effect."

Ms. Parish gave a slight smile. Convincing Mr. Morphon, Mr. Forswear, and General Carlux that things weren't as bad as they seemed was a piece of cake compared to planting the seed within Sylvia. *Why does she always have to be so analytical?* It was little wonder why Lady Cybele trusted Sylvia and her advice.

Finishing their coffee and pastries, the committee, minus a noticeably absent Mr. Morphon and Charon, made their way to the far side of the hall and waited while Sylvia rapped on the door three times. Without interaction, the large wooden door slowly swung open to Lady Cybele's office.

"Thank you all for coming in at such an early hour in our time of need," Lady Cybele said with a polite but tired smile. "Please, sit."

Several chairs were positioned around a large, highly polished conference table and the committee took their seats.

"I don't believe we need a recapitulation of last night's events at the Jinn Ball," Lady Cybele started as she took her place at the head of the table and waved the door closed. "Sylvia, we will also forgo the reading of the minutes from the last council meeting as we are not meeting under normal circumstances. Mr. Forswear, I believe Ms. Parish has surveyed the damage and has provided you with a rundown of all affected?"

"Yes ma'am, and as I was telling the others, I believe that we will continue to operate in the black and should continue producing positive earnings, once all expenses are rendered."

"Herrrhem," Sylvia cleared her throat and looked at Mr. Forswear, giving him an awkward and uneasy feeling."

"That is," continued Mr. Forswear, "assuming that the earthquakes are of natural causes. We will rebuild in a manner to protect against further damage, and the need for a larger more robust army is found to be unsubstantiated."

"I don't believe an army is ever unsubstantiated, no matter the size," interrupted General Carlux, as he sipped his overly sweet coffee mixture. "Lady Cybele, the Realm has enjoyed years of peace and tranquility due in part to the nature of our defense, which includes some of the most highly trained beast and creatures this side of the Veil. Once I whip the new troops into order, I feel that we can defend the Spring Crow Realm against any invader."

Lady Cybele nodded in agreement. "Yes, this side of the Veil... we don't know what lurks on the other side; even Charon doesn't venture past the edges, and never into another realm. The furthest he travels through any Veil is towards the other world, Leo's world."

"Yes, ma'am, but..."

"And speaking of veils, why hasn't Mr. Morphon or Charon joined us? They knew we were meeting this morning. Ms. Parish, you mentioned that you were to speak to them last night regarding Leo and Angel, I expected you to report back to me, but I didn't hear from you. I was up most of the night worrying about them. What news do you have and what was conveyed to the two at the Veil?"

Ms. Parish looked sheepishly around the table, she had forgotten to circle back with Lady Cybele to tell her that she had supposedly found the two and sent them back home, as she had told the others. "I did find the two, playing in an alleyway, and I informed them it wasn't safe and that they should make their way back to Leo's. I did tell the others as well as inform Mr. Morphon and Charon of their follies, but I must admit, I was tired and after consulting with the rest of the committee, I made my way back home and instantly fell asleep. I do apologize for any inconvenience I may have caused you."

"Apology accepted, but please don't be so forgetful in the future."

The tension in the room was becoming disagreeable when the door flung open to reveal Mr. Morphon and Charon, caked head-to-toe in dirt and grime.

"Sorry we're late," Charon spoke breathlessly, "there is a crack, a small crack, that is almost imperceptible but a crack, nonetheless. The Mountainous Veil didn't give us any trouble, but the Forest Veil was a virtual crawl. Someone didn't want to step foot into the wood and remained on the edges while I had to tromp through. It's a wonder we were able to spot it at all."

"You mean it's a wonder *I* was able to spot it," corrected Mr. Morphon.

"Yes, yes, *you* spotted it while on the inside looking out; you had a better vantage point than I."

Lady Cybele raised her hand and the argument stopped. "So, you did find a crack? If there is a crack, there is a threat. Mr. Forswear, what were you saying about natural causes? A natural cause wouldn't be able to tear a magical barrier created by the ruler of the Cardinal Realm. No, this is dark."

"There's more," continued Mr. Morphon, almost in a whisper. "Footprints." Everyone, save Lady Cybele and Ms. Parish, gave an audible gasp.

"Not to worry, the footprints were leading away from the Crow Spring, nothing coming in, so I believe we're safe. But I feel for the poor souls who ventured out last night, there is no telling what is in and on the other side of the Forest Veil," Charon informed in an attempt to calm the others.

Lady Cybele stood. "Mr. Forswear, please take your estimates to all of the contractors in the Spring Crow and begin correcting any damage that has been reported. Begin on the outside of town, with the houses, no matter what manner of creature inhabits. I expect the businesses to be done simultaneously, but begin with the houses, if you can."

"Understood, shall I ensure all are protected against future earthquake damage?"

"Yes, future damage and ensure there is adequate protection and fortification in case of a future attack of any manner."

"Future attack?" General Carlux stood, almost spilling his coffee.

"Yes, General, I believe you should ensure your army is ready for not only defense, but also devise an offensive plan for I fear we must be ready for any situation."

"We've never had an offensive course of action, only parades and defensive drills."

"Well then, General, you must consult your library and study the battles of the past. I believe they may unfortunately come in handy. Mr. Morphon, please go with the General and ensure any creature not already enlisted or working with Mr. Forswear is conscribed into the army and starts training immediately."

Mr. Forswear, Mr. Morphon, and General Carlux, armed with their marching orders, left the room while discussing their plans.

"Ms. Parish, please check on Leo and Angel, I need to ensure their safety during this time of crisis, they are more important now than ever."

Ms. Parish managed, "yes, Lady Cybele," before she exited the room with the others.

Lady Cybele waited for Ms. Parish to leave the room and shut the door with a wave. "Charon, Sylvia, I don't believe everyone was completely truthful in their tales from last night."

The two sat, looking first towards each other before back to Lady Cybele.

"Ms. Parish informed the committee that Leo and Angel were found in an alleyway and that she sent them home. Charon, you stated there are footprints leading into the Forest Veil. Sylvia, you are my most trusted confidant and Charon, I've trusted you with the protection of the Veil for as long as I can remember. Both of you have known Angel since she has been in my charge, can either of you recall how long that has been?"

Neither Sylvia nor Charon could remember a time when Angel wasn't a part of the Spring Veil.

"In that time, have you ever known Angel to be someone who did not enjoy the finer things in life? Or someone who would need to duck into an alleyway to do as she pleased? You see, she doesn't have a library or an amulet because she does not require one, and she bores easily at the thought of not having creature comforts. But I fear that while she is growing stronger and brighter with every passing day, she may have thought an adventure, or information to warn and protect her home, was in order."

Sylvia and Charon were still confused.

"You see," Lady Cybele continued, "I don't believe Angel and Leo were in an alleyway last night, but I do believe that Ms. Parish found that they were the owners of the footprints you found near the forest Charon."

"But neither Mr. Morphon nor I mentioned that the footprints weren't anywhere near the tear in the Veil."

"No, I assumed that myself."

"I can understand Leo being able to go into the Forest Veil due to his Jinn lineage, but that doesn't explain Angel," quarried Sylvia, remembering the conversation with the committee in the attic of the town hall following the latest earthquake.

"I'm afraid Ms. Parish must have found that secret too." Lady Cybele sighed. "You see, while Leo Kane is a descendant of the Jinn Knight Kane, Angel is the decedent of the original tutor, whose name was supposedly forgotten. In reality, the name was never forgotten, just hidden in plain sight. Angel was not named for the celestial attendants of the gods, but rather the celestial order is referred to as angels in remembrance of the great tutor."

Sylvia and Charon didn't dare speak for fear of missing any part of the secret.

"When the original tutor was banished for knowledge of the brothers' affairs, he accompanied Kane to the Spring Crow. Angel is the next tutor, a descendant of the most powerful magician ever known. She doesn't know the details of her ancestors, but she can traverse the Veils with little consequence, just as a Jinn. I share this with you because, as I said, I believe Ms. Parish knows and isn't forthright. I don't exactly how she discovered this, but I do know that if she is hiding these facts there is no doubt she is hiding more."

"That is amazing, I can't believe you have been hiding her here, right here under our noses the entire time. What would you like me to do?" asked Charon.

"Charon, I hesitate, but it's necessary, I need you to track Leo and Angel through the Forest Veil and ensure their safety."

"But I've never been to the outer edge of the Forest Veil, I've never tracked more than half-way through."

"That is why I hesitate, but it must be done. The Spring Crow cannot afford to lose Leo, Angel, or far worse, both. If this happens, no army in this realm or Leo's world will be able to save us."

"As you wish, Lady Cybele."

With that, Lady Cybele, very much out of character, arose and embraced Charon. "Please be careful, my friend, until we see each other again." She released Charon and he parted for his journey.

"And what would you like for me to do?" asked Sylvia?

"First, please find the two most fearsome giants that have not been enlisted into the aide of the army and post them outside the crack in the Forest Veil. Ensure they have lines of communications back to you and only you. Perhaps their mere presence can buy us time. Then, I need you to dig deeper in your library than you have ever before, I'm afraid your clipboard won't have some of the answers we need. My only request is that you find all the information you can on Theiler and Ms. Parish. This may be an impossible task, but it's one that needs to be attempted. Has he before attempted to leave the Carved Realm, has he succeeded in the past, and what world, if any, has he made his own as the Kane Jinn has made Leo's world theirs?"

"If he's never left the Carved Realm that would mean..." Sylvia gasped at the reality of time and never venturing out of one's own realm.

"I hesitate to guess the answers but if I'm correct, we are not dealing with a descendant. Accomplish your research in a place you won't be disturbed and report anything you find, positive or negative, only to me. While you are researching in your library, I'll be in my library reviewing past military strategies to help form deliberate actions needed for the army. I'm sure General Carlux will review past battles and field conditions, but I need to understand the advantages and disadvantages of the Spring Realm, the Carved Realm, and Leo's world."

"Yes, Lady Cybele, I understand and will report back."

Sylvia was on her way out through the heavy wooden door, which matched her ever-growing heavy heart, when Lady Cybele called to her one more time.

"Do be careful, my child, I fear we have enemies on all fronts." Sylvia nodded, turned, and continued without a word.

Lady Cybele opened her arms. "*Forthwith Knowledge.*" Her beautiful library appeared in the corner of her office. She entered, went deep into the back, towards the most ancient scripts located in the far corners, seldom touched out of the unnecessity of normal daily knowledge.

Unbeknownst to Lady Cybele, Ms. Parish had not left the hall, only the office and had listened to every word discussed with Charon and Sylvia. She was right in thinking there was something about that girl, and soon Theiler would give her to her to do as she wished. Imagine, the most powerful magic in all the realms would soon be hers to control.

Ms. Parish walked to Lady Cybele's library doors and quietly closed them with a faint click. Butterflies formed and fluttered through her stomach and heart as she turned her hand and magically placed a lock on the outside of the doors, twisted the single use cypher key that could not be magically duplicated in its exactness, pulled it and placed it in her pocket for safe keeping. Her amulet was bright as she thought to herself with a smile, *try to get out of that without knowing the type of magic used, old woman, or even better yet, close your library while inside and remain lost forever.*

Chapter 12

"Bower?" Leo asked. "Is that you?"

"No, child, my name is Acacia, a friend of Bower's. He's asked all of Forest Veil Grove to keep an eye on you two, and when we couldn't find you, we spread our roots through the Carved Realm in search of you.

"How did you get in? Iron John said we are surrounded by souls, a Cellar of Souls, that block our magic and that the ground itself is cursed preventing magic from escaping."

"My child, we are neither dark nor light magic, we are natural and pure. We have occupied this ground long before the ground was cursed, long before the Carved Realm existed in its current form. Like anything in nature, we live, we die, and when we die, we return to and make up the very soil beneath you. Our powers cannot interfere with the Cellar of Souls, but we can penetrate the ground from which we come and return. Why, it should be common knowledge, but we don't like to advertise the obvious."

"Can you help us?" asked Leo, his legs cramping. He wondered how Iron John had coped with the small cells for such a long time.

"But, of course."

"What about me?" blurted John, sounding both desperate and excited at the possibility of being free for the first time in a millennium.

Angel, taking pity of John and his plight, responded "Acacia, is it possible to take all three without anyone knowing?"

"If that is your wish, my lady."

Acacia, with a literal army of roots, began to churn the earth, digging and carving large tunnels beneath the dungeon, keeping a safe distance from the walls containing the Cellar of Souls. The ground barely shook as the roots, in their natural element, moved the solid ground with such proficiency that not only was the Cellar of Souls left intact, so were the surrounding walls and even the iron bars of their dungeon cages. With no warning, strong roots wrapped around Leo, Angel, and Iron John's legs and began to drag them through the dark and earthy scented tunnels while even more roots followed, covering their escape by refilling the tunnels, meticulously putting each tiny speck of dust back into the exact location from which it came.

Angel, clutching to Leo, didn't have time to catch her breath. The tunnel sped around in dizzying directions at breakneck speeds, making it impossible to focus on the roots expertly digging a wide path, while the roots behind wound their way through the furrows, filling in their travel. Finally, after the three thought they would suffocate in a winding, perpetually digging and expanding grave, Acacia unceremoniously spit the three from the tunnel, one-hundred meters outside of the Forest Veil. The wide hole from which they emerged was just as quickly filled and perfectly covered in the same rocks and soil that it originated, as if the ground was never disturbed.

Now free, Iron John was the first to reorient himself to the outside world. He didn't immediately stand, instead he remained on his back lying on the ground, pushing his great mass into the ground below. He flexed his legs, allowing them the first rest they have had in years, the joints around his knees flexed and popped in relief, a sensation he hadn't felt for as long he could remember. He then raised his arms above his shaggy head and stretched with all his might, allowing each vertebra in his strong back to expand and pop. Meanwhile, his hips flexed and the cramps he had been living with for longer than Leo and Angel could imagine began to subside. He brought his arms down beside his large frame and flexed his broad shoulders to where the shoulder blades almost touched, relaxing from the weight of so many years. While still lying, he began to unbuckle his armor, never looking for the clasp, just knowing each and every release point. When all was released, he shoved off the front plates from each limb and trunk, rolled to the opposite side, and finally rose to his knees. Iron John, now in his padded gambeson, stood without the weight of his full armor. He turned towards Leo and Angel, a grin appeared on his grizzled face while his muscles, visible form under the gambeson, rippled in the sun. He let out a triumphant laugh and scooped up Leo and Angel from their still prone positions.

Angel was the first to let out a muffled scream as she and Leo were pressed into his massive chest. Iron John was the personification of a true wild man. Not a lick of his now exposed flesh was free from matted hair, his muscles showed no atrophy from incarceration, and visible across his hair strewn face flashed the largest smile he had ever shown.

"My God," he exclaimed, "it's good to be free. Look at that, would you look at the sun, it's been so long since I've seen the sun or felt its warmth. And the trees, oh how beautiful they are. Thank you, my beautiful friends. Perhaps I was more fatigued than I realized, but now I have the energy of one hundred men," he exclaimed, while he looked over Leo and Angel's heads into the horizon, not letting the two go. He squeezed Leo and Angel, even tighter, before gently putting them back on the ground. "How can I ever repay you for this? It's such a blessing to me that you were captured. If it were not for you and your friend Acacia, I'd probably be down there forever. And Acacia," he turned towards the forest, "well, I'm not exactly sure which of you is Acacia, but thank you all, each and every one of you."

Leo and Angel stood motionless, not wanting to make any sudden moves as they knew they were in the presence of an ancient warrior. Leo cleared his throat and spoke.

"Iron John, I umm... what are you going to do now? Won't Theiler come looking for you?"

"I'm sure he will discover I'm gone sooner or later, but by that time I'll be deep in the Forest Veil," he turned, "that is, if you will permit me to take shelter in your canopy?" He addressed his question to no one in particular, towards the general direction of the forest.

"Of course, we will, Iron John. On behalf of Leo and Angel, we will provide you with shelter, but only shelter. We are not beholden but will protect a friend of the Jinn and tutor."

"Friends," smiled John. "I haven't had friends in as long as I can remember."

Tutor, thought Angel, *what tutor? Who is the tutor?*

"Friends," Iron John turned towards Leo and Angel, "if there is ever anything you need from me, anything at all, just touch your amulet and say my name three times and I'll come to your aid. It doesn't matter, a whisper or a shout, I will hear you.

Many of my powers are tied to the Carved Realm so no matter where you are and no matter how you call, I will repay your kindness." Iron John picked up his armor, which seemed to have magically cleaned and repaired itself to its former glory and buckled all into place. "Until we meet again Leo and Angel, the Forest Veil has stated it is beholden to no one, but I, on the other hand, am beholden to you." He bowed to the two, turned, and disappeared into the Forest Veil.

"That was certainly odd," Leo said, breaking the silence.

"Who was Acacia talking about? Who is the tutor? Acacia? Who were you talking about?"

Acacia provided no answer to Angel's line of questioning, but rather called her forward and into the Forest Veil. Leo followed her into the cool shade, and both were told to stop, just meters into its protective shelter.

"Beautiful children, you have shown your kindness to nature and creature alike. You could have left poor John to his suffering, but your hearts would not allow it. We have determined that we would like to give you both a small gift—the gift of nature."

Leo and Angel stood, confused, as Leo's amulet began to glow as did Angel's chest. "It is done."

"What's done?" asked Angel. "What just happened and where is the tutor?"

"You now have the gift of nature, a magic unlike any other. When the time comes, and it's required, you will have the ability to call upon and bend the elements in accordance with your needs. We trust you will not abuse this power, as it is not given freely or often. Use it wisely and only when truly required. You will know how to control this gift, when necessary. Now, you must go, go back into the Carved Realm to finish what you set out to do."

"I've seen everything we need to see, thank you very much," replied Leo.

"No, child, you have not. We've been watching and you have yet to finish your journey, your journey of enlightenment and information. You have to find the information needed to assist Spring Crow in protecting your way of life nor you in your journey of knowledge. As you leave feel free to take as much fruit as needed from our branches, but only what you need. Now go, do not delay any longer."

"What are we looking for? How will we know when we become enlightened and have the information we need?" asked Leo, more confused now than ever. Didn't they already know enough about Theiler and his soulless creations? His inquiry was met with silence.

"What tutor? Are we looking for someone else?" Angel was also met with silence.

Angel sighed as it became obvious to her that she was the only one who needed to know the answer and that the answer was not going to come. "Come on, grab some food, obviously we are going back."

The medieval stone castle, now that the two had more than a glimpse, looked more menacing than before. The first time Leo and Angel entered the structure they were bound by the strong arms of the warriors who had captured them. This time around, they were entering willingly, yet at the same time reluctantly, due to the previous encounter and were able to take in more of the immense size and structure. Not only was the fortress twice the size of the Spring Realm Town

Hall but it jutted skywards further than any building Leo had ever laid eyes on. It seemed to him that when he craned his neck, he could just see the top extending far beyond the thick clouds above. On all sides cannons and warriors guarded the single entrance, while barbed spikes grew and undulated in and out of the ground in between each guard, never appearing in once place for more than a second before disappearing again to reappear in another random location.

As Leo and Angel drew closer, they hid behind one of the cob structures closest to the fortress.

"We need a plan; I don't want to enter the same way we did last time and I only see one door in or out. Angel, do you know any spells that may help?"

"Not off the top of my head. Open your library, there must be something. What if we looked the part? Would we be able to walk in unannounced if we looked like we were meant to be here?"

"It's a thought. *Forthwith Knowledge*," Leo whispered, and his library appeared. "Library, we need to blend in and look like we belong in the fortress, how can we accomplish this task?"

The root of an Oxenbush plant, mixed in the cauldron of the soulless, drunk while envisioning your goal with the amulet in hand will lead you down the path.

"Why is it always a riddle," moaned Leo.

"Don't be so negative, it says as clear as day we need to dig up the root of the plant, boil it in one of the pots outside of a hut, and drink it while holding your amulet. It couldn't be clearer."

"What about you, you don't have an amulet?"

"I'll wait outside and keep guard."

"Like Hell you will," Leo countered, if I'm going in so are you."

"How do you plan on doing that, smarty? You pointed out the obvious, I don't have an amulet."

"Look, we're both going to make this concoction, drink it, and I'm going to keep ahold of you while we both think about getting in. If whatever happens affects us both that's great, if not then I'll figure something out while you keep an eye out for anyone from out here."

"Deal," Angel said. "There are Oxenbush plants about a hundred meters back, I'll get a root and you figure out a way to get some of the liquid from one of those cauldrons."

"How do you know what an Oxenbush plant is?"

"I have no idea," she said, "maybe I heard it from someone in the Spring Crow, but I know those are the plants we need."

Strangely, Leo knew she was right, those were Oxenbush plants, but how did he know too?

Angel went off to find the required root while Leo stood, trying to figure out how to obtain the required liquid. When Angel looked to be nothing but a speck on the outside of the forest Leo ducked into the cob hut they had been hiding behind. It was sparse, nothing but two mats on the ground and nothing else. He scoured each corner of the hut, scanning left to right, up and down, across each wall of the room. He discovered nothing in the first scan, the second scan of the second wall resulted in the same, the third the same, and in the corner of the fourth wall all he could find was the decomposing carcass of a large rat-like creature.

You have got to be kidding me, he thought as he saw Angel through a small single window, she already had the root. *I can't believe I'm doing this.*

Leo picked up the carcass, turned his head, closed his eyes, and dug the skull from the creatures decomposing body. While keeping his eyes closed, he further dug out the remnants of the brains and formed a small bowl.

"Are you ready?" whispered Angel as she made her way into the hut.

"I'm afraid so," Leo said as he raised his bowl.

"Are you out of your mind? You don't know what kind of diseases that thing is carrying, put it down. Look, we're going to go out there, drop this into a cauldron, and we're going to soak a little of your shirt in the mix. We can squeeze out the liquid from that. Geez, boys can be disgusting."

Leo dropped the skull, he wished he would have thought of that. "How did you get the root so fast?"

"I just asked, and the bush gave it to me. She wasn't very nice about it, but I put my foot down, literally, and well, to be honest, I think my foot came down too hard on her, she seemed to be in pain so she gave me the root so I would get off. I didn't mean to hurt her, and I did apologize but I don't think she was very happy with me."

"You have a way of making friends," Leo smirked. "Come on, let's get this over with."

"Wait, let's stay here until it gets darker. When it gets dark you can use your shirt, we will see what happens, and we will summon some warmer clothes again after the sun goes down."

Leo didn't argue, he knew he didn't want to go in, but he also knew that if and when they did, it would probably be better under the cover of darkness.

The two waited for what seemed like hours, barely speaking and in hushed tones, they took turns keeping an eye out, alternating between the window and the door. Each was thinking of home.

Angel longed to get back to the comfort of Lady Cybele, while Leo wished to be back in his Grandpa Joe's house, back in his own world.

When the sun began to settle, they knew it was time. Slowly, the two crept outdoors to the nearest putrid smelling cauldron. Not a soulless creature was in sight. Angel gently dropped the root into the pot, said an audible *thank you* to the not-so-nice Oxenbush, and they waited.

After a few moments Leo asked, "Do you think that's enough?"

"I don't know, your library didn't give a time for the recipe. I suppose as long as it's mixed, we should be in business. Tear off a piece of your shirt, if it doesn't work, we can give it a few more minutes."

Leo tore off two pieces of his shirt, dipped them into the liquid, and held his amulet. He gave both pieces to Angel, put a hand on his amulet, and placed the other on her shoulder.

"Squeeze the liquid in your mouth and mine at the same time, that's the only way to ensure we both drink while I'm holding you. Think of being in the castle."

Angel took a deep breath while Leo opened his mouth. Without a warning she squeezed the liquid from the shirt, they swallowed, gagged, and fell to their knees.

Nothing happened.

"Don't let go," Angel managed to say between coughs.

Seconds ticked by painfully slow until Leo's amulet began to glow. Although dim, it lit the night brighter than Leo expected. Angel's chest began to glow, similar to Leo's amulet.

"Something is happening," Angel managed to squeak.

Leo could feel it too, his clothing felt looser. He looked at Angel, her features looked sharper while simultaneously shrinking. She was growing smaller, hair appeared on her forehead and her mouth and nose grew into a fine point while her teeth jutted and sharpened against her face. Her shirt and pants began to take the shape of a long coat, a long grey-haired coat.

"Angel," Leo squeaked, "you're turning into a rat."

"You too," Angel squeaked back.

Both, in a matter of seconds, were now fully formed...rats, complete with long grey hair, claws, black pearl eyes, and strong tails.

"You have GOT to be kidding me," Angel squeaked at Leo. "What were you thinking about? You were supposed to be thinking about getting in the castle."

"I was. Well, that and I was thinking about what you said, that the carcass could have some type of disease."

"YOU WERE THINKING ABOUT THAT DISGUSTING DEAD RAT WHILE I WAS THINKING ABOUT THE CASTLE, YOU DOPE."

"Look, let's get in the castle and you can yell at me later. It's not my fault the library can't give specifics and I didn't hear you come up with a plan. We can get in like this, like the library said, it's leading us down a path so let's quit arguing, get in, and figure out how to change back," Leo squeaked in response to her outburst. He knew she was right, but he didn't want to argue a point he would obviously lose.

The two, turning towards the fortress, scampered down the rocky pathway towards the large wooden door, past the cannons, past the warriors, and easily dodging the barbed spikes by sensing the vibrations in the ground prior to their razor-like appearance. Once at the door, they easily flattened their bodies and squeezed between the bottom of the rough wood and the top of the stone path. Now inside the great fortress they both scampered to the nearest corner of the entrance, turned, and peered into the vast entrance, torch-lit compound.

Chapter 13

Inside the fortress Leo and Angel paused to catch their breath. Scampering took more energy than either had realized, and the relative safety of a corner was a welcome relief to the hazards that lay outside the protective door. As their hearts began to settle their eyes adjusted to the torch-lit foyer. Thankfully, due to the setting of the bright sun and their waiting for dusk, their vision took no time at all to take in their new surroundings.

The cavernous entrance hall was encased in Greystone blocks from floor-to-ceiling. Four rounded columns held heavy buttresses supporting a heavy block ceiling. Two stone staircases were situated opposite the heavy door leading up to a second floor while a third staircase right of the door lead downward to what Leo and Angel could only assume was the dungeon from which they had escaped. Centered between the dimly lit upward staircases was a large, ghostly glowing fireplace guarded from above by a drab stone dragon with large veiny wings stretched out as if it were ready to take flight at any moment.

"What now?" asked Angel, as much to herself as to Leo.

"Nobody will pay us any attention while we are in this form, let's move around the room to see if anything is out of the ordinary," he squeaked. "There must be something that will lead us to what we are looking for, whatever that may be."

The two scurried down the left wall, paying attention to each block they passed as to not miss an opportunity to squeeze into any opening they might not otherwise traverse. Past the stairs on the left, down the short wall, the two made their way to the front of the fireplace.

"Stop here for a second, I'm freezing," Leo instructed. "I thought this fur would block the cold but now I see why vermin create nests, this is ridiculous."

"Leo, take a closer look towards the back of the hearth."

"Gladly," Leo stated. As he did, he noticed one block missing from the back-right corner of the glowing pit.

"Why would a block be missing?" asked Angel, "I think there's something down there." "Don't be silly," Leo said. "It's just for the debris to drop through. All we are going to find down there is cinder and ashes."

"Look closer at the logs, do they look like they are actually burning? I don't think it produces ash."

Leo looked with a critical eye. The stack of logs was neither burning hot as expected nor producing embers or ash. Instead the eerie glow produced little warmth but no waste, as if its sole purpose was to prevent investigation by prying eyes. He turned to face Angel, as he did, he could have sworn he saw the dragon guarding the hearth follow him with his eyes but attributed the movement to shadows playing tricks.

"Come on Leo, if the fire was real it would produce ashes, then I could believe the brick was missing for the purposes of cleaning. As it stands, I don't believe it, I think it's a small opening and the fire is only meant as a diversion. You know, hiding something in plain sight as to not draw attention."

Leo considered this but as he did, he couldn't shake the feeling the stone dragon guardian continued watching them. "Why would someone need to hide something in plain sight, especially in the center of a room... the center of a room where the eyes are initially drawn due to the fire?"

"Exactly, nobody would expect it. I'm checking it out. Are you coming?"

Leo hesitated. *Did the tip of the dragon's wing fold?*

"What's the worst that could happen?" questioned Angel. "We end up in a pile of ashes and we come right back out. We said we were going to look for anything out of the ordinary and I think a hole built to serve an unneeded purpose is out of the ordinary. So, are you coming or not?"

"Okay, okay, you win. But for the record, it's a waste of time and I think we should keep looking. Perhaps something is upstairs, or even down by the dungeon."

"If you insist on scaling those steps as a rat, be my guest. Or perhaps you would prefer to make your way back down to the dungeon. That was fun wasn't it?" Angel's squeaky tone dripped in sarcasm.

"I said you win. Go on, I'll be right behind you."

Angel, ensuring not to singe her fur on the glowing fire, made her way to the back of the fireplace and disappeared into the hole. Leo took a deep breath and followed.

In their current form, the two easily traversed the small chamber provided by the removed block. As they moved forward the small tunnel sloped steeply downward, deeper into the solid walls of the fortress. Leo used his claws to dig into the stone in order not to slip deep into the bowels of the unknown.

"I told you this was just for ashes." Leo complained.

"Then why aren't there any ashes on the stone? This is something else." Angel retorted.

Leo had to admit, if it was used for its appeared purpose it would be caked with grey soot and ashes. He looked up from contemplating the tunnel floor just before smacking his snout into a wall directly in front of him. Angel was no longer in front, rather, she was now scurrying down a sudden left turn.

"I told you this was hiding something. Who would put a turn in a chute? Nothing would get past."

Leo had to admit she was right and followed her as the tunnel began to wind left, another left, and a third left. The tunnel was corkscrewing downward in ninety-degree angels deep into the heart of the fortress.

Angel, now far ahead, called out, "Hurry up; I knew this was hiding something."

Leo finally arrived at the end of the dizzying corkscrew and jumped in shock. He wasn't prepared to see Angel transformed back in her true form.

It's little wonder small animals run from us, he thought, "she looks like a giant.

When Leo fully emerged from the tunnel, he began to feel odd. First his fur and tail began to take the shape of his coat and pants, he slowly began to lose his tail and his once-useful claws began to transform back into his familiar hands and fingers. After only a few seconds he was transformed back into his human form. Leo patted himself down and remembered back to the words of his library.

The treacherous path will once again reveal your true nature. Your soul will return to the body of birth, making the treacherous path both deadly and revealing.

"I knew I was right, look." Angel motioned her arms around the dark, corridor-shaped room with a smile, "I knew something was off about that fireplace."

"Yeah, but where are we now? I mean, I'm thankful that we are back to normal but remember what my library said, something about the path being deadly."

Angel, focusing on her own excitement, had momentarily forgotten the warning. As the prospect of additional danger sunk in, she turned towards Leo, her shoulders rounded, and she wore a defeated look. "Why can't we just walk in, talk to someone in charge and say 'Look, who do you think you are trying to destroy the Spring Realm? What do you have to gain and why can't you just leave us in peace?' My God, why does everyone have to be so cynical and power hungry all the time?"

Leo now knew that when Angel got on a roll it was best to let her finish.

"Look at the trees we met, they aren't power hungry; they just live their lives and let others live theirs. Iron John just wanted to be left alone, why can't more people be like him? And you, why you were just mourning Joe, I mean your Grandpa Joe; you didn't ask for this but here we are in the bottom of a giant fortress after we've been turned to rats," her voice began to raise, "which I still blame you, by the way, looking for God knows what and NOW there is some unknown danger, possibly deadly danger ahead, and we have no idea what we are facing."

Leo and Angel didn't have to wait long to figure out the danger as her raising voice ending in an all-out yell of frustration, causing a stir.

Leo took a few steps forward and stood beside Angel, both stared in wonder down the long, now brighter but still dim corridor. On each side, separated by large stone pillars, were iron bars large enough to accommodate several hundred men. Faint glows emanated from the foreboding cages.

"Shhhh..." warned Leo, "something is down here with us."

"Great," exclaimed Angel. "Just come out and do your worst."

A ball of fire erupted from the first cage on their right. Then, down the corridor, the last cage on the left also erupted in fire. The light from the great fire was bright enough that the two could now clearly see there were twelve cages in all, six per side, and an iron door at rest at the end of the gauntlet.

"Dang it, Angel, now look what you've done."

"It's not my fault, I get emotional sometimes, and we've been through a lot." Angel lowered her tone out of fear. "What do you think it is?"

"When we went through the fireplace, I swore that the dragon above was looking at me, and right after you entered, before I went in, I swear one of its wing tips folded down a bit."

"And you are just telling me now? What if we missed something up top?"

"It was dark; I thought my eyes were playing tricks on me."

There was a crash on the bars in the cage to the right closest to the two, while another bolt of fire shot out from the cage just beyond. Angel jumped toward Leo, Leo grabbed her, and the two could clearly see the scaled beast. It rested its broad body on the iron bars, its black scales heaving with every breath it took. Enormous, leathery wings ran from the tips of the beast's shoulders and folded down into a point above a muscular tail. The beast turned its head and stared into the very souls of the unwelcomed guests. The face was unlike anything Leo and Angel had ever seen; a demonic reptilian face perched upon a thick neck of pulsating spikes. It dug its sharp front claws into the stone below, making an ungodly scraping noise, and flashed a black tongue against sharpened, stained teeth.

"Dragon," yelled Angel, releasing Leo and running towards the direction they entered.

She scratched and clawed at the tiny opening the two entered but it was of no use, she was much too large to return the way she came.

"What do you do with dragons in the Spring Crow?" yelled Leo.

Angel paid him no attention as she continued to search for an escape, any escape.

"Angel!" Leo caught her by the shoulders and turned her to face him. "What do you do with dragons in the Spring Crow?"

"Dragons in the Spring Crow are part of the community, not gigantic fire-breathing beasts."

Leo thought hard. They obviously couldn't escape from the way they came, there had to be a way past the twelve cages to the door beyond.

The cage to their right began to bang, louder and louder, a similar looking dragon emerged from its depths and began ramming the iron bars, bending them little-by-little with each lunge of his great girth.

This time it was Leo who grabbed for Angel, holding on for dear life. The beast caused a stir amongst the other dragons and now all were fully awake, banging on their doors, breathing fire in the air all around.

The cage to the right broke free from the stone floor, only the top of the iron bars remained fixed in the ceiling.

"Ask your library," screamed Angel.

It was too late, the dragon, with one final blow to the iron bars, broke free from his enclosure with such force that he slammed into the cage opposite, bending those bars further as well. He shook off the rough landing, turned towards the two, and began his charge.

Leo and Angel raced to the right of the corridor, but the dragon was much too quick, much quicker than its massive size would suggest. He lunged towards the two as Leo pushed Angel aside. Leo ducked from the massive demon-like teeth just in time as they sunk into the stone wall behind. Angel, picking herself up off the floor screamed, turning the dragon's attention towards her. Without thinking, she began to run the length of the corridor straight into the awaiting fiery inferno.

"Angel," screamed Leo, his amulet now glowing hot against his skin. She skidded to a halt and turned just in time to avoid the hot breath of the next dragon in line, who was now almost free from his cage.

Leo closed his eyes, pictured the warrior's weapons as clear as day, right where he left them in his memory on the shelf in his father's garage next to his sports equipment, including his baseball bat. Not a fraction of a second later Leo stood, amulet glowing, holding an aluminum baseball bat.

"Do something," Angel pleaded as she was now trapped between eleven fire breathing dragons attempting their escape and the freed dragon who was turning to charge.

Leo, forgetting anything and everything, allowed his adrenaline to take control. With one hand, he grabbed the tail of the dragon and pulled himself onto the giant beast. Running up the back of the scaled monster, he made his way to the shoulders, where he swung with all his might at the leathery wing of the creature, regrouped, and swung again, this time at the neck. He took a third swing while continuing his climb and sunk a blow into the dragon's eye.

Never will you enter, never will you escape, a morsel but a meal none the less, Leo heard as he geared for a fourth swing.

"Shut up," he yelled at Angel as the dragon turned from Angel towards the direction of the third blow as Leo landed a fourth.

"I didn't say anything."

You will make a tasty treat, young blood.

"Stop talking," Leo shouted as he swung a fifth time, again striking the same sinister eye.

So, you want something to eat, I'll give you something to eat, how about an aluminum sandwich, he thought as he landed a sixth blow.

The dragon paused. *How dare attempt to speak to me like the Master.*

Leo heard the voice in his head. Nobody was in the room but he and Angel, save the dragons.

I asked you a question, answer or I'll use the bones of the little treat in front of me to pick her own flesh from my teeth.

Leo hesitated mid-swing, the hit landed but didn't have the same impact as before. *You can hear my thoughts?* Leo internalized.

We communicate with the souls of our Masters. What type of Knight are you that have the soul of a Master? Leo heard as the dragon crept closer to Angel, seconds ticking by. *Very well, keep your secret to yourself, while I enjoy my snack.*

Kane, Knight of Kane, Leo began yelling over and over in his head. He was proud to be Grandpa Joe's grandson, and tried desperately to remember exactly who and what Lady Cybele told him he was, while trying to stop the beast from advancing further. He raised the baseball bat once again, prepared to fight to the finish.

The rattling of cages stopped, the fiery breath from all sides died down to a dull flame and now gently illuminated the corridor and all the cages within.

Kane, Leo heard, as the dragon dropped to his front knees and bowed its daemon head. Angel froze, not knowing whether to run or hide.

We have not encountered a Jinn Knight, other than Master Theiler, in many lifetimes. Please forgive me, Master Kane, for not recognizing you by the scent of your blood. I now recognize and I beg for your mercy.'

My mercy? Leo now realizing that he was communicating with the dragon telepathically. *Don't eat me and I'll forgive you.*

And the girl? Leo heard the voice of the dragon while its great mass shifted slightly underneath him.

No! Not her either.

As you wish.

Leo slid down the front of the kneeling dragon and cautiously faced his perceived enemy; the corridor grew silent, only the breath of the dragons and the panting of Angel were heard.

Angel ran to Leo, embracing him as if seeking shelter, and momentarily forgot about the dangerous beast before them.

"What's going on, why did it stop?" she questioned.

"You can't hear him?" Leo asked.

"Hear who?"

"The dragon, he's communicating with me. He said I have a soul like the Master, his master, Theiler."

Leo thought hard and carefully as not to put their lives in any further danger. "Sir, please, tell us your name and why you are down here." He repeated the words aloud for Angel's benefit and hoped he could concentrate on both his thought and speech. He understood that it was easy to speak without truly thinking and he was determined not to make that mistake.

Master Kane, I have gone by many names, Serenque by birth, Decimation throughout the Realm, and my enemies simply called me The Assassin.

"We will call you Serenque, if that is agreeable to you," Leo thought and spoke carefully.

Yes, Master Kane, as you wish.

"What's going on Leo, talk to me," pleaded Angel, still unsure of what was happening and continuing to fear for her life.

"It's okay, Angel, I believe Serenque serves the Jinn Knights, specifically Theiler, but I don't believe he will harm us." Leo turned and addressed the ferocious looking, but now slightly more docile, beast. "Serenque, who is down here and why? How have you come to be trapped in this place?"

Prior to the Leader of Elysium and the realms banishing the three Jinn we lived in relative peace, wandering the countryside and hills. We were acquaintances of all three, Theiler, Garaile, and Kane and allowed all the Leaders sons to walk amongst us with no concern for their safety.

"So, you know of the Jinn history?"

We witnessed the Jinn fight, but we felt that it was merely the fighting of brothers. Perhaps, in hindsight, the fighting of brothers differs between the types of beast, dragons and Jinn. We now know that Jinn, or any human like creature, can be the most cunning and evil of beast.

"You think I'm a beast?"

Serenque gave a low growl. *Of course, Jinn are beast, all creatures are beast, but the Jinn... when the fighting became fierce enough for the Cardinal Leader to banish his sons, Theiler was sent to our realm and refused to leave, he controls the realm with an iron fist. Theiler had the opportunity to move between this and another world but didn't take advantage, rather, he split our peaceful realm, taking the souls of all the inhabitants he could and the rest... the rest he flayed or imprisoned as a warning to all those who attempted to stand up to his cruelty.*

Leo thought back to Iron John and his imprisonment.

Some survived, much like us, but we were ultimately incarcerated by the souls he returned to his warriors. There were too many souls under his control, we fought great battles but, in the end, we bowed to the Master, the master whose soul matches yours. When we could no longer fight, we were led down into a great pit, walls and cages were built around us, and only the room at the far corner indicated past freedom.

"Can you tell us what's in the room?" Leo thought carefully and spoke gently.

Nobody knows. Nobody ever goes in; nobody ever comes out. Our lot in life is to protect its contents with our fiery breath and mere presence—it is not to contemplate the content or purpose. But you, Master Kane, cannot be denied by us, you are Jinn.

Leo passed the story to Angel as Serenque communicated it.

"Oh, poor things," softened Angel. "How long have you been down here? Have you eaten?"

Serenque eyed here.

The unspoken stare startled Angel. "No, I mean... I don't mean me. Stop looking at me like that. What I meant was we don't have much, only what the forest provided, but we are willing to share."

Angel pulled various fruits out of her satchel and laid a growing pile before Serenque.

While Angel was busy feeding her new friend, Leo went cage-to-cage surveying the damage and, working with each dragon released the remaining into the great corridor. At first all were skeptical of his Jinn presence, but when Leo reassured them through the return of his thoughts all seemed to begin to trust.

Angel continued pulling fruit from her satchel, much more fruit than she had initially taken, in fact, enough to form twelve piles each nearly the height of the cages and provide plenty for each beast to eat his fill—he first sustenance any had had for as long as they could remember. All would have preferred meat and fat but all assured Leo he and Angel were safe.

Once Angel had finished the feeding she turned to Leo. "Where did you get that club?"

"I was imagining the warrior's weapons, just like you said, and I pictured them clear as day on a shelf right next to my baseball bat. I must have been too focused on my bat rather than the weapons because this is what appeared."

"You mean you summoned that from your world?"

"Yeah, I suppose I did."

"You can't do that."

"What do you mean I can't do that? Here it is." Leo eyed the bat.

"It can't be done," she now said more as an inquiry than accusation.

"Well I didn't know; did I break a rule? Should I put it back?"

"No, I mean you can't do that, as it's impossible. You can't bring something from another world into this world unless it comes with you across the Veil. Nobody, not even the most powerful amongst us, can summon an item that hasn't been brought in across the Veil or gathered and stored from one of the realms."

Leo thought about his for a moment. "Well, perhaps it was mixed up with one of the weapons, or maybe a warrior had a club that just looks like my bat."

"That's extremely doubtful, nothing in the realms look like that," she pointed at the bat. "I admit, it worked... but I'd put it back before it draws attention. Although," she hesitated, "remember how you did it and we can ask Lady Cybele about it later if we remember."

Angel returned her attention to the Serenque. "How will you continue to survive down here? We need to find a way to free all of you." Forgetting her fear and scratching Serenque's great spiked neck, near where an ear would normally be.

How in the world does she do it? thought Leo.

She is kind and has powers beyond her knowledge, communicated Serenque, as he turned his head towards her hand, *to include the power of compassion and forgiveness, something not seen in the Carved Realm for a very long time. Allow her to continue to explore and use her powers without question.*

Was Serenque starting to purr? Leo had never heard of a dragon purring.

Go forth into the room beyond, we will make no attempt to stop you. All we ask is that whatever you find you use in an attempt to bring our realm back to its former glory.

"Angel, we need to go, we need to discover what is beyond the door, to see if we can find anything that will help us discover Theiler's plans for the Spring Crow."

"What about Serenque and the others?"

Leo had almost forgotten; they couldn't leave the dragons trapped the same as they were when they arrived. Sure, Serenque did try to kill them but now leaving the twelve—in what amounted to a tomb—was no longer an option. In doing so, he would be no better than Theiler.

"Angel, do you still have the strip of cloth that we dipped into the cauldron?"

Angel hadn't thought of it, but she must have had the cloth, she didn't remember dropping it when they morphed. She searched the floor and found the two still damp pieces of cloth next to the small opening they arrived.

"Here they are, what do you want me to do?"

"Tear them into strips and wrap a piece of fruit in each. Let the dragons eat them, maybe something will happen."

"Why didn't I think of that? The library didn't say we could only use the potion once. Okay, think of how they can get out while I get everything ready," instructed Angel as she began tearing the cloth into equal pieces. She carefully wrapped twelve fruit in the still damp cloth and hand fed each of the dragons while Leo closed his eyes, imagined climbing through the small opening, and grasped his amulet.

The transformation began slowly, but once started, it was a remarkable sight. One-by-one, the dragons began to morph; their scales turning into exoskeletons, their legs and claws doubling, and fine hair began to cover their now shell-like bodies. Great eyes appeared on their heads while their strong, sharp teeth turned into grinding venomous jaws. Each had transformed into great, fierce spiders. Large enough to make Leo take a hesitant step back, but small enough to traverse the opening from which they arrived.

Thank you, Master Kane.

Until we meet again, Leo perceived in his mind as the twelve, led by Serenque, disappeared into the wall through the opening.

The last to leave turned and eyed Leo, giving him an uneasy feeling, which he attributed to the fearsome features of the transformed beast. All was quiet and only Leo and Angel remained in the great corridor.

"Why spiders?" questioned Angel while giving a shiver. "That's almost as bad as dragons."

"I don't know. I just thought of the quickest and easiest way to get back up the chute, and I remembered an old song I heard as a kid, "The Itsy-Bitsy Spider."

"The what?"

"Never mind, it's just something from where I'm from."

Angel turned her attention away from Leo, satisfied with his other world explanation. "Are you ready?" she asked as she faced the now unguarded door and stared.

"As ready as I'll ever be."

The two walked the length of the now empty and nearly black corridor no longer lit by dragon's breath. Their footfalls echoing with each step, signaling their proximity the closer they drew to the opposite end. Leo opened the unguarded door and the two entered into the room to the unknown.

Chapter 14

The Spring Crow was buzzing with activity. Mr. Forswear had formed a team of abled-bodied repair beasts; creatures of all types with any building experience were busily hammering, sawing, and correcting any damage caused by the latest tremor. Meanwhile, General Carlux, accompanied by Mr. Morphon and with the help of his library, was actively training all other creatures whom had no knowledge of construction in the art of both offensive and defensive warfare.

While the rest of the Spring Crow council carried out their assigned duties, Lady Cybele settled into her favorite leather and wool wingback armchair, which sat behind her gold leaf encrusted oak desk. Once settled, she summoned a silver fountain pen and parchment to jot down ideas and thoughts. While Sylvia, who had already delivered the guards to the Forest Veil as instructed, safely researched powers associated with remaining with one's own realm, in her own library.

Lady Cybele was determined to discover what Theiler had planned for her home. Armed with her rudimentary but irreplaceable supplies, which she would later store in her memory, and further armed with her impeccable mind to memorize facts and history, she was prepared to work out the past. She resolved to determine what, if anything, Theiler could accomplish now that there was a tear in the veil separating his realm from theirs.

Lady Cybele's library was not a simple book containing all the wisdom passed from generation to generation, as was Leo's. She understood and accepted that she was not as powerful as the boy, and her information could not be condensed into a simple tome. Although it was impossible to condense her collection of books, maps, globes, and almanacs, she did have the ability to live through the past via her vast collection. A benefit of knowledge and, to her chagrin, knowledge gained through many years of both trial and age.

From her seat, she had access to any of her books with just a flick of her wrist and a touch of her amulet; she began with a few preparations that would seem as a waste to most scholars. For what was required, in order to find the exact information she was looking for, she knew that she would need to start from the beginning. She thought carefully of the past, how the once young and sweet boys grew older, powerful, vile, and vindictive. These were trying times to say the least, and the last straw came when three powerful armies, one controlled by each brother, fought to the death of many, if not most, under their control. A fact that she purposely neglected to share with Leo, as she felt he was not ready for such truths.

She closed her eyes and focused on Theiler, the middle child, somehow forgotten with no real special place in the heart of anyone. Low self-esteem, jealously, a feeling of inadequacy, and division... division... if the middle child, Theiler, was capable of anything, it was creating division to seek attention. Young, quiet, brooding, yet capable, of interjecting himself in the most vulgar of manner, using the interjections to divide while he later sat back to revel in his deeds. Causing strife and division became Theiler's identity, no longer silently suffering, he found comfort in the misery of others.

As Theiler grew older, his identity became clearer and his formation of an army of weak-minded individuals was an easy step in his process. His army of creatures, all seeking something more than their lot in life, were stripped of their souls, taunted and tortured by Theiler until they were his to control. Some would call it Stockholm syndrome, Theiler called it *easy*. Lady Cybele reflected on these faceless foot-soldiers and remembered their strengths and weaknesses. Every one of Theiler's soldiers had the capability and means to stand against Garaile and Kane's armies psychologically, but had neither the brute force of the eldest nor the cunning of the youngest.

Lady Cybele thought to the great battle between the three brothers, not a creature in the Cardinal Realm was left unaffected by its bloody aftermath and the warrior, the divider, and the cunning ravaged the once calm and peaceful world. Garaile sliced and diced his way through the Realm in attempt to win his father's favor. Kane, who she instructed Charon to tell Leo was the people's soldier, was promised freedom but controlled his army through the prospect of a peace that would never come. Finally, Theiler, who twisted the words and therefore the armies of both brothers in order to turn one against the other, dividing both in an attempt take ultimate control of the Cardinal Realm.

Lady Cybele opened her eyes and thought to herself, *if we are meant to repeat a past that nobody understands that is where Theiler will start, dividing the Crow Spring prior to his final quest to conquer and control all.* She rose from her chair. Although she could summon the required books, she decided that this particular ancient text deserved a personal visit, these were some of her most valuable possessions and if hindsight were really twenty-twenty, she would need to be sure of their exact location, their touch, and their knowledge. She walked past multiple polished hardwood shelves, her footsteps not making a sound on the deep velvet carpet underneath, until she came to the furthest reaches of her library. There, she pulled open the glass covering encasing the antique and placed her hand on its spine.

"My how I've missed you, Stepmother," Lady Cybele jumped at the sound of a familiar but long-lost voice. "You must miss me, too, if you are going through so much trouble to discover ancient secrets buried in those dusty manuals." Lady Cybele's hand dropped from her the ancient tome and instinctively clutched her amulet.

"Theiler," she whispered, turning towards the visible golden orb suspended in her library. "You've grown in power, yet are still a scared little boy. What else could explain how you entered into my sanctuary and why you would attempt such a fool thing."

"This scared little boy knows of your spies and their capabilities, dear mother. Did you really think sending children was such a good idea? I'm sure their souls will be easily manipulated. and not only will I have two new warriors, I'll be surrounded by family... that is until I'm finished playing with them."

This confirmed Lady Cybele's suspicions; Ms. Parish was aware of Angel's capabilities and she was playing her knowledge against the Crow Spring. Thankfully, Theiler on the other hand, did not know that his insider was marked, a nugget of information Lady Cybele would keep to herself.

"My dear Theiler, whatever do you mean?" Lady Cybele needed as much information as she could glean without raising suspicions that she, in reality, did not know the status of Leo and Angel, as Theiler believed. "Who would be foolish enough to travel outside of the Spring Crow and how could such a thing be accomplished? Doesn't the Veil protect your Realm from ours?"

"Don't be foolish. I know of the Jinn and Tutor crossing the Forest Veil and their—soon to be doomed—attempt at saving the Spring Crow. Children... their inexperience is my greatest asset, their use of magic that does not belong in the Carved Realm is like a beacon. I've been tracking their every move and my warriors are waiting to bring them to me."

Lady Cybele knew Theiler was right, unless Leo and Angel stopped using magic or started using dark magic—perish the thought—the two would easily be found and captured. She needed to discover Theiler's plan to ultimately conquer the Spring Crow and she knew she was on the right track. If Theiler took the time to appear to her, to provide threats and cause worry to throw her off the trail and divide her from her goal, she knew she needed to finish her research to inform the council.

"Theiler, my poor boy," Lady Cybele was playing to his belief he was the forgotten son, "how long has it been? I know we will meet again in the near future, and I truly hope you realize that your father would not approve. In fact, I believe he will, unfortunately, continue your banishment because you have yet to understand his true wishes. It will definitely break his heart."

Theiler laughed. "I'm no longer worried about approval. I'm strong enough on my own to build an army from the Spring Crow as well as mine, and with my new warriors, I will be strong enough to take not only Spring Crow, but all realms. Goodbye, Stepmother. I wish I could say I'm sorry for your son, or should I say many-greats grandson, but all is fair in war and I'll be happy to welcome him when I control his soul." The golden orb vanished, leaving Lady Cybele alone in her library.

She knew she needed to work quickly, to review and relive the past contained in the ancient text in order to warn the others of the fight to come. While the appearance of Theiler confirmed her suspicions and made time of the essence, if she rushed to conclusions, she would not serve the Realm or the council appropriately. She turned her attention back to the ancient book and placed her hand on the spine to remove it from its sacred place, and she returned to her desk. Instinctively, she opened the book to exact location, placed her left hand on its fragile pages, and placed her pen on the parchment. She closed her eyes and her amulet began to glow once again.

Lady Cybele found herself living through the past, walking unseen amongst the population where she dwelled long ago, in a time only a very few remember. The Cardinal Realm smelled of fresh lavender and the ground below her was a light sand color, peppered with few rocks. Beyond, laid green fields where she knew she would find Theiler practicing his craft with his war ax—a gift from his father. As she drew closer, she studied him carefully, spinning the device with accuracy and determination, slicing the air around him with a soft hiss. Alone, as usual, his focus was unbroken, and his form was impeccable.

After a few minutes Theiler paused, as if carefully considering his actions, and brought the blade of the ax to the tip of his left index finger. Without pause, he made a small slice in his finger, allowing his royal blood to drip on the bit and slowly run down the cheek of the ax. Smearing the royal blood, he kneeled down, he placed the ax in the grass before him while keeping both hands on the haft and grip.

Lady Cybele drew closer in an attempt to view the scene in its entirety, to discover what was happening in this poor child's mind that kept him isolated from everyone save his monstrous interactions with his brothers. Slowly, as a wisp of smoke rolls off a snuffed candle, a white-gold light flowed from the ax into Theiler, as if he were taking the energy out of the seemingly inanimate object. Theiler remained with his eyes closed for five, ten, then twenty minutes, never moving a muscle, save the inaudible movements of his lips. Finally, the same wisp of smoke— now red and black—flowed from Theiler back into the ax, completing the ritual.

He's charged the item with dark magic, realized Lady Cybele, *why would he need an item with dark magic when he can perform most anything he needs without?*

Theiler rose, lifting the war ax with him, and circled the ground where the single drop of yet dried blood dripped from the bit into the grass. He raised the ax, plunged it into the soft soil, and raised it again, as if he had calmly been gathering firewood. The split began to grow in length and a dozen new wisps of red and black smoke emerged from the crevice, forming into human like figures before closing again, leaving barely detectable cracks. Before the wisps of smoke could fully form into human form, Theiler, with one expert swing of his ax, sliced through the center of each with a single blow, simultaneously catching the dissipating smoke carved away by the weapon. He placed this dissipated red and black wisp into a hunting bag he had slung across his back and waited patiently for the figures to fully form.

"My God," gasped Lady Cybele under her breath, "he's creating life from the blood of his blood and the very life forces from the ground we walk, from the very nature we were birthed. Worse, he's taking their poor souls before they have a chance to exercise their own free will... Eidolon. This type of magic is inexcusable; he has obviously been training in the dark arts during his extensive time in self-isolation, we should have ensured his inclusion rather than allow him to exercise his own excommunication. If he is continuing this practice today, how many souls does he now possess and how large is the split expanded each time he practices Eidolon? Large enough to shake and crack the Spring Crow... large enough for his ever-expanding army to traverse?"

Lady Cybele removed her hand from the ancient text, now armed with the knowledge that Theiler's war ax is imbibed with dark powers, powers that were now being used to form an army in which Theiler controlled the very souls. She looked down at the parchment, covered in automatic writing of notes she knew she took, but never remembers writing when living through the past. Upon re-reading and memorizing the notes she knew what she must do, she must warn the council, prepare the army, and ensure the safety of Leo and Angel.

Lady Cybele removed the book from her desk and replaced it in the glass enclosure at the end of her library. Returning to her desk, she imagined her memory place and stored the parchments in case she or anyone else may ever need them again in the future and made her way to the wooden double doors. She pushed on the now closed doors... nothing. She pushed harder... still nothing. Becoming frantic, she thrust her shoulder into the door, but it would not budge. She was trapped with no way to call for help.

"Is anybody out there? Help! Open the doors!"

She knew all that would normally be in the hall during this time of the day were preparing the Spring Crow for a possible invasion, and that other than herself, no one in the Spring Crow was powerful enough to receive a message from beyond the confines of a personal library. She was trapped unless... if Theiler, one of the three Jinn brothers, was powerful enough perhaps another Jinn would be as well. She needed to warn Leo and Angel and send a signal for help. Lady Cybele opened her palm and formed a communications orb.

Chapter 15

Leo pushed the now unguarded door, which gave a low and moaning groan. Sunlight peaked through the slowly widening crack until the door fully swung open. Leo and Angel, staring into the blinding sunlight, stepped through as the door suddenly slammed shut behind them. There before them in a field of green grass, in polished silver armor unlike any other they had seen on the other Carved Realm warriors, stood a human-like creature with a large battle ax.

"I see I was correct in my choice of dragons," said the mysterious figure, facing away from the two. "Only Jinn would be allowed to pass, but I wasn't expecting nor believed there would another as rumored, until now. You, young lady, must be the power behind your escape from the Oubliette. I must say, that was a surprise twist indeed, bravo." The figure calmly spoke as he turned and raised a sweeping hand. "Welcome to my realm."

The figure, larger and more beautifully clad than that of the other warriors, gave Leo and Angel a smile. Unlike the rest, he had a fully formed and rather handsome face. His long black hair framed a strong and rugged appearance, without a blemish nor scar to give hint to his identity. Underneath the polished silver armor, the two could tell he was strong, physically much stronger than either had ever seen in a human-like form, and his demeanor seemed calm, almost trancelike.

"I do hope you had a pleasant chat with Serenque, he can be intimidating when you first encounter him but once you get to know him... he can be terrifying. Unless, of course, you are his master, you are one of his masters, aren't you?" Theiler directed the question towards Leo.

"I'm no one's master, I'm..."

"I'm fully aware of who you are brother, or in this case, nephew. My, how my little brother Kane must have let himself go during his journeys. Why he would venture out of his Realm is beyond me." Theiler gave a sharp breath between teeth and tongue. "All in an attempt to live a life outside of his realm in search for knowledge. Kane was always in the pursuit of knowledge, to his own detriment. My, I can only imagine how he aged, grew old and wrinkled, and ultimately passed in agonizing old age. And you, the final Kane in his un-glorious lineage, what a disappointment to see an unarmed boy sent to do the deeds of the Jinn."

"I'll have you know he's more powerful than you know, he's..."

"Silence, you. The old Jinn is dead, and I know you, I know you better than you know yourself. Yes, you have no idea who you are, what you are. I bet you would like to understand, wouldn't you? I bet you would love the answers to the questions you've had nagging in the back of your mind. I'll start simply, with what I know to be your first question. I am your blood, your future, your Jinn ancestor. I am the almighty Theiler."

Theiler began walking towards the two. His every step was made with purpose, no energy lost in his fluid movements. He stopped, lifting his ax, eyed the two, and sunk the tip gently into the ground before them. The ground gave way with a slight shake, a small tear formed in the carpeted green, and a single wisp of red and black smoke slowly rose forming a figure right before their eyes. Just as easily as Theiler split the soil, he swung his ax towards the smoke, carving the soul of the partially formed being and placed it in the smooth leather bag slung around his armor.

Leo and Angel, now both understanding how the Veil had been cracked after millennium of ground splitting slices curtesy of Theiler's war ax, coupled by the reality that his army was hand made by his own design, didn't have another opportunity to ask questions. A figure came from behind and roughly swept the two off their feet, holding them in his vice-like grip.

"I believe you met my second in command earlier, Sir Necro, so no introductions will be necessary. "

"You can't do this to us, we have rights, we don't even belong here." yelled Angel while kicking and wrestling to free herself.

"Of course, you don't belong here, you're obviously trespassing, aren't you? Necro, I believe the cells in the center of the fortress will be a better fit for our guests; I wouldn't want them wasting away in the dungeon as I may want to visit again after I'm ruler of the Spring Crow. I can always use new soldiers who are familiar with new territory." Theiler laughed as he delivered his confident closing remark before turning and walking away, leaving the two in the capable hands of his second in command.

"I can't believe we fell for that, look at us, were back in captivity as if we were criminals," lamented Angel.

"Well, we did come into his realm, break into his fortress, and free his dragons," reminded Leo."

"What the hell is the matter with you? Whose side are you on?"

"The Spring Crow, of course, I'm just saying..."

"You're just saying we belong here. I should have known, you're just like your ancestor Kane and it wouldn't surprise me if you gladly accepted a position in Theiler's army. Why, I bet he'd replace Necro with you, *oh nephew*, and before you know it you will be the second in charge." Angel's tone dripped with sarcasm.

"What are you talking about? Why would I ever want to be in cahoots with Theiler and how am I being just like Kane? You nor anyone else in the Spring Crow will tell me what Kane did."

"Kane played both sides, you idiot." Angel was yelling again. "I told you he was too smart for his own good, didn't I."

"Played both sides?"

"Of course. All three brothers wanted to take over all realms, including Kane, but Kane wasn't as strong as his brothers and he knew it. He was smart, perhaps too smart. He tolerated their torture, both physically and mentally, witnessed his mother's torture at the hand of both, but he always sided with one brother or another when it suited him."

"Why wouldn't he just pick a side, or better yet, walk away? What did he have to gain?"

"Gain? The realms and all of Eidolon, of course. By playing both sides without his brother's knowledge he would be on the side of the victor. Once victorious he could concentrate his energy on one rather than two enemies. You've heard the saying, the enemy of my enemy is my friend, and Kane was both friends and enemy to both. Now, thousands of years later, you're going down that same path aren't you… taking Theiler's side."

"Calm down Angel, I'm not taking any sides; I'm just trying to be logical. I don't want to see the Spring Crow fall to Theiler or anyone else for that matter. I'm just trying to be practical, trying to figure out how we can get out of here and get back to the Spring Crow. Eventually, I'd like to get back to my world too."

"You want to leave me?" whispered Angel, her emotions switching faster than Leo could keep up.

"N… no," Leo began to stammer, but quickly gained confidence. "I like being around you and I really like the Spring Crow, it's just I need to get back to school, to my dad, to my real life."

"So, once this is over… it's over?" she trailed off.

"Again, no. I'll visit but I can't stay in this fortress for all my life and neither can you. We just need to be practical and I don't know if magic alone will get us out of this situation."

Magic is just what happened next. A golden orb appeared in the corner of the cell, a stark contrast to the cold stone walls surrounding the two.

"Leo, thank God I've found you," Lady Cybele's voice echoed against the stone. "You and Angel must return to the Spring Crow as Theiler is attempting to widen the crack in the Veil and bring his soulless warriors through."

"We know," answered Leo. "You need to warn General Carlux and the others."

"I can't, Ms. Parish has locked me in my library, and the only two powerful enough to communicate or receive communications from within are you and Theiler. You need to hurry."

"We can't, we're imprisoned too. Can't you just turn your library off or close it?"

"Not while I'm inside, there is the possibility I would disappear with the library and never be able to recall it again. There is the likelihood that I could be trapped forever with no possible way of coming back. You and Angel are our only hope; you must escape and warn the others before it's too late." The Golden Orb flickered as Lady Cybele quickly gave her warning. "Your magic in the Carved Realm is being tracked, you mustn't rely on your powers, no matter innocent you use them." With the final warning the orb flickered again and disappeared.

"What did she mean; Ms. Parish locked her in her library? Why would she do that?" asked Angel.

"That doesn't matter right now, what matters is figuring out how to get out of here and back to the Spring Crow, releasing Lady Cybele, and letting the rest of the Committee know what's coming. We can figure out why Ms. Parish would do what she did later."

Angel studied their cell. Much like the dungeon it was encased in thick grey stone but, while small, it was not nearly as cramped. An iron gate separated them from the outside, which was guarded by two large hairy gargoyles each carrying wooden clubs tipped with rust colored spikes. Each hideous and odorous gargoyle wore a blank expression on his face.

"I don't think our guards are going to give you the same respect Serenque did," remarked Angel. "We need to put a plan together so we can somehow overpower them the next time they open the gate."

"Look around," replied Leo. "I don't think this cell is used very often, and how do you suppose we can overpower gargoyles?"

"Okay, maybe you're right, we need to outsmart them. Any ideas?"

"As a matter-of-fact, I do. Lady Cybele is right, we've been relying on magic far too much and it makes sense that we may be tracked by our magic. Think about it, Theiler must have known we were in the dungeon and that somehow, we disappeared. He also knew that we were with Serenque and that I was able to get past him. Everything we have done so far has involved magic. What if we did used magic again but didn't use it to escape? What if we only use it as a means to an end, a way forward but not the ultimate end?"

"I'm not following. Use magic, but not use magic? What do you have in mind?"

"Warriors brought us in, why shouldn't one take us out?" Leo clutched his amulet. In Theiler's smugness, he neglected to remove it from the young Jinn. "Iron John, Iron John, Iron John."

On the far side of the Carved Realm, now most of the way through the Forest Veil, Charon was making his way through the thick brush and had completed his transformation from his suave Spring Crow appearance into the skeletal form he despised. His skin stretched tight, uncomfortably tight, and the black barbed wire that always appeared cut deep into his mouth and eyes, stretching them further each step he took towards the Carved Realm. The maggots that always accompanied his puss-filled infected intestines were beginning to itch, and his strong muscles tore with each movement.

Charon hated this form. He hated looking and feeling this way when he knew deep in his heart that he was something—someone— different all together and that when strangers saw him, they couldn't see his true form, his true intentions, and his true heart. When he was in his Spring Crow

173

form, he always made it a point to dress his best and to ensure his appearance was above reproach. Now, his finely tailored suit was once again a simple black cloak draped across his shoulders and side. He was alone in his powers to cross the Veil and no one, save the Jinn or someone born of higher powers such as the ancestors of the all-powerful tutor, could traverse the Veils without transformation. Even if he were not the only who could cross, Charon knew he was the only citizen among all in the Spring Realm who could handle such a transformation and still keep any form of sanity. It was up to him, and only him, to track the children.

"Who dares enter my forest without my permission?" Charon heard a booming voice coming from the distance. Rushing upon him Charon could see a man, clad in armor, looking as though he may cause an unnecessary delay in his quest.

Iron John, free again and determined to maintain his freedom, was upon Charon much quicker than Charon had anticipated. "State your name and your business before I cut you down like the devil you are."

Charon could say nothing, he only stood knowing that he could little defend himself from a warrior in his present condition.

"I see, you are a soulless creature, escaped from the Carved Realm. Creature, how did you come to regain what little life you have left? Speak lest I ensure your soul never has a body which to return."

Charon remained calm, calmer than he expected, and raised a lone boney finger.

Iron John, sensing no danger but remaining at the ready to strike if provoked, allowed Charon a moment, but decided it would be a very brief moment.

Charon, seeing no other way for communication, slowly, as to not startle the warrior with sudden movements, kneeled down and picked up a small stick. He brushed his hand on the forest floor to reveal smooth soil and began to write.

I'm seeking two children; I fear that they may be in danger.

"Not even children would be fool enough to venture into the Carved Realm, you must be mistaken, go back to from where you came."

These are two special children—teenagers— kind and powerful children of interest to many. Charon continued to write.

"I do have two friends, my only friends. Tell me what your business with these children."

Charon could see little choice; he must give away his identity, possibly his life, in order to gain knowledge needed to rescue Leo and Angel.

Sir Leo and Lady Angel, Jinn and Tutor. Both are in danger. I have come from the Spring Crow in order to ensure their safe passage home. Charon was scrawling in the soil as quick as he could.

"Jinn and Tutor? Leo and Angel? Why didn't you say so," Iron John exclaimed as he raised Charon from his kneeling position and patted him gruffly on the shoulder. "I hope I didn't scare you, man; I haven't had much luck in the past with creatures I don't know. The name is John, Iron John, but you can just call me John. What did you say your name was?"

Charon stung a bit from the creature comment but brushed it off and kneeled down once again to write.

Charon, Keeper of the Veils.

Charon rose slowly, hoping to avoid another friendly, but harsh, pat on the back.

"Well now, Charon, last I saw Leo and Angel they were just beyond the opening of the forest, not far from where we are now. I'm sure they are safe and ..."

Iron Johns broad muscular chest began to thump, his heart attempting to escape from within and pounding forcefully into his chest plate. Charon looked at him with eyes wide from both the barbed wire pulling them back in their sockets and curiosity.

"I'm being summoned, something that hasn't happened for as long as I can remember," Iron John informed Charon. "Leo is calling, he needs my help."

Charon, momentarily forgetting he was in the presence of a dangerous warrior, grabbed Iron John by his large arm, pointed to himself, and then towards the far side of the Forest Veil.

"You want to come too? In your condition?" Charon nodded feverishly to convey his desires.

"Well, if I mistook you for a soulless creature perhaps others may too. Can you pull that cloak up over your head in order to blend in?"

Charon covered his head with the cloak and pointed towards the far side again.

"Okay, Okay, you can come along but don't make a sound."

Unable to make a sound, Charon just glared at Iron John—still hurt over the soulless creature comment—as the warrior had already begun onward to the fortress.

Charon and Iron John sped to the edge of the Veil, past the cob houses, and into the heart of the Carved Realm. Charon kept his hood from his cloak on—covering the majority of his face—and acquired a chain for his waist, in order to better blend in and not to be recognized as a creature with his soul intact. Iron John walked with the stride of a warrior and was, of course, not challenged by any of the soulless creatures along the way. He did, however, keep a keen eye out for other warriors who may recognize him as warriors unlike themselves.

"I feel Leo's presence close; it's coming from the fortress. We need to find a way to get in," Iron John stopped and stated matter-of-fact.

Charon nodded in agreement and made a walking motion with his right index and middle finger.

"Perhaps I could walk right in; warriors are in and out of the fortress quite a bit, but no other creatures venture in. I'll have to cause a diversion while you sneak in, I can follow after. When I get close to the fortress, duck behind the nearest hut to the entrance and wait, you will know when it's time. Run in and close the entrance behind you so as not to draw suspicion."

Charon, again, nodded in agreement.

The two continued through the town, drawing closer to the fortress with no hindrance from the Carved Realm inhabitants.

"Duck behind that hut when it's time," pointed Iron John to a nearby cob structure before he ran off out of sight.

Charon waited. In his opinion, he waited far too long... minutes turned into an hour, an hour into two. *It will be dark soon; did I miss the sign?* he thought. *How am I to know when to make my attempt?*

Without warning, the guards furthest away from the entrance began to run to the far side of the fortress, followed shortly thereafter by those closest to the door. There was now a straight shot, free from guards and traps, directly to the entrance. Charon, stiff from waiting, sprinted towards the fortress. His tight skin and stiff joints loosening ever so slightly with every long stride he took.

When he made it to the heavy wooden door, he threw his full weight into it and swung it open, while taking just a second to look back at the commotion now occurring in the Realm. A great fire engulfed multiple cob structures and the warrior guards were frantically attempting to extinguish the blaze before it spread. With his glance complete, Charon closed the heavy door behind him, safe in the empty, great fortress hall.

Minutes passed, then another hour. *Why does he insist on taking so long to do anything?* Charon thought to himself. It was dark now, and after another hour, the door slowly opened and in walked a warrior.

"Charon, it's me," said a familiar voice.

Charon emerged from the shadows, raising his arms to Iron John in a manner to convey his displeasure of being made to wait for more than four hours.

"Yeah, about that… I'm a little out of practice with flint and steel and do you know how hard it is to find flint? There is almost nothing around here except plain old rocks, anthracite, and dirt. I had to search everywhere. Once I got my hands on some flint, I needed to ensure I would start a fire that would get their attention. Pretty good, eh? I knew if I set any ordinary hut on fire the guards wouldn't care. I mean, come on, who cares about the soulless? But if I found a guard's home or something else of importance, I knew we'd be in business. I found a weapon cache, so I grabbed a new sword and then set the rest ablaze. Like I said, pretty good."

Charon put both hands on Iron Johns shoulders, getting him to refocus.

"Right, I can feel Leo summoning from the center of the building. If I remember correctly there is a bastille close by."

Chapter 16

"Do you hear anything? Angel asked Leo, who was sitting crouched on the floor nearest to the bars of their cell. "Is there any movement from the guards? Is anyone coming?

"Nothing yet, but Iron John said he would come if summoned, I don't think he has a reason to lie to us."

"He's a warrior from the Carved Realm," snapped Angel, becoming agitated again. "For all we know he was created by Theiler, his soul was stripped, and he was brainwashed like the rest, just like Necro. Furthermore, they could be friends and are sitting in a tavern right now laughing about our fates."

"Boy, for someone who normally sees the good in everyone, you sure are negative right now."

"Negative? I've traveled through a dirty forest, was sent to a dungeon, dragged through the middle of the earth, drank an awful concoction, turned into a filthy rat, and was cornered by a dragon."

"But you're only looking at the negative, why we..."

"We? You dragged me through this and now we are trapped again. This is all your fault Leo Kane."

"It was your idea to come here, I had no idea what was in store for us when we crossed the Forest Veil. I didn't even know what the Veil was until a few short days ago."

"Great, blame me, it's all my fault, it's always my fault." Angel continued in a sing-song voice while mimicking those in the Spring Crow, "Angel doesn't have a library. Angel doesn't have an amulet. There must be something wrong with Angel because she's not perfect like everyone else."

"Angel, please, calm down. I'm not blaming anyone, and you have the biggest heart of anyone I've ever met. Look, if it wasn't for your thoughtfulness and kindness to nature, to the trees and Iron John, we may not have found how Theiler is using his weapon to split the Veil and the realms. Why, you even knew to feed Serenque to prevent him from eating you."

"Eating me?"

"Long story, but the point is, you need to keep following your heart and being who you are, and not worrying about if you're good enough for everyone else. You are better than everyone else."

"You don't care about my heart, you only care about you and helping yourself."

"Listen to yourself Angel, this isn't you. What did Theiler say before Necro brought us here?"

"Don't change the subject."

Leo continued, "He said you would feel as he feels, and you would advance his desires. He touched you; he is using you to get to me, to tear us apart. He knows that as long as we're together on this and working as a team we are harder to beat, and we can get back to the Spring Crow."

"He's doing nothing of the sort, it's you and your..." Angel paused.

"I'm right, aren't I?"

"I don't know what's come over me," her demeanor changing. "I feel so angry. Leo, what's happening to me?" Angel looked at Leo with pleading eyes.

"Concentrate on good things, things like Lady Cybele watching over you, your new friends Bower and Acacia, even Serenque seemed smitten with you. How can you be angry when you have touched the lives of creatures unlike yourself? Like, how you've befriended me and were a friend to my Grandpa Joe."

Angel's chest gave a soft glow, so soft that Leo didn't notice at first. He took this as a sign she was coming back around.

"Listen," Angel stopped him from his thoughts and changed the subject before Leo had a chance to finish processing his next sentence. She heard shuffling outside of the cell and came to the cell bars next to Leo. "Look, the gargoyles are kneeling."

Leo realized Angel was right and forgot about the argument; the large hairy gargoyles were all turning towards the entrance and kneeling.

"I do hope the accommodations are adequate, after all, it's not every day we get trespassers, especially of your caliber," Theiler said with a laugh as he entered the cell, followed closely behind by Necro.

"We didn't do anything wrong, let us out of here." demanded Angel.

"Why, that's spoken like a child. I expected more from someone of your lineage," retorted Theiler.

"And why do people keep saying stuff like that?"

"You really have led a sheltered life in the Spring Crow haven't you, child. All the lies and secrets Lady Charon has kept from you. You have nearly as much power as the Jinn, you would go far in the Carved Realm, my girl, very far."

"Don't listen to him," interrupted Leo, "he's trying to divide us again, just like he did when he touched you."

"Ah, there is the Kane I'd been waiting for, you and your kind always did figure out other's powers quicker than you could decipher your own. You would do well here too; in fact, I believe Necro will train you well when the time comes, when your soul is mine."

"Our souls will never be yours; we will fight you with everything we have," yelled Leo, now understanding more of Theiler's plan.

"In time, no one, no man or beast, can save their soul from my will. Come Necro, let's give these two some space to think about their future. Either way they choose, they will be a part of our family."

Theiler, followed closely by Necro, turned and walked past the still kneeling gargoyles. As they reached the last gargoyle Necro turned to him, "If they attempt anything, make sure they hurt."

"Yes, Sir Necro, as you wish."

Again alone, only guarded by the gargoyles, Leo and Angel huddled from both fear and the need for solitude in the far corner of their stone cell.

"What a hypocrite," whispered Angel. "He pretends to be such a good-mannered person but in reality, he's a double-dealing, deceitful hypocrite."

"He's using his manners to throw us off; he's attempting to gain our trust and give us promises of being great in the Carved Realm. It's a game and we need to be sure that when we make it back to the Spring Crow, we warn the others of his game, not to trust him, and to steer clear of his weapons.

"He's going to enter the Spring Crow through the crack in the Forest Veil, just as we thought, and he's going to have his army behind him but far enough behind as to not draw suspicion. Without Lady Cybele to ensure everyone is informed of his presence, he's planning on drawing everyone in with his fake good-natured personality, he's going to tell everyone what they want to hear, divide everyone with false truths, and gain trust while turning the town against one another."

"Turn us against each other?"

"Yes, then once in—once everyone trusts him, and only him—that's when he will summon his army to cross, when everyone's guard is down, he will then carve our friends' souls without a fight."

"Oh... Oh!" Angel didn't take long to understand. "The Spring Crow is gearing up for a battle but if he wins their minds there won't be a battle, we will fall right into his trap."

"Exactly! That's why we need to get out of here and back to the Spring Crow, so we can ensure there is a battle, a great battle, such a great battle that he won't be able to talk his way into an easy victory."

For the next twenty minutes, Leo and Angel spoke in hushed tones as not to give away their knowledge of Theiler's plot and powers to divide. Angel had determined that the first thing she would do when they arrived at the Spring Crow was to free Lady Cybele from her library, while it was Leo's responsibility to find General Carlux and warn the army of the impending battle.

"Do you think I should advise General Carlux that a surprise attack would be best, or should I leave it up to him?"

"Don't be daft Leo, you have information that he can use, that his army can use. Give him everything he can use to give his army the advantage, don't rely on him to come up with a battle plan out of thin air. The more information he has, the better he can protect his troops and the better the troops can protect the Spring Crow."

Leo and Angel continued discussing their plans to perfect their responsibilities when, or rather if, they escaped their current situation when a gruff voice penetrated their hushed tones.

"Sir Necro, we weren't informed that you would be back so quickly," spoke the largest gargoyle.

A warrior, whose identity was hard to determine in the dim light of the bastille, spoke in a harsh tone. "Theiler wants these two now, it's time that they learn how a true ruler conducts business. Release them to me, I'll take it from here. Go!"

The head gargoyle relayed the command to the portly and vastly hairier gargoyle charged with guarding the entrance to the cell. In turn, the portly gargoyle produced a skeleton key from his thick shag and twisted it in the lock, opening the iron gate with a creak. Leo and Angel froze, unaware of what was to come next, only aware of Necro coming their way to once again ensnare them in his vice-like grasp.

As he came closer, their fighting instinct took over and as they began to struggle, they were greeted by a familiar voice whispering. "Good, keep fighting, make it look real. Act like you don't want me to take you."

"Iron John?" Leo whispered back, suddenly realizing what was happening.

"Yes, you summoned me, didn't you? Now come on, put up a fight to make it look good, I need to get you two somewhere safe."

Leo and Angel put up a fierce fight. In reality, they fought as hard as they normally would under worse circumstances. Iron John pulled no punches when roughly grabbing the two, throwing one over each shoulder.

"Shut the door behind us," commanded Iron John. "The next time you see these two they will be real Carved Realm warriors."

The laughter of the gargoyles was heard in the background as Iron John walked straight out of the bastille as the head gargoyle closed the door behind as instructed.

Once clear of the bastille and its guardians, Iron John put the two down and looked at them as if to ask, "What next?"

"How, I mean, you look nothing like Necro, how did you get away with that?" asked Angel.

"It's a known fact that gargoyles are some of the best guardians, that's why in some worlds they are placed on buildings as protectors. What is little known is that they are extremely near-sighted. Once removed from their perch atop buildings and down on the ground they can't tell one person from the next. I figured as long as a confident warrior walked in, they would assume I belonged. I had no idea they would mistake me for Necro, wait until he finds out." Iron John smiled. "Come on, we need to get your friend and get out of here."

"Friend?" Leo asked, but not before Angel let out a shriek before covering her mouth to muffle the sound.

Charon appeared from the shadows in his full Carved Realm glory. Angel had never seen Charon in this state.

"Charon," Leo kept his whisper as low as he could in his excitement, "boy am I glad to see you."

"Charon?" questioned Angel wide eyed, mouth agape. "What happened to you?"

"I'll explain later," answered Leo. "We need a plan to get out of here."

"You're Jinn, summon a spell that will transport us through the Veil," suggested Iron John.

"We can't, we think Theiler is tracking us through our magic, magic that isn't familiar with the Carved Realm. If we continue to use our powers, he's sure to track us down again, just like how he knew we were with Serenque," Leo explained. "John, how did you and Charon get in?"

"I just walked right in; who here would stop a warrior such as myself?" he stated proudly, letting his chest rise a bit.

"Then that's how we get out. If we were back in my world, we wouldn't be able to rely on magic but perhaps a little trickery is in order."

The three stared back at Leo.

"Don't you see? Just like you freed us from the cell, that's how you are going to get us out of the fortress. Put us back over your shoulders and pretend we are your prisoners. If anyone asks, tell them you are on official Carved Realm business, directed personally by Theiler. Charon, follow behind and act like you are doing Iron Johns bidding. It's the only way."

"That's too simple Leo," protested Angel, "we can't rely on just walking out, that will never work."

"Do you have a better plan?"

Back on the broad shoulders of Iron John, Leo and Angel allowed themselves to be carried though the fortress, down the dimly lit grey corridors, and finally into the entrance hall. Charon followed closely behind, keeping an eye out for anyone who could be following. Iron John paused at the great door, their last barrier between them and the relative freedom of the outside.

The cool night air felt warm in comparison to the cold, damp quarters they had just sneaked from. Iron John stepped with purpose as Charon followed, keeping his head down as to not draw suspicion to his disfigured but soulful facial features.

"I think a straight shot to the crack in the Forest Veil is the best option," said Iron John as they made their way through the ever more densely populated Carved Realm square, "once we get to the veil you three run and don't stop until you reach your Realm."

"What about you?" Angel spoke in a low tone in order to prevent any of the now thicker soulless creatures from overhearing. "You can't stay here, what if you're caught and punished for helping us escape?"

"Don't worry about me, I'll keep an eye on things here and if it gets too heated, if the army is planning to move, I'll get word to you."

The four quickly and quietly made it through the populated area and to the edge of the Forest Veil, Iron John gently lowered the two and gave his back a stretch.

"I can't believe that worked, I can't believe we weren't tracked," Angel broke the silence.

"Magic can't solve everything," replied Leo. "Sometimes you have to think of solutions that would work in other worlds where magic doesn't exist as you know it. Finding solutions to problems, without the use of magic, is an everyday occurrence in my world. Granted, it's not every day we have to escape from a prison but understanding Theiler would expect us to use magic, not using magic was really the only solution."

"But you called for Iron John."

"Yeah," interjected Iron John, "Theiler must have known I was on my way."

"Not necessarily," explained Leo. "You're from the Carved Realm, in fact, you've been here for so long you are a part of the Realm. Theiler is looking for magic foreign to this realm, I only used your capabilities, not mine, to ask for your help."

"What about Lady Cybele's communication orb?" asked Angel.

"I'm hoping that because we didn't use our magic and it originated from the Spring Crow, Theiler won't believe we used it as a means to escape. He's watching us, not her. He may know there was something up but nothing we could use to escape. He's specifically tracking our use and, as far as he knows, we haven't used any magic because, well, we haven't."

"That sounds too simple, but I can't argue the results," Angel gave in. "Come on, we need to get through the Veil and warn the Spring Crow."

"Are you sure you won't come with us?" Leo turned his attention back to Iron John. "The Spring Crow army could really use an experienced warrior and I'm sure General Carlux will welcome you to his contingent."

"Don't worry about me, someone needs to stay back and keep an eye on things, to give a warning when Theiler is on the move. When it's time to fight, you will find me on the side of your General, I look after those who look after me. Take care Leo and Angel, my friends." Iron John turned to Charon with a smile and took Charon's shoulder in his large hand. "Until we meet again... new friend." Iron John turned and made his way back from the direction they came, disappearing into the night.

Chapter 17

Racing through the Forest Veil the trio didn't speak a word, each were wading deep within their own thoughts of discoveries, thoughts that swirled around Theiler's assumed plot, the future of the Spring Crow, and thoughts regarding their own self. The only sound that penetrated their movement was their quick footfalls on the soft forest floor.

As Charon approached the threshold of the Spring Crow, he began to morph into his normal dapper self, clothes clean and features chiseled once again. The three slowed to a quick walk, now panting from their sprint, Charon finally broke the silence, "Lady Cybele should have additional information for us and needs to be warned about Theiler's intent. He mustn't be allowed to enter without warning. We need to think of a way to save our home"

Now at the edge of the Forest Veil the three took a knee to quickly discuss the details of their plan while continuing to catch their breath. Realizing Charon was unaware of Lady Cybele's entrapment, Angel quickly stepped in and filled in the details. "Ms. Parish trapped Lady Cybele in her library, she hasn't had a chance to pass what she knows, the Spring Crow is sitting defenseless."

"What do you mean, trapped?" Charon asked, eyes wide.

"Somehow, Ms. Parish closed the doors on Lady Cybele and locked her in her own library. She can't leave and she can't make the library disappear because she may go with it," Angel explained.

"How do you know this?" queried Charon.

"She sent a communications orb to us while we were trapped in the fortress," answered Angel.

Charon looked both bewildered and impressed. "She sent a communications orb, while trapped in her library in the Spring Crow, over to you two, while trapped in the Carved Realm, and you were able to retrieve and use it? That's absolutely amazing."

"It helps us understand what we may be up against now that we're back, but it doesn't help us in warning everyone, I can't create magic like that." Said Leo.

"General Carlux has been conscribing able-bodied creatures into the army," Charon said. "They may be a ragtag bunch of giants and trolls, but it's more defense than we had a few days ago and if we do somehow get the upper hand, we will need as much offensive support as we can get."

"I'm not so sure," interjected Leo. "If Ms. Parish is working for Theiler, she has probably spread lies to General Carlux, lies that would convince him we aren't in danger. She's going to lay the foundation of deceit that Theiler will build upon."

"And if General Carlux believes those lies and he is convinced we aren't in danger he won't be training the army adequately," Angel said, finishing Leo's thought.

"This is worse than I thought," Charon said. "I can't believe Ms. Parish would do something like this right here in the Spring Crow. She's always been so giving to the community and has even worked her way up within the council."

"Speaking of Ms. Parish," Leo said, "we need you to try to find her and find out what she knows. She's probably in hiding, possibly on the outskirts of one of the Veils. No one in the Spring Crow will attempt to look for her there and if she thinks you're in the Carved Realm she will feel safe. Look for her in all three Veils and ensure she can't contact Theiler again, otherwise she may warn him."

"I'm going to work out how to free Lady Cybele, she's the closest thing I have to family and we need her to convince the rest of the Spring Crow that we are truly in danger," said Angel. "She almost always uses her library from Town Hall so it shouldn't be too hard to find."

Time was of the essence and they needed to ensure their steps were carefully thought out prior to execution. Once the three were convinced their plan needed no further discussion, they silently nodded to each other as if to say, 'Godspeed' and each sprinted towards their intended goal.

Chapter 18

Angel, now alone for the first time in days, felt the absence of her constant and comforting companion. *How did he pull that, what did he call it, "bat" from his world into the Carved Realm? That's impossible, nobody can bring something in that hasn't been brought in before. Even the items stored in his memory place aren't really physically in his world.* Her thoughts shifted quickly back towards Lady Cybele, the only family she had ever known, now trapped in what was supposed to be a safe place, a safe place made into an uncertain prison. *If Lady Cybele were to shutter her library while inside, she could disappear forever, and if she didn't escape from her library the Spring Crow could do the same.* Angel ran harder, ignoring the pain coursing through her legs, until she finally arrived at the entrance to the Town Hall.

Angel slowed as she approached the large wooden doors leading into the hall she knew awaited on the opposite side. What would she find, she wondered? She placed her hand on the door, expecting the worse.

"Angel," came an excited shout from behind, startling the already frazzled girl. Sylvia had arrived at the Town Hall just seconds after her. "I just have to tell Lady Cybele of the information

I've found. Why, it's such a fascinating story of how creatures, human-like creatures, can be formed from the very ground we walk. And you won't believe one of the creatures he made."

"Sylvia, you almost gave me a heart attack. Where have you been.?"

"I've been in my library as Lady Cybele requested. You're never going to believe what I found regarding Theiler and... wait a minute... I was told you were... that you traversed the crack in the Forest Veil and that you may be in trouble. Oh, I'm so glad that you're okay. Lady Cybele is going to be so excited to see you; she was worried to death."

"We have bigger problems," interrupted Angel. "Ms. Parish trapped Lady Cybele in her library, and we need to get her out in order to warn the Spring Crow of Theiler's plan to attack."

"Attack the Spring Crow? Why, that's ridiculous! We have an army, what does he have?"

"You already have the pieces; all you need is to put them in place."

Sylvia gave Angel a quizzical look, not fully understanding the meaning, and Angel wasn't going to give away everything she knew until she was sure whom she could trust. Lady Cybele would know.

"Follow me, once we free Lady Cybele, I'll fill you in."

The two entered the Town Hall. Angel was being cautious, not knowing the true whereabouts of Ms. Parish, and Sylvia bursting in as she would on any given day.

"The doors are just closed, she's not trapped. Lady Cybele just wanted her privacy, we shouldn't disturb her." Sylvia turned back towards the door as Angel caught her shoulder.

"No, Lady Cybele contacted us in the Carved Realm, she can't open the doors. Look, a lock has been put on the outside. Why would there be a lock on the outside of her library when all she would need to secure it is to latch the doors from within?"

Angel pulled on the doors with all her might, leaning every ounce of weight into her effort. Sylvia, now grasping the situation, tried to help by pulling on the doors as well.

"Stand back," ordered Sylvia. Touching her amulet, she ordered, *Sluiter Augury*. Her amulet began to glow white hot.

"Ouch," Sylvia yelled jumping back from the door and rubbing the slight burn on her chest left by the amulet. "What kind of magic is this that I can't undo? Who did you say put this in place?"

"Never mind that, if the magic can't be undone perhaps it can be destroyed?"

"What could possibly destroy what can't be undone? Perhaps Lady Cybele was mistaken about you, I though you understood magic and its innerworkings. Why, it would take less time for the lock and everything around it to corrode and degrade than it would to break this spell."

"That's it! Sylvia, you're a genius. Stand back, I've not attempted this before."

Angel placed both hands on the lock and concentrated on the powers granted to her by Acacia, the power of nature... power that would last long after both the Spring Crow and Carved Realm were long forgotten to time.

The lock casing, internal pins and cam began to patina, as if to age before Sylvia's eyes. The patina turned to corrosion and oxidation, slowly but visibly crumbling within Angels hands.

Sylvia watched in awe as Angel withdrew her hands from where the lock had once been. All that remained was a small pile of oxidized rust on the library threshold and a prominent amber stain on Angel's outstretched palms. Angel wasted no time in yanking open the heavy library doors, revealing a distraught Lady Cybele, pacing between the vast shelves.

"Angel, I'm so relieved to see you," Lady Cybele exclaimed, as she embraced her ward in a loving hug. Angel, longing for family, gladly returned the gesture of motherly love.

"Lady Cybele, how did this happen? Who would dare such a thing?" questioned Sylvia.

"Sylvia, my trusted confidant, Ms. Parish isn't whom she seems. I never imagined that we would have a traitor in our midst, but I was blind. Ms. Parish is under the influence of Theiler's deceit and she must be stopped before she causes further damage."

"Ms. Parish? Where is she now?" asked Sylvia.

"We believe she thinks Charon is still in the Carved Realm, so we think she's taken refuge out in one of the Veils. She doesn't know Charon returned with Leo and I, so we sent Charon to track her," replied Angel.

"And Leo?" queried Lady Cybele.

"He's making his way to General Carlux to warn him that a battle is imminent. We must ensure General Carlux believes Leo. There is no telling what damage Ms. Parish has already caused and I believe I know how he has formed his army, an army vastly devoted to Theiler."

Lady Cybele turned towards her library. "I can repair the door at a later time. *Complete*," Lady Cybele ordered, and watched her library disappear. "Come, we must hurry, Ms. Parish has a head start."

"*Kaleso*," ordered Sylvia as she touched her amulet. Seconds later the three could hear the clip-clop of Sylvia's horse drawn carriage as it pulled to the front. "Come on, I'll fill you in on what I found regarding Theiler and his love."

Chapter 19

Leo ran, his lungs and legs burning well beyond mortal pain as he closed the distance from the Forest Veil to the parade grounds where he knew General Carlux would be training his army. He felt as though he would collapse at any moment but kept his frantic pace, knowing he could not rest until he delivered his message, much like Pheidippides carrying his message to Athens.

When Leo arrived at the parade grounds, he found it unguarded. Passing by the empty guard station he continued his sprint to the General's headquarters and burst in.

"General Carlux," Leo managed to announce breathlessly, "Theiler can cross the Forest Veil and he's on his way. He plans to cross alone but his army will be close behind, ready to pounce on any weaknesses he creates." Leo found the nearest chair and sat, head between his legs, panting.

The headquarters was empty, save for General Carlux, drinking another fully sugared coffee, talking calmly with Lieutenant Demrofinu and Mr. Morphon about the night's movements.

"Don't be ridiculous my boy, Ms. Parish came by earlier and informed us that Lady Cybele had found nothing to suggest that we were in any danger. In fact, I've already finished with our nightly drills and have sent the soldiers either home or to the Crow's Beak pub to celebrate a hard night's work."

"The pub. How long ago?"

"Not more than fifteen minutes or so I suppose. Why, it is early morning after all, I wouldn't dream of sending them before dawn, that would be irresponsible to say the least."

"You need to call them back. Angel, Charon, and I just escaped the Carved Realm and Theiler is planning on entering the Spring Crow at any moment; he's going to divide us, give us a false sense of security, and then bring his army in to destroy us."

"But according to Ms. Parish..."

"Ms. Parish is working with Theiler. Don't you see? He needed someone who we trusted to put his plan into action, she's not who you think she is," Leo said.

"I've known Ms. Parish for years, she's a wonderful woman, wouldn't hurt a fly," General Carlux replied, clearly becoming agitated.

"That's exactly what I'm trying to tell you, that's exactly what she would have you believe... what she would have everyone believe. She trapped Lady Charon in her library, told you not to expect Theiler, and now she has gone into hiding to bide her time until Theiler arrives. Charon is tracking her as we speak."

General Carlux had now clearly lost his temper. "This is nonsense and I won't hear any more of it. There is no danger, if there were Lady Cybele would warn me."

"Calm down, boy," Mr. Morphon finally chimed in, "Ms. Parish assured us."

"You have to listen to me," argued Leo.

"I'd listen to Sir Leo, if I were you," Lady Cybele stated matter-of-fact as she strode into the headquarters, followed closely by Angel and Sylvia.

"Lady Cybele, what perfect timing" the General greeted her as he stood, pushing away from his desk and nearly knocking over his drink. "Please help me explain to this young man that we have nothing to worry about, that the army doesn't need to be on call at all times."

"I'm afraid I can't do that, General. It appears that we have a traitor in our realm and if we don't act quickly—and soberly—we may soon find ourselves under the spell of our enemy."

"But Ms. Parish came by and said..."

"Ms. Parish isn't who she claimed to be," interrupted Sylvia. We think she may be a creation of the Carved Realm, dedicated to Theiler."

"That's preposterous," General Carlux interjected.

"No, it's true," pleaded Sylvia. "Theiler may have created her, cleaved her soul through Eidolon but in her case, he didn't torture her soul. He showed her what she considered love to convince her to love him back. Somehow, if he created her, he created a Gadaseer and knew he could use her to his advantage. After he cleaved, warped and turned her soul he returned it to her, and she's been his follower ever since."

"So that's how you believe she came to the Spring Crow? It should be impossible to traverse the Veils, but another Gadaseer? No, I don't believe it," the General retorted while turning his back.

"Charon crosses all the time," countered Sylvia, "what I don't understand is how we didn't know."

"Charon has stated that he turns into something other than his outer self," General Carlux turned to face Lady Cybele once again and continued his argument. "I've never witnessed it personally, but he has stated it's terrifying. If Ms. Parish morphed into what Charon describes we would have known."

"We haven't worked that out yet, but you have to believe us, she did cross," said Leo in another attempt to convince the General.

"General Carlux, I have walked through the memories of Theiler in my own library and can attest to the fact that he does create life and does indeed practice Eidolon. He can, and will, cross the Forest Veil through the damage he has caused. He is coming, and sooner rather than later," informed Lady Cybele, growing tired of the General's constant defense.

General Carlux gave with a sigh, "Lieutenant Demrofinu, please recall all the soldiers from their homes and the Crow's Beak."

"But, sir, the men..."

"Didn't you hear what Lady Cybele just said? Theiler is practicing Eidolon and has found a way across the protection of the Veil. Gather the men immediately."

"Yes, sir," replied Lieutenant Demrofinu as he hastily gathered his belongings and sped out the still open door.

"Leo, I'm sorry I doubted you," General Carlux stated while turning his attention back to Leo. "What did you see? What did you and Angel experience in the Carved Realm? Don't leave any details out, we need to know exactly what you know if we are to stand a chance at defeating Theiler.

Chapter 20

Charon had just morphed back to his gentlemanly self when he was asked to once again travel through the Veils in order to track down Ms. Parish. He took pride in his appearance, but he took greater pride in his home, the Spring Crow. He and the teens had just crossed back through Forest Veil so he decided that the best option would be the Mountain Veil, north of the Spring Crow.

The journey through the foothills started with a loose path Charon had walked many times before in his travels. As the suns began to rise on the Spring Crow, the path became steeper and started to gently rise a few meters above the level of the realm. He pressed onward, up as the gentle rise began to become steep, quickly rising to several hundred meters above the realm. The warm suns heated his now exposed and morphed muscles and he paused, for what he assumed would be long enough to wipe the sweat from his brow. As he paused, he turned towards the Spring Crow. Soldiers, hundreds of soldiers, were pouring out of their homes and the Crow's Beak towards the parade grounds.

Charon didn't like going too far into any veil, but the Mountain Veil was his least favorite of the three. There was no place to hide as there was in the Forest Veil and he didn't have control of a reliable mode of transportation as he did in the Water Veil. With only his feet to guide him through the ever-growing rocky terrain, he also knew of the stories passed down from his Gadaseer ancestors.

According to the Gadaseer's of the past, the Mountain Veil was the home to the Ringing Rocks. Legend had it that the rocks appear in the fields void of all vegetation and are composed of a substance unknown to any man or creature from any of the known worlds or realms. Charon had never ventured far enough into the Mountain Veil to encounter such a rock but today he knew that he had to go further than he had ever before in order to ensure all ground was covered in his search for Ms. Parish.

As Charon climbed higher into the veil his skeletal foot, void of his normal polished shoe, struck a rock and suddenly a series of audible occult-like sounds began to ring in his ears. He could hear the stones but could not make out their warning, and pressed on, higher into the Veil. Ignoring the subtle ringing which continued in his ears and the stretching muscles in his face, arms, and body, he scanned the terrain. *Void of all vegetation, just like the stories*, he thought. As he scanned, he hit upon another rock, which this time bounced away from him and hit a second. A chain reaction erupted, and a bright green light appeared like a fire in the sky immediately in front of him.

"Who dares disturb our slumber", Charon heard as he fell still.

Who's there? Charon thought as the barbed wire stretching his mouth was tight enough now to prevent speech.

"Repent for crossing into territory sacred to the Jinn Master, repent and save your soul."

Charon began to back slowly, *If you can hear me, I am Charon, I have been sent by the*

*decedent of the Kane Jinn in search of someone
who may seek to do harm to the Spring Crow.*

The light in the sky shone brighter, hotter.
"We are the protectors of the Veil, none who pass
shall cause harm to any realm. You say that you
were sent by Jinn but have come into our sight and
shall pay the price."

I've been sent by the Jinn, Charon thought
in reply. *If you are the protectors of this veil and
the realms tell me, have you seen a lady from the
Spring Crow in your veil and why does she seek to
do harm to the realm?*

"You shall see for yourself that no living
being has entered from your realm, only from the
realm of the original Jinn," the flame replied,
leaping closer to Charon. "When you turn your
head towards your home, to meet your Kane Jinn,
let all who will listen that not all is what it seems,
and not all are whom them seem. Take no steps
further and turn back. When you come to the
realization of our words a new battle will open."
The flame flickered out of sight back into its rocky
form, still singing in Charon's ears.

Charon, wasting no time and careful with
his step, began his journey down the Mountain Veil
as quick as his bony legs would move. He didn't
understand the warning, but he needed to get back.
Nobody from the Spring Crow had been to this
part of the Veil and maybe Lady Cybele would
understand what he had heard.

Chapter 21

Theiler, alone in his chamber, closed his eyes, taking a moment to remember... his father hated him, his brothers hated him, and he was an outcast and a loner. He'd show his father that he was not to be forgotten, that he alone would rule the Carved Realm, the Spring Crow, and eventually all the realms of Elysium to include his father's beloved Cardinal Realm.

Without a special place in the heart of his father, Theiler would turn to his mother for solitude, only to be rejected by her as well. *Mother,* he thought, *what a weak-minded foolish woman, only existing to serve father and his will.* His mind drifted away from his weak mother, but this memory provided a gateway back to his younger days. He vividly remembered the day he and his brothers came into their powers, the day after he received the only gift he had ever received—his war ax. Theiler, eyes now fluttering, drifted into a dream filled dark slumber.

"Leave me alone," yelled Theiler's younger brother Kane. "Can't you see I'm trying to read?"

"Come on Kane, you can't really be interested in those old books Father gave you. Wouldn't you rather practice with a real weapon?"

"I said leave me alone. You go swing your ax around all you want but I'm not interested. Why do you have to be so annoying?"

"What do you think you're going to do with books? You need to learn to fight, you can't learn that from a book." Theiler said.

"When I'm controlling both dark and light you will change your tune," replied Kane as he attempted to continue his studies.

"You won't control anything, you're an embarrassment, too weak and Father knows it too. That's why he didn't present you with anything useful, because he knows you will never be useful."

Theiler left Kane to his book but not before swinging the ax in his direction, causing the younger Jinn to flinch at its proximity.

Theiler laughing, left his younger brother and walked through the fields and into the forest surrounding the Cardinal Realm, swinging his ax at all manner of life and continuing to laugh each time he sliced into a defenseless creature. *Stupid things*, he thought to himself, *some creatures don't have the good sense to move... I'll give them a reason to move.*

Theiler eventually came upon the eldest brother Garaile in an opening, swinging his broadsword through the air with expert skill and timing, its edge singing with every stroke. Theiler knew Garaile had only just received his gift of the sword but marveled with jealousy at how well his older brother had already begun to master its use.

"Garaile," called Theiler, "would you care to practice with someone who can give you a real challenge rather than slicing away foolishly through the air?"

Garaile eyed his younger brother with a smirk. "That weapon is too much for you, I don't know what father was thinking, you're too weak for such a weapon but if you insist."

Garaile wasted no time in attacking his younger brother, easily maneuvering past Theiler's broad and clumsy swings, thrusting his sword to ensure the smallest of cuts were just deep enough to cause the weaker brother pain.

"Take it easy, it's just practice," shouted Theiler as his brother cut him once again, placing a small gash in his stomach.

"How do you ever expect to be a ruler if you can't fight? Take your ax and go home, or better yet, throw it in the river. You'll never amount to anything." Garaile's words cut deeper than his sword.

I'll show them, thought Theiler as he walked away, wounded both physically and mentally, rejected by one brother and defeated by another. "I'll defeat them one-by-one, one day I'll rule all of Elysium. I'll tell Father that Garaile and Kane are attempting to learn the dark arts and while he's punishing them, I'll earn his favor. I'll learn to control this weapon; I'll learn to create from chaos."

"Mother," Theiler's dream state suddenly flashed to himself as a child with the only person he felt would understand him, "one day when I am the ruler of Elysium and all its realms, I will ensure you never have to depend on anyone ever again."

"Theiler, I'm bound to your father; you know I could never leave King Acadamel, he's the most important being in all of Elysium. Besides, do you really think he would leave such a responsibility of a kingdom to just anyone?"

"Mother, he won't live forever, but I on the other hand will find a way."

"What are you saying? Are you plotting against your father, the king?" His dream state mother was on him in a flash.

"Of course not, Mother, you know I'm only looking after your best interest for the future."

"You're plotting against the king. Your brothers wouldn't do such a thing. What would the other mothers think? Oh, how I wish I had never had a child."

The words, though a dream, cut deeper than any rejection or brutality his brothers could manage.

"Master."

Theiler heard a sandy voice on the distant wind, yet it seemed to be coming from his mother's still moving lips. The young Theiler didn't understand, was someone talking to him through her? What kind of magic had taken over?

"Master."

There was the voice, yet again. Theiler woke with a jolt.

"Master, the prisoners have escaped," informed a small gargoyle standing in Theiler's chamber unannounced, shaking with fear.

"How dare you intrude into my presence," Theiler spat. "Who sent you?"

"Master, the young Jinn and his companion have snuck past the guards, they are nowhere to be found in the Carved Realm," the gargoyle informed while shaking with fear.

"That's impossible, I would have sensed their magic," growled Theiler.

"No magic, Sire, a warrior representing himself as Sir Necro removed the two on your behalf."

"None of my warriors would dare masquerade as Necro nor defy my order. Tell the truth gargoyle, who tricked your mind?" Theiler reached for the War Ax resting close to his side.

"It is true, Sire, a warrior clad as Necro released the prisoners and, along with a servant, carried them from the Bastille."

"The tutor in the Oubliette, did she release another? Was the Jinn not her only rescue?" Theiler wondered, now realizing his chamber of souls surrounding the Oubliette was also in peril. "Iron John," Theiler said while pacing in the gargoyle's direction, the small gargoyle now backing slowly towards the door. "Where is the one who defies me?"

"Sire," the gargoyle stammered, "Iron John has escaped as well."

With the speed no mortal could match, Theiler wielded his war ax, the gargoyle's blood spilled to the floor.

Emerging from his chambers, war ax in hand, Theiler screamed, "Get me Necro! The time for war is now!" He again yelled. "No time for fun; no time for the route of deception. We attack immediately with speed, force, and violence," he silently whispered to himself.

Warriors lined in columns formation, formed as far as the eye could see throughout the Carved Realm. Sir Necro, at the head of the formation, looked over Master Theiler's creations with contempt. All created in the same manner as he, but none as devoted to Theiler. He had no compassion for their fate, most would die in the takeover of the Spring Crow but no matter, he would sit on Theiler's right, to advise his rule.

Behind the warriors, creatures of every shape and size stood at the ready, prepared to give their lives in the name of Theiler. The remaining soulless creatures gathered, yet further behind in a gaggle of unholy darkness, heads bowed, and fists clenched. They, like the warriors and animal-like beings, were charged with ensuring that the unfortunate survivors were tortured until their souls could be cleaved and harvested by the Master.

Theiler arrived from the rear, parting the waves of creatures and warriors without compassion, slicing his way through with his dark magic and war ax. Taking his place of leadership in front of Necro, he eyed his second. "I trust all is prepared, that no warrior or creature dare defy my orders lest you, yourself, taste my wrath."

"All is prepared, Master. Blood will be shed to bring about the birth of an expanded Carved Realm in your honor," Necro replied with a bow.

"Bring the strongest of the creatures to the front and arm them with the sturdiest steel you can afford, slash the Forest Veil alongside the crack I have prepared. Once the army has passed, leave half of the creatures behind with one-hundred warriors to finish the Forest Veil. I want no reminder of my Father's barrier. You, my trusted warrior, must stay behind to ensure none return out of cowardness and slay those who do. Acadamel will see who is the strongest of his sons"

The largest of Theiler's creatures, Minotaurs, giant gargoyles, manticores and the like, armed with sturdy weapons, formed a loose formation spread at the head of the warriors. Empty eyes looked upon the forest, ready to destroy all in their path. Upon Theiler's command, the unholy army began their march into the forest, weaving a path of destruction through the crack in the Forest Veil.

Chapter 22

"Alright, men, hold those lines. Nothing gets through the forest without our knowledge," Mr. Forswear barked his orders to the creatures guarding the Veil. "I have it on good authority from Lieutenant Demrofinu that we are to expect intruders and you have the distinct honor of being the Spring Crow's first line of defense."

All manner of creatures not conscribed to General Carlux were now standing guard, prepared to give their lives in defense of their homes, their families, and their way of life. Mr. Forswear, under the advice of Lieutenant Demrofinu, aligned the creatures towards the Forest Veil in a line formation, which stretched the length of the area. On the break in the Veil, he reinforced the formation with additional creatures behind. All carried the weapon of his own choosing, be it farming instruments or typical sword and shield, each was comfortable with his choice.

"Mr. Forswear, how are the men? Do you need my assistance with anything?" called out Charon, who was making his way down from the Mountain Veil.

"I think we have it under control Charon. I pity the forces who try to get through our defenses," Mr. Forswear stated as he motioned a sweeping hand over his men. "How did it go on the mountain, any signs of Ms. Parish?"

"Unfortunately, no," Charon said. "However, I did encounter what I thought to be just stories from my past. The Ringing Rocks are very much real. They passed on that Ms. Parish was not in the Veil and that the only thing that did pass was from the realm of the original Jinn. I was hoping to find her, if nothing more than to question her. As you know, I never knew my family, so I've never known another Gadaseer. I'm curious to see how she transforms when she crosses between realms."

"The Ringing Rocks," Lady Cybele stated. "Yes, the stories make sense now. All veils have protection and that protection will only appear when needed. What else did they say?"

Charon thought for a moment, "When we realize what they say is true, a new battle will take place."

"Hmmm..." Mr. Forswear jumped in. "I don't believe it. I know for a fact she's from the Spring Crow; perhaps, she's fled back to the Carved Realm. I doubt we see her showing her face again." He considered his last remark, "It's too bad. I've known her for years and I would have never imagined she would throw herself in with the likes of Theiler."

"No matter where she might be from, I don't believe she had a choice," said Charon. "She may have been created by Theiler and when he discovered she was Gadaseer his power over Eidolon was too much for her to withstand. In addition, if her soul was tortured and then shown any form of kindness, what was she to do and believe? Once her soul was returned, she trusted him implicitly. I'm sure she loves him with all her heart. What I'd like to know is how she became a Gadaseer; the trait is normally passed down through the generations. I feared the trait could one day end with me."

"Regardless of how it happened, we're in a mess now, aren't we?" Mr. Forswear turned back towards the beast guarding the veil while continuing to address Charon. "You've seen what we're up against. What do you think our odds are?"

Charon forcefully exhaled, "I'm not going to lie to you, I don't know if anyone really was in the Mountain Veil, regardless, your men are up against trained warriors, bloodthirsty trained warriors. When Theiler decides to come through the Veil, and he will come, your lines will serve as a temporary pause along his path but nothing more." Charon felt he was being too honest. "With the size of your forces, I'm sure most will battle with heart, as fierce as possible, and live to reap the rewards of a glorious victory."

Mr. Forswear, emotions now mixed between pride and fear, decided pride must win out and turned to his men. Placing a hand on his glowing amulet, his voice boomed out to his ad hoc force with conviction, "Neighbors and friends, I understand your fears and that you are hyper-aware of what is to come. I seek your help to guide us to victory. I implore and challenge you to communicate all actions, fight with determination, and use every magical and physical power the Spring Realm has given you. I'm honored to join you in the battle to come."

He removed his hand from his amulet and turned back towards Charon, "They are fighting for the realm, their home. If they believe in our cause, I must truly believe as well."

"Well said, my friend," Charon gave a friendly squeeze to Mr. Forswear's arm. "I need to check on Leo and Angel. I'll be back when you need me."

Charon found Leo and Angel, who had excused themselves from Lady Cybele, General Carlux, and Mr. Morphon, talking alone in the distance while watching the army slowly gathering under the direction of the general.

"Leo, it's time to put on your armor," Charon placed his hand on Leo's shoulder in a fatherly manner.

Stunned, Leo replied in a slightly embarrassed tone, "I don't know how to fight and I don't have armor. I didn't take any from the warriors and I didn't think to store any in my memory place."

"You're kidding me about the fighting part, right?" interjected Angel. "Not more than twenty-four hours ago, you climbed onto the back of a dragon and started beating him with a metal rod."

"Baseball bat," corrected Leo.

"Whatever it was, you pulled it from your world without it ever being in ours. You can fight and you have powers, yet unknown."

"You pulled something from your world into ours?" Charon eyed Leo with awe, "Nobody can do that, it's impossible."

"I didn't know I wasn't supposed to pull the bat; if I had known, I wouldn't have."

"No, it's not that you shouldn't have, it's that you shouldn't have been able to. This is, actually, a wonderful turn of events. If you feel you can use a weapon, the weapon of your choosing, I'd continue with it," Charon said with a smile. "Come on, you do have armor? Let's go try it on," Charon began to walk away from the army. "Oh, and you come, too, Angel. Lady Cybele left something for you as well."

In the unsurprisingly well-kept attic at Grandpa Joe's house—now Leo's house, from what he had been told—Charon lifted the lid of a well-worn steamer trunk. Of all the times Leo was at Grandpa Joe's he had never ventured up into the attic, not even as a curious kid. Grandpa Joe had kept him so well entertained with his stories of adventure that he didn't feel the need to wander or further explore. Now, Leo knew those stories were tales of his grandpa's past and of Leo's future responsibilities.

"It's been some time since Joe wore this and we may have to alter it slightly, but this is going to work perfectly." Charon grinned as he lifted what appeared to be a fifteenth century helmet from the trunk.

"It's beautiful," gasped Angel.

It truly was, thought Leo. The helmet was capable of enclosing the full head via hinged plates that folded backwards to allow both access and protection, while additional plates extended downwards to protect the neck. A visor completed the defenses and the entire piece was polished to a black shine.

"Put it on," urged Charon. "Let's see how it fits."

Leo, never attempting to put on armor, found the various pieces and parts intimidating but fairly simple. Unlike medieval armor of years past, Grandpa Joe had ensured his armor was lightweight and pliable when required but still offered all the protection suitable for a warrior going into battle.

"It's a little big," Leo commented, his hands and arms not long enough for the gauntlets covering his arms and his chest swimming in the cuirass.

"Not a problem, let me handle it." Angel's chest began to glow. "*Modekleidervosfit.*" The suit of armor shrunk down to a perfect fit.

"Still feel the need to dress me I see," joked Leo. Angel blushed and turned towards Charon so he wouldn't see.

"You mentioned Lady Cybele left something for me?" she said.

"And so, I did. Look in the bottom of the trunk; I think you will find it already fits."

Angel peered into the—what she thought was empty—trunk and pulled out beautiful golden chainmail hauberks along with matching breast plates, helmet, and all the other accouterments that would protect her during battle.

"It's beautiful," whispered Angel. "Why would Lady Cybele leave this for me? She doesn't owe me anything; it's I who owe her for watching over me for so many years."

"Why don't you ask her yourself," Charon grinned and motioned his head towards the attic door where now stood Lady Cybele.

"My dear, Angel Dianna, over the past few days you have proven yourself to be wise, gentle, and brave. You have a mind like no other and a heart that hasn't been seen in many lifetimes. I'm sure you have often wondered why you, and you alone, do not have access to a library nor an amulet."

"I just thought that I didn't deserve what the others had. I know I'm different and everyone else knows it too."

"You're right, you are different," Lady Cybele smiled. "You have ancestors like no other in all of the realms. You are the descendant of the original tutor, banned from the Cardinal Realm for the knowledge of the family secrets. In your blood flows the power of the most powerful magician ever known. You have no need for a library or amulet for that matter, your power comes from within," Lady Cybele explained as she touched her own heart.

"I can't be a descendant of the tutor, I'm not special and everyone knows it," argued Angel. "If I were so special, why wasn't I told?"

"The original tutor vowed secrecy in order to ensure that his descendants didn't become hungry for power, as did his pupils, the Jinn. We agreed that when the time was right and a descendant pure of heart and spirit revealed him or herself, the secret would be revealed," Lady Cybele beamed. "We've been waiting a long time for you, my dear."

"That's what Acacia and the others were talking about." Angel sat on a sturdy wooden box in the corner in order to steady herself from her wobbling legs. "We kept hearing about someone special, the tutor; I had no idea they were talking about me."

"Of course not, how could you, my dear? You never let your pride get in the way of your heart and what needs to be accomplished. Think back to your early childhood... you were easily bored, had no library, yet naturally picked up magical ways, and have no amulet but still have power. Much like the Jinn your ancestors trained, you are a special person amongst the realms."

"I hate to break this up, and trust me, I do want to hear all about this when we can, but we need to arm up and join the others before it's too late," Charon brought everyone back to the moment at hand.

"Quite right, sir," Lady Cybele smiled. "Choose your weapons wisely and meet me and Charon at the Forest Veil, we will be waiting for you with General Carlux. I'm sure he would be proud to have both of you leading the defense of our great realm alongside him."

The two were now alone in Leo's attic, dressed for battle and getting used to the surprisingly pliable, yet sturdy armor that would protect them in their first major battle. Leo finally broke the silence that was awkwardly hanging between them.

"It sounds like our families go back quite a way, doesn't it?"

"I suppose, it's just a lot to take in. I mean, over the past few days I didn't know who I was and thought I didn't fit in. Lady Cybele and Charon are the only ones who consistently treated me like I belong and now, I'm still not sure I belong."

"Of course, you belong. There must have been a reason the original tutor chose to stay in the Spring Crow, to stay with Lady Cybele. He must have seen something in her and the Realm that guided his decision. It's up to you to continue what he started."

"Speaking of Lady Cybele," Angel said, "exactly how old is she?"

"I was wondering the same thing," Leo smiled back at Angel`.

"I guess we need to choose our weapons if we are going to help General Carlux," Angel closed her eyes and her chest momentarily gave a faint glow. In her hands appeared a crossbow and on her back a quiver of arrows that she had taken from one of the soldiers Bower and his friends had detained in the forest.

"I'm not so sure I can use any of the weapons in my memory space, I've not trained on anything. I wish we had more time, time for me to learn how to handle a sword like the other Jinn before me—like Grandpa Joe must have trained."

"What about that bat club thingy you used on Serenque? Poor dragon, he never saw it coming.

In fact, Charon believes you should stick with what you are comfortable with."

"First, I didn't know he would turn out to be our friend, so you have to let that go. Second, it's not a weapon, it won't last more than five minutes against a steel sword."

"Get it anyways. If you can bring something into our world from yours, who's to say we can't also give it a little something extra?" Angel winked.

From his memory place, the shelf in his father's garage, Leo pulled the aluminum baseball bat as his amulet glowed under his armor.

"Okay, now hold it tight and close your eyes." Angel looked around the attic and spied a sewing kit on an old trunk. "Eyes still closed?"

"Yes, now hurry up, the others are waiting on us."

Angel pulled a sewing needle from the kit and pricked Leo on his left thumb, drawing a bead of dark red blood.

"Are you crazy? What was that for?" Leo blurted, opened his eyes, and glared at Angel. "How is that going to help?"

"Trust me, we can imbibe your weapon of choice with your essence, just as Theiler did... at least I think... put a drop of the blood on the bat thingy and repeat after me."

Leo put a single drop on the grip of the bat and waited for Angel's instructions.

Angel began to chant, "*Profora alminio lux chalyva.*"

"*Perform aluminum lux chevy,*" repeated Leo.

"No, not at all correct. We are going to have to work on your spells. Let's do this one word at a time and I'll enunciate. Repeat after me and make sure you place a hand on your amulet this time. "*ProFORMa.*"

"*ProFORMa*," Leo repeated while clutching both the bat and amulet.

"*AlmiNIO.*"

"*AlmiNIO.*"

"*Lux.*"

"*Lux.*"

"*ChaLEEva.*"

"*ChaLEEva,*" Leo finished.

The bat began to vibrate, growing in both length and form. What was once an average aluminum baseball bat, transformed to a light, but strong, steel club, gleaming in the dimly lit attic.

"There," she said, "now you have a weapon you are used to wielding and we've ensured its light enough for you to use continuously, but strong enough to stand up to any weapon in the realm."

Leo raised the bat and took a few swings. It was now slightly larger, but somehow lighter and sturdier. It felt natural in his hands and easy to swing, even in the armor that clad and protected him.

"Wow, thanks, Angel. How did you do that?"

"I'm full of what I thought were useless spells, I guess they have a use after all. And don't thank me yet. If we do go into battle you are going to be going up against an army who has been training, and who has been brainwashed by Theiler. They will stop at nothing to ensure his will is done, otherwise they will perish at his hands and their souls will be lost forever."

"It's now or never, I suppose. But first, I think a weapon should have a name, what do you think?" asked Leo.

"You don't see me naming my arrows, do you?"

"No, but I think it should be named. What do you think about Levience?"

"I think we need to go," Angel replied.

"I think it has a cool name, like defiance only better." Leo placed Levience in the scabbard attached to his left, easy access from across his body with his dominant right hand. "We need to get out there with the others."

"Hey," Angel stopped and came face to face with Leo, "if we get separated or if something happens to one or both of us..."

"Nothing is going to happen. General Carlux and the army will protect us; we just need to do our part too."

"Seriously, listen to me. If something happens, I just want you to know that I'm glad you crossed the veil into the Spring Crow. This is as much your home as it is mine, and I'm... I mean I..."

"I'm glad I met you, too, Angel."

Suddenly, the two could hear yelling coming from the distance. A great crash violently shook the house around them. Both rushed to the only window in the dimly lit attic, wiped off a light layer of dust, and peered out. There, in the distance, was Serenque quickly approaching and skidding to a halt. Leo and Angel rushed down the stairs, out of the house, and ran full speed towards the panicked crowd that had gathered around their winged friend.

"Wait," yelled Angel as she broke through the crowd as they were gathering for an attack on the beast, "he's our friend. Don't hurt him."

Leo reassured the gathering forces, "He's okay, he's here to help."

From atop the dragon's back slid a warrior that gave the ever-growing crowd pause, a large wild warrior obviously not from the Spring Crow. Iron John, stretching his muscular legs, scooped up Angel and Leo in one of his aggressive but friendly hugs.

"John," Leo managed to gasp from his compressed lungs, "what are you two doing here? You should be watching the Carved Realm."

"I've seen all that needs to be seen. Theiler is no longer coming alone, his forces have gathered, and they are on their way through the Forest Veil as we speak. The only way to warn you was to use his own way through; I don't believe Theiler knows just how far his path stretches up as well as out."

Lady Cybele, watching from a distance, parted the crowd, placed her hand on the neck of Serenque, and turned towards Iron John with a tired smile. "Sir Johnathan, it's been a long time."

"Lady Cybele," Iron John knelt as he spoke, "it's been much too long."

"Rise, Johnathan, what news do you bring us from the Carved Realm?"

"Gather your forces, my lady, the time for battle is now."

Chapter 23

The Spring Crow was eerily quiet once the excitement of Serenque and Iron John's arrival had passed. Lady Cybele ordered anyone not involved with the battle to lock themselves in their houses and to ensure they had weapons to protect themselves in case of the worst. Those who could not defend themselves were escorted into the town hall, where a protective spell began below the polished chrysoprase streets and rose above the heliotrope hall. The hall and homes were further protected by the few soldiers General Carlux could spare. The streets were silent and still, save the occasional fiery snort from an old mare too weak to charge into battle and the gentle rustle of leaves of the wind. All the shops up and down the square were locked tight and windows boarded in hopes of saving their wares and façade. Not a single man, woman, or beast breathed easy.

The square lay in the middle of the Spring Crow, nestled in the triad of the once considered unbreakable protection between the Mountain Veil to the north, the Water Veil to the west running north to south west, and the Forest Veil from north to south east, was now under the pressure of a heartless enemy from the west.—an enemy hellbent to separate their world, and their very souls.

What seemed like thousands of Spring Crow soldiers, both volunteers and conscribes, stood in multiple formations at the westward edge of the Forest Veil, shifting uncomfortably in their ever-growing hotter suits of armor, weapons at the ready. Sweat dripped from under their helmets and down their backs as the suns beat down. The formations were so close in ranks that both man and beast could feel the breath of their brethren on the back of their necks. Somewhere from the back of the formation a lone flute played. Everything and everyone were silent.

Leo and Angel stood with Iron John at the head of the first formation, Charon took his place slightly behind to the left, while General Carlux walked amongst his army. Mr. Forswear and Mr. Morphon tended to the needs of the soldiers and beasts, handing out water and giving silent encouragement where needed. Sylvia continued to consult her library from the rear. Lady Cybele ensured she remained at the head of, not only Leo and Angel, but of all present.

It started with a mere rustling of the leaves from the Forest Veil. What seemed like a cooling summer breeze slowly became harsh and then violent. The trees of the forest put up no fight, some were unceremoniously cut down with a single blow from behind, while others were brutally hacked away to clear a wide swath capable of supporting the movement of Theiler's vast army. The rancid smell of the death and destruction followed Theiler's army as it leapt from the Veil. En masse, the strongest of Theiler's creatures and warriors broke through the Forest Veil into the

Spring Crow. Theiler's army moved as one, not caring who or what was in the way, and only considered one thought... to destroy. On finally witnessing the size and power of the Carved Realm, one by one and then groups of many from the Spring Crow army turned and fled towards the protection of Town Hall.

"Hold those lines! Charge while they are still in the veil," shouted General Carlux now directly in front of Lady Cybele, attempting to lead his dwindling army in the defense of the Spring Crow. As the general shouted, he grabbed the shoulders of the men fleeing around him in an attempt to redirect their momentum. "We must protect our livelihood; don't let them penetrate any further past the Veil."

Leo, following the lead of General Carlux, moved between the fleeing men shouting words of encouragement. As the Spring Crow's lines of defense continued to break, he charged towards the nearest Carved Realm warrior, swinging his bat furiously at anything that came within striking distance. All around he could hear the clash of steel on armor, both offensive and defensive. Those who did not flee for the assumed safety of Town Hall fought ferociously in an attempt to protect their families and homes. Those who did flee were cut down from behind in a flurry of the Carved Realm's warriors' wrath.

As Leo worked furiously in the defense of his new home, he turned towards the north and witnessed a bloodthirsty gargoyle, much larger than he had seen in the Carved Realm, pounce on a fleeing conscribe, biting into his exposed neck, and draining him of blood and life. Knowing it was too late, Leo rushed behind the gargoyle and struck with all his might onto the creature's right ear, bringing the gargoyle momentarily to his knees. The creature returned to his feet and continued towards the remaining men who continued to run in fright. Leo realized all too well that he was ill-equipped to be a true warrior; brute force and anger were all he could rely on. As he wildly swung Levience, a hand grasped his armor and pulled him away from a troll a split second before the beast's club was to make contact with his skull.

"Leo, you need to get to a safe place," yelled Iron John who, yet again, protected Leo from a warrior appearing from behind. "You are going to get yourself killed out here. Take Serenque and Angel and get to the other side of the Spring Crow. We will find you when we can."

"I can't leave now. I'm staying and that's all there..."

Iron John hoisted Leo to his shoulder and stormed off to find Angel, who was fighting her own battle with a Minotaur, who easily turned and kicked at each of Angel's blows.

"Come on, you," Iron John scooped Angel to his opposite shoulder and simultaneously vaulted over the Minotaur, now collapsing under Iron John's great weight. Running with the two draped over his shoulders, he broke through the battle and whistled for Serenque, who arrived in a matter of seconds.

Iron John shrugged the two onto Serenque's back. "Take these two to the edge of the Water Veil. I'll come for them when I can."

Serenque lifted off over the carnage below. As he turned east towards the Veil, Leo and Angel could see that only a portion of Theiler's army had crossed, with the remaining forces allowing the first wave to weaken the Spring Crow. The portion of Theiler's army that remained in the Carved Realm beyond the Forest Veil stretched as far as the two could see. From their vantage point on Serenque, Leo could make out giant lizard-like creatures as well as humanoid ape, additional dragons, and the thousands upon thousands of Carved Realm warriors biding their time. In each, he could tell that their soul was no longer their own and they only survived to carry out the biddings of their master.

"We need to warn the others," yelled Leo over the cold wind rushing by. "When the rest of the army breaks through, Spring Crow will be crushed."

Serenque landed on the shores next to the water, shook the two off his wide back, spread his wings and without a thought or word, only a nod, took flight to rejoin the defenses.

"I can't believe he said I need to learn how to fight," said Leo as he removed his helmet and threw it to the ground where is spun to a halt. "Listen, you can hear it, you can actually hear the battle from here. We need to get back and help.

Leo was right; from a distance to the west, Angel could hear the ravages of war, the low rumble of thousands of foot soldiers, and the agonizing screams of the injured and dying.

"If you don't know how to fight then figure something out, open your library, what are your strengths?" ordered Angel. "There's a reason Iron John took us away; there's a reason Theiler wanted us for his army. We need to find Theiler's weakness, and quickly, before it's too late."

Leo concentrated as hard as he had ever concentrated on anything in his life, touched his amulet, and spoke the words, "*Forthwith knowledge.*"

Leo found himself without his library; instead, in a green field, the smell of lavender surrounding him. Confused, he took a tentative step forward but stopped when he realized a young Theiler was kneeling only a few feet in before him. Theiler did not seem to notice the second Jinn in his presence, but Leo did notice the blood-smeared war ax lying before Theiler.

Wisp of smoke rose, and light flowed from the ax to Theiler and back as he spoke low and deliberately. "*Pfader, etz emconte dolo guis tz amini famil tulitin. Rizquten me perferr etz guis aminiJinn abb, conarmis, sunamis, meumsed om mitt Elysium.*"

Leo stood, not daring to move, drifting his eyes over the kneeling Theiler. In the distance he saw a woman, dressed in a dark amber dress, a black trench cape around her shoulders.

Instinctively he reached for his amulet. When Leo opened his eyes, the Spring Crow suns were beginning to set over the Forest Veil, the cool wind blowing from the east over the nearby water chilled him to his core.

"What the Hell was that about," demanded Angel. "You've been standing in that same spot clutching your library for more than three hours."

"I saw him. I mean, I saw Theiler, but he was younger. And I think I saw Lady Cybele, but I can't be sure. I know how he is creating his army; I know what his goal is, and I think I know how to stop him, but I need to face him."

"Face him? He's a trained warrior. What can you possibly do that someone else can't? I mean, I appreciate your bravery, but we need to concentrate on warning the others of the second wave and I'm afraid that we've been here so long we might be too late."

Leo listened, he could hear and understand Angel's concern. The battle had stopped. Were they too late? Had the Spring Crow already fallen to Theiler's army? "There is one more thing," Leo eyed Angel, "and it's something I can't do without your help. Theiler did something similar with his war ax that you had me do with my bat, but I didn't understand the words. What do these words mean?"

Leo repeated and pronounced Theiler's incantation as best he could, "Is it possible to enchant an object more than once?"

Angel thought for a moment. "It roughly translates, 'Fathers scorn and pain, blood of family brought to life. Through my blade and Jinn blood carve souls from the below, my weapons to control, so I might take my rightful seat over all of Elysium.' It's a very dark spell, but we may be able to alter it."

Angel had no idea where the knowledge of the enchantment came, probably passed down through her bloodline from the original tutor, but she knew exactly what the words meant. "Theiler enchanted his ax to not only take life but to also create life, that's what we saw when we were in the Carved Realm. He's playing God. Without his war ax he is nothing, he's connected everything he is, and all his powers, to a single object. You need to get that ax," she explained.

"What about multiple enchantments?"

"Sure, it happens all the time," she eyed Leo. "What are you thinking?"

"I don't want anything to take life, but if I can return life, break souls free from their loyalty to Theiler... that would be a start.

"I've got just the thing," smiled Angel, "but we need to act quickly."

"And one more thing..."

"You already said 'one more thing'" replied Angel.

"Okay, the last thing. You need to use an enchantment from the days of the original tutor to match the power of the magic in Theiler's weapon... old magic."

"That is going to be a little more difficult," Angel sighed as she took Leo's hand and guided him in a kneeling position, Levience sitting between tutor and Jinn.

Angel placed both her and Leo's hands on Levience, closed her eyes, and let the glow from her chest provide comforting warmth throughout her body. "*Tz lammp deturaccen infecterfer busCarluxi tzis addpaci anim. Dominit ult impeveoustuum prasidpreber tzum preccidium prabeerium tzm busCarluxi sutz.*"

Warm blue smoke flowed from Angel's fingertips, into Levience, and back into Leo's arms entering his body. He felt the warmth emanating from Angel and his amulet began to glow dark blue as the smoke filled his veins.

When both ceased to glow, Angel opened her eyes. Levience appeared the same and she hoped her inner knowledge of the old language was adequate to provide the force and protection Leo would need.

"What did you say?" Leo spoke as his brought his eyes up and to meet Angel's.

"I asked that Levience burn for you, to strike down your enemies, bring peace to those who need peace, and to offer you protection. Basically, I asked that it burn as a torch, cut down your enemy, bring souls to peace, provide you, it's master, ultimate control as well as protection from your enemies."

"I hadn't thought about protection."

"I know," she answered, her eyes still locked on his, "but I did."

Leo was the first to stand, holding Levience to his right. It didn't feel any different. "How will I know if it worked?"

"The only thing we can test now is if it will burn as requested. You don't need to touch your amulet for this one, just concentrate on the enemy and think '*deturaccen*'... wait, let me give you the pronunciation... Detur-A-Ken."

Leo brought Levience before him, gripping it tightly in both hands. "*Deturaccen.*" The weapon burned with dark hot blue flames, causing Leo to nearly drop it from shock. The flames had no effect on him, but he could tell that the weapon would bring either peace or destruction to anything, or anyone, it came in contact with.

"We need to go Leo. Think about Levience as normal again, the flame will disappear."

Leo did as he was instructed, and the weapon retook its former state.

"I hope we're not too late, we've been here for far too long," Angel worried aloud.

"No, we're not too late. If Theiler was here, he would have found us by now, so the rest of the army must not have come through yet. I'm the only one who can stop him, to him it's personal, Jinn on Jinn. Come on, we have a long way back to the edge of the forest."

Night had fallen by the time the two had reached the west side of town on their way to the forest. Well before reaching the forest, they could see pockets of the Spring Crow's army receiving treatment for wounds by those that were not too injured to assist.

Angel took no time in lending a much-needed hand in mending broken bones, burns, and battle wounds cut deep into man and beast. She knelt down beside a giant whose breath came in short bursts, blood trickled from the corner of his large mouth. Assessing the gaping hole, she placed her hand over his left lung and, in a gentle voice, requested the giant expel all the air from his lungs. Using her new powers of nature, she sealed the punctured lung with the giant's own muscle and skin by causing a thin sheet of his own life forces to regrow, to allow precious oxygen to once again flow through his massive chest.

"I don't have time to complete the healing process but that will ease the pain," she gently spoke as she rose from her position. "There are many others who need my help, rest comfortably and I'll be back to check on you." She squeezed the giant's large hand as he gave her a grateful smile.

Lady Cybele, seeing Angel's compassion, stared with wonder at the precious gift her ward had been bestowed. *The power to heal,* she thought to herself, *nature looks with fondness on this child.* She turned to an equally impressed Leo, who was standing just meters from Angel. "Go further west towards the forest; there are many that need your help. Angel will assist me in making as many as comfortable as possible. Go, ensure the survivors are brought here for care."

Leo was not expecting the scene of bloodshed he witnessed at the edge of the forest. In the first wave, no clear victor was evident; bodies from the two armies littered the field in red, green, and dark grey blood from the various men, creatures, and enemy warriors. Leo moved through the carnage, stepping lightly as not to desecrate the fallen nor further injure any who may have survived. In the deafly silence he heard an otherworldly moan. Turning, he looked down. There before him lay a warrior of the Carved Realm, barely clinging to what little life remained.

"Kill me now, lest I rise up and strike you down, Spring Crow foe," the figure seethed through compressed lips.

Leo continued to gaze on the warrior with tears in his eyes. *This man, this literally tortured soul, could he be freed from his pain? Will Levience take life as well as restore peace as requested?* Leo wondered. Raising Levience, he thought the word, *Deturaccen*. The sword lit with a beautiful fiery blue hue.

The warrior, upon seeing this, grew wide-eyed and terrified at the prospect of losing what soul he had.

"Stay still," are the only words Leo spoke as he placed the tip of Levience on the warrior's stuttering chest.

The warrior grew still. Silver wisps of smoke slowly, then more evident, streamed out from his mouth as if a banner were being pulled. The wisps moved this way and that before settling in as a shadow of a human figure.

"Thank you," it spoke when fully formed. "You have freed me from my bonds and have given me free will as well as a choice. The choice to remain as your companion or henceforth return from which I came." It smiled at Leo. "I choose to return to my home." With that, the silvery wisps slowly seeped into the ground below.

Leo stood in stunned silence, Levience grew dark. He composed himself and continued to search for survivors, enemy as well as friend, restoring whom he could and closing the eyes of those he could not. In all he was successful in restoring scores of the Spring Crow army, who made their way back towards the town square, and relieved the suffering of many Carved Realm Warriors as well. All warriors returned from which they came save one, a warrior called Frederick. A dark figure that once restored, pledged his eternal gratitude to the kindness of the Jinn.

Leo, along with his new companion Frederick, continued to search for survivors until it seemed all hope was lost. As he was preparing to return to the wounded in the rear, he spied a familiar form. There, beneath the crushing weight of a manticore lay Iron John, wounded but very much alive.

"Help me move this beast from him," exclaimed a frantic Leo to Frederick. "Don't worry John, I can help, I can ensure you are better."

"Don't," exclaimed John. "I've seen what that weapon can do and I'm not sure where my soul would take me. My soul is capable of resisting Theiler but I'm not so sure it can resist itself. Just get me to my feet and back to the others. I'll rest there."

Leo, Iron John, and their new companion, Frederick, followed the surviving Spring Crow army back to the town square, leaving behind the wake of death.

The three arrived back in the Spring Crow center to find Angel and Lady Cybele comforting the last of the injured. Huddled next to the two were Charon, Mr. Morphon, Mr. Forswear, and Sylvia. Through the dim of night, General Carlux could barely be seen in the distance, making his way towards Leo.

"Leo, victory is ours," exclaimed General Carlux. "We lost a lot of good men, but the battle is over. I pray to all of Eidolon that the Spring Crow never see a battle such as that again."

"General," Leo began, "that was the first wave. When Serenque was taking us east we could see that less than a tenth of Theiler's army had come, the rest are biding their time, waiting for us to weaken. I fear they won't have to wait long."

General Carlux regarded Leo's warning somberly. "I'll instruct my men to rest while they can. It will be a fitful night for most, but I assure you we will be ready to continue." With that, he left Leo to brief his men.

Chapter 24

The next morning the Spring Crow army, now less than half of its former glory, ate in silence, with their sustenance provided by the temporarily opened Magpie Bakery. All thoughts swirling on the events of the previous night; man, and beast alike, knew what the new day had in store.

General Carlux, drinking his hot sugary coffee, sat with Lieutenant Demrofinu and his army's newest member, Frederick, to discuss tactics while the rest of the council questioned Leo and Angel on exactly what they witnessed from above.

"Look," said Angel as she took a stick from the ground and drew a rough map. "Theiler's army has carved a path through the forest and sent a fraction of his army through. Now that the path is clear and we are weakened he's going to send the rest, it's only a matter of time."

"She's right, that's exactly what I saw too," Leo interjected between slow bites of breakfast, which consisted of ginger sugar tarts.

The previous night's search and recovery efforts took a lot out of Leo and he wasn't much for talking on this bright and, on any other day, beautiful morning. Angel, on the other hand, seemed full of life and energy. All night she had put her use of nature to the test, and it appeared that not only did her new powers of magic help heal the wounded, it also helped heal her soul.

Leo knew his powers over nature probably had some effect on his being, but due to the fact he used Levience and didn't lay 'hands on' to any of the souls he freed, he doubted it had the full effect. Still, he was pacified by the good deeds he accomplished but tired nonetheless.

"Lady Cybele," Charon, sitting peculiarly close to Sylvia, spoke up, "I believe it's time we gathered the forces and made our way back to the battlefield. I'm afraid if we delay too long, we may find ourselves fighting within the confines of town."

"I agree, Charon," Lady Cybele replied as she arose from her seated position. Though weary and tired, Lady Cybele never faltered in her graceful manner of movement or word. "General Carlux," she called, "please have your men finish their meals quickly, we must not allow Theiler's army the benefit of surprise. We must be at the ready to meet the foe on our doorstep."

Once the order had been given, those who could fight took to their feet and, with weapons in hand, made their way back to the western field of the Forest Veil. Those who were still injured but willing to continue the fight made their way, albeit more slowly, behind. Serenque, who was a needed addition to the Spring Crow army, carried Lieutenant Demrofinu into the morning sky in order to scout the incoming enemy.

The Spring Crow army, complete with man and beast, formed a defensive posture and lay in wait for the oncoming forces. They did not have to wait for long, Charon was correct in his opinion not to delay.

"Forces arriving from both the left and the right," Lieutenant Demrofinu called from high above, loud enough for General Carlux to hear and bark his orders.

"Stand fast men, don't let anyone past you or onward into town; we don't want to fight door-to-door, keep them in the open." He turned to Charon, Mr. Morphon and Mr. Forswear. "Gentlemen, it's been a privilege to have you in our army. My men trust you as they do me; it would be my great honor if you would lead the defense on both the left and right. Charon and I will remain center while Lady Cybele and Angel protect the injured. Charon, ensure Leo is protected by Iron John and battles with him wherever he goes. Keep Frederick as close by as possible. Hurry back before the enemy breaks through. If everything we have heard is true, and I have no doubt that it is, Theiler will be looking for Leo."

"And Sylvia?" asked Charon.

"Find her on your way to Iron John but do so quickly, ensure she stays in town with the wounded. In addition, we need her to continue to consult her library, perhaps she can find more information on Ms. Parish. She is still out there somewhere, and we have no idea what she is capable of. Hurry."

Charon took off like a bolt, finding both Iron John and Sylvia while Mr. Morphon and Forswear made their way to the flanks. Without argument, Lady Cybele and Angel dropped back to tend to the wounded while simultaneously understanding the unspoken responsibility that they would be the last defense against any enemy forces.

No sooner had Charon returned, than the first of Theiler's army broke through the now ragged and scorched Forest Veil. The Veil, taking no sides, made no attempt to defend itself from the onslaught, instead choosing to take the destruction in stride, knowing in due time nature again would take its course in regrowth.

Theiler's army came en masse. Many more soulless creatures than before leapt from the ragged forest and attacked with weapons, claws, and feverishly gnashing teeth.

"Through on the right," yelled General Carlux at the first sign of a chimera leaping from the forest, fangs and claws gleaming in the morning suns. Part lion and part dragon, its soul had also been carved by Theiler, who did not discriminate on the type of creature he kept under his control. Its wings spread with each nimble leap as it pounced on the first Spring Crow victim, a man shrouded in fine armor, armor that would momentarily protect him from the chimera's claws, but not long enough.

"Hold fast," ordered General Carlux, but his orders drowned in the chaos that ensured as his army again drew back at the second onslaught of Carved Realm warriors.

Leo held the gleaming blue Levience aloft as he went into his second attempt at battle. Although untrained, his heart and confidence had grown since his arrival in the Spring Crow merely weeks ago. He, with Iron John, broke the ranks of men falling back and charged into the thick of the ever-growing enemy.

"Follow us," shouted Iron John as he drew his sword and followed Leo into the morning battle, "for the Spring Crow."

Arrows passed Leo so closely he could hear them tear through the cool morning air. Levience deflected arrows passing too close, curtesy of Angel's protection spell.

Upon seeing the young Jinn and his companion Iron John, followed closely by Frederick, the Spring Crow army momentarily paused before yelling and turning to follow him back into the field of battle.

A dark-faced warrior approached Leo from behind. Sensing the danger, Iron John, with catlike agility under his heavy armor, lunged forward and took the figure by the gut, spilling his life on the soaked midmorning dew.

All amulets in the Spring Crow glowed around the necks of the brave men and creatures, their weapons shown with gore, and their tattered spirits began to fade. Theiler's army was massive; more than ten times the size of the Spring Crow. Not even Serenque was immune to the arrows and ordinance aimed skyward by the creatures below.

Leo continued to charge forward with multiple swings of Levience, which tore at both man and beast, freeing the souls who wished peace and slaying those who were too far lost for redemption. Under his armor he was coated in sweat while the blood of his enemies penetrated the slightest opening in his protection, mixing in an unholy concoction of carnage.

Theiler's army, under the constant strain of attack, began to part at the center of the battle. Leo, looking up from the ghastly troll he had just slain, was the first to spot him. There he was, Theiler, riding atop a dragon Leo recognized from the fortress. Similar to size and breed of Serenque, he carried his master as Theiler whipped the beast into a frenzy.

"Get behind me," ordered Frederick, "he's after your soul and the soul of all in the Spring Crow. If he defeats to you, he defeats everyone."

Leo followed Charon and Frederick to the left flank, south of their former position, lashing out at all who dare confront them. Iron John followed closely behind, turning his back occasionally to thwart the attempts of the enemy to take the three from the rear.

Further to the north, Theiler dismounted his dragon and, without a word, cut down Spring Crow creatures with impunity. Each who dared to face him, one-on-one or in forces of many, had their armor sliced through by the magic of his war ax.

"Find the Jinn," Theiler said. "Bring him to me." He screamed as he remounted his dragon to survey for Leo.

To the east, Theiler's army had begun penetrating the perimeter of the Spring Crow square. Lady Cybele and Angel, abandoning their attempts at comforting the wounded, began to battle with both magic and weapons. Lady Cybele, never losing her composure, was capable of forming blasts of air, knocking down dozens of warriors while Angel took aim with her crossbow and took down intruders one-by-one.

"We two cannot protect the Spring Crow alone, I'll hold back as many as I can while you heal the best of our injured. Go quickly, I won't be able to hold them for more than a few minutes," ordered Lady Cybele as she summoned another blast of hot, thick air, blowing back the advancing forces.

Angel wasted no time. Storing her bow, she began to heal the largest of the giants first, taking precious time to ensure their wounds healed adequately to continue fighting, before moving further west to additional creatures and men.

"Take them alive," Lady Cybele heard from above. "They will be our latest addition," ordered Theiler now soaring above the two.

Upon hearing the master's order, the dark warriors doubled their efforts. Advancing from the center, right, and left, the enemy overcame and overtook Lady Cybele and her powers. Ripping the amulet from her neck, a gargoyle held it up and victoriously screamed, "Go after the girl."

Mr. Morphon was joined by Mr. Forswear from the north and Lieutenant Demrofinu, now back on the ground, fought the southern forces while General Carlux and Charon continued to battle in the north, the last location they had spotted Theiler. All five kept an eye on the horizon for Theiler to reappear, all wanting to sight him, yet fearing they would.

The warriors were much quicker than the two councilmen, who were not accustomed to warfare. As they fought valiantly, it was clear that they were losing ground. Double-, sometimes triple-teamed, the only advantage the two had was fighting to save their home and fight they did.

Serenque, who had not retaken flight, spotted Mr. Morphon whom was surrounded and beaten back by a squad of trolls, each violently swinging their clubs only to barely miss destroying the man. With a flick of his tail, Serenque knocked back the advancing enemy only to be struck from the right by a lance, penetrating deep into his side. Serenque, momentarily stunned, shot fire in the direction from where the offending weapon flew, scorching the earth and owner with his hot breath.

Serenque's defense gave Mr. Morphon time to glance up, there, in the distance speeding towards the trio was Theiler.

Sensing one of his own, Serenque turned to face the enemy as he the second dragon descended from above and skidded to a halt. Theiler dismounted, stepped aside, and allowed the two former companions to entangle in fiery warfare.

The two beasts collided, causing the very ground below all in battle to violently shake. "Wygum, I should have known that of all who were tortured you would be the one to turn on the young Jinn," Serenque spoke to his former friend.

"It is you who has turned on the Jinn Master," Wygum replied as he raged towards the injured Serenque, lance still penetrating his right.

The two fought, scraping claw against claw, teeth gnashing on necks, fire scorching the hardened scales of their devil-like appearance.

Wygum, sensing Serenque's injury, worked his way to his left, Serenque's right, and drove the lance further into his former companions wound. Flicking his powerful tail and wrapping his leathery wings around Serenque, he continued to hold the beast and beat the lance until he buried the shaft into Serenque's thick hide.

Serenque released a blast of fiery air, but it was no match for Wygum, who was all too familiar with fire. Serenque began to succumb to his injury. Although he valiantly continued the fight, his will and powers weaned.

Theiler, sensing the defeat of his traitorous former sentry, smiled as he relentlessly brought his war ax down on all who dared confront him. He continued to scan for Leo, smelling the air around him for the familiar family bloodline.

"There," he smiled to himself, eyes steely and calm. "The foolish boy is coming to me."

The battle raged on around Leo as he continued to make his way south. Unbeknownst to him, Theiler was slashing his way north to confront his young nephew.

Leo, still followed closely by Frederick and Charon, had little clue that Theiler was making his way towards him. The three continued fighting for their lives, for the Spring Crow. Lieutenant Demrofinu, battling close by, witnessing Theiler on the move and seeing Leo in the distance, knew Leo was no match for Theiler. Even with Levience burning bright, the young Jinn was ill-equipped to battle a seasoned warrior without assistance.

Leo, now semi-expertly wielding Levience, was the first of the three to spot Theiler charging forward. His war ax seemed larger, more powerful than Leo remembered from the courtyard in the Carved Realm. The weapon gleamed through the blood splatter that dripped down from its bit and cheek, matching the blood matted in the ferocious Theiler's hair. Close behind he spotted Lieutenant Demrofinu, charging the foe from the rear.

Theiler rushed closer to his bloodline, quickly closing the gap with every lunge forward. It was the closest he had been since the field of green in the fortress, where he should have ordered Necro to personally guard the young Jinn and the tutor. Theiler could feel the surge of victory coursing through his cold veins. Finally, he would have the Jinn Kane bloodline and soul for himself.

Leo pulled ahead of Charon and Frederick, who were protecting both themselves and Leo on all sides with the expertise of seasoned warriors. Raising Levience, praying for both protection and destruction, he was nearly upon Theiler when the unthinkable happened.

Lieutenant Demrofinu reached Theiler first from behind and landed a crushing blow on the distracted foe, briefly bringing Theiler to his knees. Unaccustomed to being off guard, Theiler quickly regained his footing and turned towards the offending lieutenant.

"That was the last mistake you will ever make in your short life," Theiler growled as he slashed his ax sideways at the nimble Lieutenant.

Lieutenant Demrofinu parried and followed the ax with his own sword, nicking Theiler's dominant hand but not disarming the warrior. Not to be outdone, Theiler recovered and punched the lieutenant with a force that took the breath away from the young man. With one last breathless attempt at survival, Lieutenant Demrofinu lunged forward with his sword, his aim was true but blocked once again by Theiler's quick action. Though the defensive maneuver was quick, it was not quick enough to prevent, yet another deep gash on his wrist, exposing tendon and muscle through the injury.

Theiler, unamused with the Spring Crow army's second in command, raised his weapon and spun, taking the head of his foe in one clean move, not bothering to carve the soul.

"No," screamed Leo and he closed the last few steps between he and Theiler, bringing the full weight of Levience down on to the Theiler's injured side. Levience's hot flame scorched through Theiler's protective armor, burning the warrior's flesh.

Charon and Frederick, ceasing the opportunity to attack the weakened Theiler, raced past Leo and flanked their opponent.

Theiler turned towards the two, raised his uninjured hand and with a flick of the wrist sent the well-trained men flying back, landing in a heap. He turned his attention back towards Leo.

"Now, I shall teach you a lesson in humility, a lesson I thought I taught my brother Kane long ago. Prepare to join me as my slave in both realms forever."

Theiler sliced the air before Leo, just grazing the breastplate protecting his ever-faster beating heart. Bringing his ax back while dodging an untrained roughhouse swing from Levience he lunged forward, slamming the butt of his weapon into the plackart protecting the young Jinn's sternum and knocking him backwards.

"First, I'll carve the soul of the tutor while you watch," snarled Theiler as he swung and purposely missed the faltering Leo, "then I'll ensure my stepmother suffers before you." He swung again, this time slicing towards Leo's leg as Leo struggled to maintain balance.

Leo, not as quick to his feet as he would have liked, instinctively thrust Levience before his face, just in time to catch a crushing blow from Theiler. The two struggled while their weapons sizzled, entwined in an unholy bloodline bond.

To the west, Angel had rejoined the fight, protecting herself, as well as watching over the injured, from those who sought to take her into captivity and destroy the wounded members of the Spring Crow army. Her arrows flew straight and true, tearing through any whom attempted violence.

I need to draw their attention from the town, she thought as she let another arrow fly from her endless supply summoned from her memory place. *The injured won't be able to protect themselves if they catch me, and I can't protect both myself and them.* She started south and the warriors followed, taking every opportunity to inch closer, fighting amongst themselves to be the one to capture the tutor and win favor of their master.

As Angel made her way up a ridge separating the town from the main battle, she witnessed a sight she hoped she would never encounter. There, at no more than fifty meters, stood Theiler and Leo, locked in a mythical duel. She knew she needed to act quickly, to do something... anything, but what? What could she do that a Jinn Knight could not?

A familiar voice rang out, "Angel. Angel, come to me; we need to break Leo free." It was Iron John, who had managed to evade the same fate as Charon and Frederick.

"John," she breathed hard and fast, "Theiler is distracted, and Leo needs that ax. This is as close as he's ever going to get, can you break the bond between the weapons?"

"I'll do my best, but what about you?"

"Once the bond is broken, you will need to move away quickly. I only have once chance at stopping Theiler before he realizes what is happening. Now, please, go."

Iron John breathed deep. All of his years of training, years of torture, and years of captivity had led him to this point, a point to where he could help his first real two friends. He began with a jog, and then burst into a sprint while pulling his sword. By the time he reached Theiler, he was in full tilt, allowing his great girth to carry him. Bringing his sword between Theiler's war ax and Levience, he knocked Levience from the unskilled hands of Leo and the war ax from the injured Theiler. His momentum continued, bringing his full weight into Theiler, knocking the warrior away from Leo.

Levience, no longer in the hands of its owner, lost its fiery glow and lay in the field next to the war ax. Angel, seeing her only chance, knelt to the ground, closed her eyes, placed both hands into the bloody soil, and envisioned her goal.

"Nature, hear my plea, hold fast, hold tight."

Iron John, following Angel's instructions, broke from Theiler just as he was recovering from the crushing blow. Theiler, rising to full height, moved slowly as if trying to run through a watery bog. Roots grew like tentacles from the ground and entangled the warrior's feet, legs, and quickly ran up to his waist and chest, holding him fast. Without his ax all he could do is struggle under the great power.

"Now, Leo," yelled Angel, still kneeling, "whatever you know, whatever you need to do, you need to do it now."

Leo, blinking and not believing what he saw, snapped from his momentary trance and retrieve the war ax. He knew its power was from Jinn blood, his ancestor's blood, and he hoped he was right in believing. He raised the ax above his head and, with a glance at a wide-eyed Theiler, brought it crashing down into the earth before him as he has seen Theiler do.

Leo was right.

Theiler's army, no matter their position or action, halted in place. Even the mighty Wygum turned his attention from Serenque to watch as their master struggled in the clutches of nature's strangle.

Wisps of souls arose from the ground. They came slowly as if they were the smoke from a snuffed candle rising skyward. More and more wisps seeped from the ground, both greeting and scolding the Carved Realm warriors.

Theiler's army dropped their weapons and greeting the wispy souls as long but not forgotten friends. Each warrior followed and faded with the haze of souls back to the earth from which they came so long ago. Free at last.

As the warriors returned to the earth another more sinister vapor arose from the crevice created by the ax, a vapor that formed into a ghoul never before seen by any in all the realms. Without a word, the ghoul slowly made its way to Theiler and stroked the warriors face. Theiler, who had never shown the emotion of fear now wore it in his panic-stricken eyes. Before Theiler could make another sound, the ghoul enveloped him and slowly began to melt into the depths of the world below. Before disappearing completely, the ghoul turned towards Leo and pointed a shadowy finger in the boy's direction and disappeared.

Chapter 25

It had been a full month in the Spring Crow before things began to become somewhat normal again. Levience was safely recovered from the field of battle and stored in Leo's memory, the armor polished and returned to the attic, and all wounds, save the memories, healed.

A fitting tribute to all of the fallen was conducted and a heroes' cemetery was created at the edge of the former Forest Veil, now just a beautiful regrown, albeit magical forest, where the majority of the battle had taken place. In the heart of the cemetery was a memorial to Lieutenant Demrofinu, whose bravery knew no bounds, who sacrificed his life along with so many others in the defense of the Spring Crow.

The Spring Crow decided that the enemy warriors also deserved a fitting burial, after all, their souls were not theirs to control and they had fought valiantly as well. To the west of the forest, in the newly expanded Spring Crow territory, an equally beautiful cemetery and memorial park was erected in order to never forget their enemies in war.

The Town Hall, though untouched by the actual battle, was given a facelift as well. The once cracked and broken unity fountain was split into thirds in order to make room for a fourth figure.

Now, holding hands with the three polished figures, was that of a beast, a symbol of all creatures who fought bravely in defense of the realm.

Serenque was given a position within the Spring Crow army and became the personal protector of General Carlux. His friend, foe, and now acquaintance, Wygum, was forgiven for his actions. Through no fault of his own, his soul torn between the two Jinn, was now free and charged with guarding the outer edges of the newly expanded Spring Crow.

"Sir Leonardo, can I see you in my library for a moment," called Lady Cybele from the steps of the Town Hall where Leo and Angel sat, enjoying treats from the Magpie Bakery compliments of Clivelhorn. "I won't keep him more than a moment, Lady Angel Dianna."

Leo had not been in Lady Cybele's library since his first day in the Spring Crow. Now accustomed to the realm and all its splendor and nuances, he had a better appreciation for the splendor of her library.

"Please, have a seat," Lady Cybele summoned two wing-back chairs which magically appeared facing each other on an ornate Middle Eastern styled rug. "I'm sure you have many questions."

"Well," began Leo, "Angel told me that I shouldn't be able to pull items from my world into the realms, that it's impossible to bring something in that hasn't been brought before. How did I get Levience through?"

"Magic comes in all forms and not everyone, to include the tutor or myself, can understand all aspects. From what I have been able to piece together my son, Kane, absorbed knowledge of your world's magic and passed the traits down through generations. By crossing the Veil and allowing himself to become engrossed in both worlds he gained the ability to meld the two."

"So, it's in my genes?"

"From what I can understand, yes. The knowledge of the tutor has been passed down, why not the knowledge of the Jinn as well? Theiler did not take advantage of this, instead choosing to stay in the Carved Realm in order to prolong his life and the grief of others. Thankfully, Kane did not choose this same path."

"Speaking of Theiler, how did he create a Gadaseer when he created Ms. Parish and why was she able to cross without changing?"

"Theiler's magic was dark and I'm still working out the details of how he created a Gadaseer, if he created her at all. Dark magic is not something I enjoy researching, it's highly addictive. I will eventually make my way to the answer, but it will take time. As for the crossing without changing, her soul was already dark. While she did not change in outward appearance, I am assuming her soul grew even more hideous when she came to us. This is the only reason I can assume she had such little problem in spreading her lies."

Leo understood, some answers would have to wait.

"I have something for you, and there are some final things I'd like to discuss before you return to your world."

"Return? But I thought I could stay here? I have my grandpa's house, friends, and Angel is teaching me more and more about magic—I'm just now getting the pronunciations correct."

"You must return, it's the way of the Kane Knights, the Kane Jinn, and what my son would have wanted. You have a walker's spirit; you know that as well as I."

Leo recalled walking through the memories of Theiler in his own library, he also thought back on being able to cross the veil without harm.

"Can I come back whenever I wish?"

"You can, but I caution you, as I did your grandfather, Sir Joseph, as you travel back and forth it becomes more difficult with each passing year to keep your secrets. Which reminds me, this is for you." With a flick of her wrist she produced an envelope sealed in black wax.

Scrawled across was his name. "Can I read it now?"

"Please do, I'm sure you will have questions. I'll do my best to answer what I can honestly. All other questions you have—and you will have others—will be answered in time."

Leo cracked the wax protection and began to read the words of Grandpa Joe:

10 January 2007.

My Dearest Grandson Leo,

Today is your sixth birthday and I must say you are turning into a fine young man. It was not long ago that I had the heartbreaking responsibility to watch over you while your father arranged for your mother's funeral. It was a beautiful ceremony, but no boy should be without a mother. My wife, your grandmother, passed well before her time as well but I would like to introduce you to your many-great, great grandmother, Lady Cybele.

Leo looked up at Lady Cybele. She had mentioned her son Kane, how did he overlook the obvious?

"Please Leo, go on," she insisted.

By now, I have passed, and the responsibilities of the Kane Jinn Lineage have passed to you. Your father is a good man, a hardworking man, but after discussing our lineage with him he has no desire to carry on the family work. It is up to you to maintain the dignity of the Kane name. Keep your father safe and listen to what he has to say, he is educated in the ways of our earthly world as you should be as well.

Your life has no doubt changed in wonderful ways, ways I will probably never know but am familiar. Treat the Spring Crow as your home and protect the realm from all those who would seek it harm.

There is family waiting for you, but that family does not honor the Jinn lineage as the Kane have learned to honor. You will face trials and tribulation, but I know you, with the help of your extended Spring Realm family, will overcome all obstacles.

Everything I held dear in the Spring Crow is now yours. You may share this information with your father, but I caution you to keep the Realm and its secrets just that, a secret from all others.

My dear Leo, you will be a powerful Jinn Knight, just like those before you. Use this power to maintain peace, learn your craft, and always remember that I am eternally proud of you and your father.

Until we meet again, Grandpa Joe.

Leo looked up from the letter with a tear in his eye, folded it neatly and returned it to the time worn envelope.

"Grandmother?"

"Yes, Sir Leonardo. I am truly the mother of Kane, third wife of Acadamel, and I chose to accompany my son upon his banishment. I've longed to tell you, but it was not my place, I agreed with Sir Joseph that when the time was right, I would welcome you into our home."

"And Angel?"

"The tutor saw great things in my son Kane, and of all the Jinn Knights knew that Kane would be a great scholar as well as a great warrior. Hence, all inhabitants of the Spring Crow were granted a library, just like the original book of knowledge granted to Kane from his father."

"How long do I have? I mean, how long until I have to return?"

"In a week's time Charon will escort you through the Veil once again, where you will be delivered back to your world. It will seem as very little time has passed whatsoever."

"If almost no time has passed why can't I stay?" argued Leo.

"As you get older you will be able to spend more time as your Grandpa Joseph spent time. For now, at your age, you run the risk of being missed for any period of time. We must protect the realm as your grandfather wished."

The week went by with a flourish of activity. Leo spent long hours with Angel, learning the ways of the Jinn, magic, and of her life before his arrival in the Spring Crow. When he wasn't with Angel, he spent time with his library and between those activities he visited with Charon at the Troll Tavern, where Leo had grown accustomed to the pickled sow's ear.

Sylvia joined Leo and Charon twice during the week. She couldn't get over the fact that, no matter how hard she studied the past, present, and tried to predict the future, she could not find any useful information regarding Ms. Parish other than she was created in the former Carved Realm and her soul was cleaved through Eidolon. Her whereabouts unknown to all of both the new and old Spring Crow.

When he was in private, Leo would spend hours going through his grandfather's belongings, remembering the stories and tall tales he would tell when Leo was younger. The tales came to life each day in the Spring Crow and Leo now understood the stories of adventure. Stories he would someday write and hopefully pass on himself.

The morning of day seven came in a flash. Now, standing on the shore of the Watery Veil, he waited as Charon released the small vessel from its mooring and waited for Leo to say his farewells.

"Leo, my boy, next time you're here we're going to turn you into a fine warrior," exclaimed General Carlux. "Let me know when you're in town, we will start training immediately."

"Not so fast," interrupted Sylvia, "I want him to show me the proper ways to advance my library so I can study history in a more expeditious fashion," she winked at Leo as she put her hands on his shoulders, embraced him, and spun him around to be face-to-face with Angel.

"I'm not going to cry," she said as she wiped her cheek with the sleeve of her dress. "You have to tell me all about your adventures in your world when you return." She, like Sylvia, hugged Leo tight and said, "Be safe out there."

"Don't do anything I wouldn't do," called out Mr. Morphon.

"Yeah, be careful, we've heard stories of your world," chimed in Mr. Forswear.

"Don't forget about us, you hear," waved Frederick, the Spring Crow's newest appointed Planning Commissioner.

As Leo stepped onto the beautiful gold railing boat Angel, from the front of the gathered crowed, placed one foot on the boat, steadied herself, and kissed him on the cheek. "Come back in one piece," she said as she carefully stepped back onto the shore.

Charon pushed off and thus began Leo's next journey, the return.

Chapter 26 – Epilogue

Ms. Parish, with free reign high upon the mountain at the distant end of the Abrog Realm, many miles north of the Mountain Veil separating it from the Spring Crow, peered through her syncoscope, a viewing device much like a telescope summoned through her powers. She watched as Leo said his goodbyes to his friends in the Spring Crow and her eyes widened when she witnessed from a distance Angel peck Leo on the cheek.

"She's smitten with the boy," she smiled. "Perhaps we can interrupt his world as well as influence her in our goal." She turned to the warrior on her right, knowing he had witnessed the same. "What do you make of the recent events?"

"I knew brother was a fool, but never did I believe that he could not conquer a Kane," growled Garaile in his low graveled tone. "In retrospect, I believe that this will be beneficial. I expected Theiler to rule the Spring Crow and have only one brother to battle but now," he gave the slightest hint of an out of the ordinary smile. "Now it's just a matter of destroying the weak Kane bloodline before I'm ruler of the three banished realms and can set my sights on the Cardinal Realm.

Michael Sloan

Michael enlisted in the United States Air Force in 1996 and retired after a 24-year career. He currently lives in Florida with his loving wife.

Made in the USA
Columbia, SC
06 September 2020